FISHING
THE MUSE

To Peggy

Enjoy the Read

FISHING THE MUSE

Al Sorci

To order additional copies of this book, contact:
Xlibris Corporation
1-888-795-4274
www.Xlibris.com
Orders@Xlibris.com
19175

For my family and friends.

PROLOGUE

When Ford Sinclair dropped out he did it like he did everything else . . . *masterfully*. That was twenty years ago, and still his whereabouts remain a mystery.

Investigators of various kinds, hired by various people for a variety of reasons, have beat the proverbial bushes in the hope of flushing Sinclair out into the open. The most recent to take on the challenge was television's *Unsolved Mysteries*—hosted by Robert Stack, the actor, who, incidentally, had crossed paths with his prime-time prey back in the late-1970s; during Sinclair's brief yet highly-regarded Hollywood Period. But in the end even the erstwhile portrayer of Elliot Ness came up empty in his pursuit of the elusive Ford Buster Sinclair.

Dead-ends in every direction. A vanishing act that would have turned the Great Houdini green with envy. Howard Hughes, with all that money to hide behind, paled by comparison. Because as it happened: One minute Sinclair was there, and the next, for no apparent reason, he wasn't. No warning, no valediction, not so much as an "abracadabra" before he pulled off the grand show-stopper of all tricks.

Suspicions of foul play were laid to rest early. With talk of a kidnapping (and fears of worse) flying around, a letter arrived at *The New York Times* building in New York City on April 21, 1980. It was addressed to a Mr. Arthur Brimm, then editor of the paper's Arts and Leisure section, and a longtime Sinclair enthusiast. As printed in the next day's edition, the letter read, simply:

> To whom it may concern;
>
> Gone fishing.
>
> > Sincerely,
> > Ford Sinclair

Handwriting experts from the F.B.I. verified that it was, indeed, penned by Sinclair. Postmarked 17 April, Mexico City. And from there the trail had quickly grown cold. The temperature dropping steadily as the days turned into weeks, then months, and years—until two decades lay dormant, encased behind murky layers of frozen silence.

Others, however, have come forward on Sinclair's behalf. A proxy of lawyers and accountants: hired guns who tend the financial affairs—family support, royalties, taxes, etc.—while at the same time insisting they have absolutely no idea where their client is, or what he may be up to. "As far as we know," they say, "Mister Sinclair is on vacation. And does not wish to be disturbed."

Whether or not their ignorance is genuine continues to be a matter of debate. But there is no question as to the validity of their representation. They speak with Sinclair's full (if detached) authorization. A claim that cannot be made by certain professional journalists, who, over the years, have taken the liberty of sharing their particular insights on the subject.

What is, to date, considered the "definitive" Sinclair biography was written by none other than the fore-mentioned Arthur Brimm. Published in 1985, *Ford Sinclair: Half a Life* chronicles its dashing protagonist pre-birth to post-powder. And although unauthorized, Brimm's research proves painstaking. The accounts—drawn from in-depth interviews with many who played principle roles in the Sinclair saga—paint a most fascinating portrait of the man.

The book's front jacket features a photograph of Sinclair, at forty, taken only a few weeks before he made his unceremonious exit. It shows a square-lined, classically handsome face. Piercing blue eyes backlit by an intense, inner fire. Intimidating, to say the least.

On the back jacket the negative of the same photo. Dark. Haunting, like a cold black ghost. A rather symbolic effect insomuch as the image appears, appropriately enough, to be on the verge of receding entirely into the realm of exclusive shadow.

The big picture, however, lies between the covers. Bone-white pages stamped with a curious and thematic mix of extraordinary achievement and chronic dissatisfaction—a paradox which alternately fuels the imagination and boggles the mind. There's Sinclair the artist: the musician, the poet, the painter, the filmmaker. Then there's Sinclair the man: the introvert, the wanderer, the exasperation, the relentlessly restless soul.

And, finally, Ford Sinclair . . . the fugitive fisherman.

CHAPTER ONE

The song was there—in my head.

But as it passed through my lips, and into the trumpet, it got tragically lost in translation. Out came the brassy butchering of Mary's little lamb.

Mr. Crino recoiled from the slaughter. His hands raised in self-defense.

"Woody, please," he begged me. "Stop!"

I lowered the horn. The music teacher exhaled a sigh of relief.

"Not so good, huh?" As if I had to ask.

Mr. Crino was clearly baffled. "Have you been practicing at all?"

"Yes," I answered. "Every night, religiously." And that was the sad truth. I'd spent countless hours in the barn on our family dairy farm in Bird in Hand, Pennsylvania, after the cows had been fed and put in their stalls for the night, blowing that secondhand trumpet out the upstairs hayloft door until my lips were chapped and my fingers sore. Honking in the moonlight, in desperation, and, evidently, in vain.

Mr. Crino shook his gray head. "Then I'm sorry," he said, a note of defeat in his voice as he reached into the seat pocket of his Hagar slacks. "I'm afraid you just don't have what it takes." He pulled out his wallet. He removed six ten dollar bills: the amount I'd paid for a month's worth of private lessons. "Here—" he pushed the cash towards me "—here's your money. Take it back."

"But—"

"No. No buts. Believe me, you'll be doing us both a big favor."

But I didn't want the money. I wanted to play! To share with the world the song in my heart.

"Please, Woody," Mr. Crino insisted, forcing the reimbursement into my hand. "Have mercy."

Mercy?

What about me? It seemed I was the hapless butt of some cosmic joke. A prisoner. Behind bars of unmerciful fate . . . .

It all started in 1933 with my great-grandfather, Woodrow Wilson Washborn the 1st, who had passed the farm of his Scottish immigrant boyhood dreams down to my grandfather, Woodrow Wilson Washborn II, who, in turn, had bequeathed the land to my father, Woodrow Wilson Washborn III. Which meant that I, Woodrow Wilson Washborn IV, at the dawn of the new millennium, was next in line to inherit the whole milk-sopped seventy-five acre shebang.

A prospect I dreaded almost as much as death itself.

Still, the dutiful son, I went through the motions: the daily milkings (of better than one hundred dull-eyed holsteins), the baling of hay, the endless shoveling of manure, the mundane mending of fences. And with every post I held steady, while my father swung the big hammer, I felt it was me being pounded into the ground, inch by grudging inch, every torturous blow planting me a little deeper.

I tried to fight it. When the Bird in Hand Community Theatre held auditions I was there, always; the try-outs for their revival of Arthur Miller's *Death of a Salesman* no exception.

After weeks of rehearsing in front of my bedroom mirror, I was confident that the meaty role of Biff Loman would be mine. This time I was determined to have what it took.

So there I stood, alone on the stage in the basement of the Town Grange, emblazoned by a single spotlight, a white hot circle—at that moment the very center of the universe—surrounded by darkness, only the red glow of the EXIT sign on the far back wall. The room empty but for Doc Carney and Miss Delripple seated on folding chairs in the front row. Their breathing the only sound as I began Biff's eloquently-dissatisfied monologue.

"Pop," I recited, "get this now, will you?" So far, so good. "Every time I . . ." Suddenly, inexplicably, my mind seized-up. "I . . . uh . . ." My heart started to pound. My legs weakened and shook. It was as if all the blood in my body had gone straight to my head. My ears deaf to everything except the crazy throbbing of my pulse.

I spoke louder in a frantic attempt to hear my voice above the internal uproar. "Today I realized something about myself. And I . . . uh . . ." *Damn it!* I knew the words. Hell, I knew the whole damn play by heart. What was more I'd lived it, was living it. A son intent not to follow in his father footsteps. That was me!

So why couldn't I get it out?

Drenched in a cold flop-sweat, I stopped to regroup. "I'm sorry," I said to the vague silhouettes in charge of the casting. "Can I start again?"

"You know, Woody," replied Miss Delripple, "the part of Biff Loman in really quite demanding. Perhaps you should set your sights a little lower."

I sagged.

"How low?"

This time it was Doc Carney who answered.

"We still need someone to help out with the parking."

I refused to surrender. If I didn't have a musical bone in my entire body, or the stage presence to be an actor, then I would find some other way to express myself, artistically.

When I saw a notice posted on the community bulletin board at our local A&P offering painting lessons at the Bird in Hand Public Library, I was quick to sign-up. I bought an assortment of brushes, watercolors, an easel, and a thick ream of heavyweight 36x24 inch paper . . . . Thus equipped, and fueled by a raw enthusiasm, I assumed the position—on Tuesday and Thursday nights—behind the easel in the library's classroom for Adult Education.

There were ten of us in the class; under the no-nonsense tutelage of Mrs. Lillian Kincade, former director of the Lancaster County Counsel for the Visual Arts, now retired. A tall, refined, wisp of a woman, it was rumored that the widow Kincade had, in her long ago youth, been something of a bohemian party gal in New York's Greenwich Village heyday. But from where I stood it was hard to image the lady a free-spirit. She approached our work with all the seriousness of a highbrowed critic at a major exhibition. Her M.O. was quite deliberate: she would move from one student to the next, look over a shoulder, and appraise (objectively, she'd promised) the painting-in-progress.

At least that's how she operated in respect to my classmates. To me she never said a word—just a reserved, passing glance at what I was doing as she hastened evasively down the line. No comments, no suggestions, no critique of technique or prospective. Nothing. Which I took as a positive sign. Her silence a rather discreet affirmation of my unfolding talent.

No news was good news, I figured.

So it went . . .

The first two weeks were spent on still life. We painted a wicker cornucopia of assorted fruits, a glass vase filled with different kinds of flowers, a table setting, an old wooden hobby-horse borrowed from the children's reading wing.

Although a bit timid at the beginning, my brush strokes became increasingly bolder. I honestly believed I was getting the hang of it. I swiped and swooshed and jabbed at that textured paper like a young man possessed. With every swirl of those fine nylon bristles I created colors never before seen: not-quite-banana yellows, almost-lilac blues, remotely-woodlike browns. My palate was a veritable, albeit unintentional, testament to polychromatic invention.

I was having a ball.

With the third week came a special treat—a live model: Sally

Jo Ferguson, the reigning Miss Bird in Hand, so crowned at the annual Farm Festival the previous summer. A few years younger than me, Sally Jo was bound for Penn State in the fall, and was posing now to earn some extra money to help cover the costs of the required textbooks she would need to continue her education.

College. A rite of passage I had never experienced. Although, grade-wise, having graduated from B-in-H High with a solid 3.0 GPA, I could have gotten into some very respectable universities. But the schools I was inclined to attend—each with an impressive Arts program—were predictably deemed impractical by my father, who's first (and only) choice was the Pennsylvania School of Agriculture, where, he'd decided, I could earn my degree in Animal Husbandry. Which would then be put to good use on the farm.

Anyhow, rather than major in all things bovine, I opted to forgo formal academia altogether. Cow U.? No thank you.

Of course the budding freshman Sally Jo did not pose for us in the nude. Ha! Now that would have turned our little town upside-down, good Christian folk that we were. Had word of a bared breast leaked out, well, that library would've been stormed like Doctor Frankenstein's castle.

No. Sally Jo's wonderful curves were kept entirely under the wraps of a throat-high, ankle-length, pink on blue polka-dotted Easter frock.

Then again who was I to complain? She was a pretty, willing subject; that was all that mattered.

At Mrs. Kincade's direction the model took a seat on a tall stool. She sat up straight, perfectly still with her hands folded chaste on her lap; and the class, arranged in a circle around her, went to work.

Having a front view, I concentrated primarily on the face. The smooth flesh-tones and delicate lines, watery green eyes . . .

The image was there—to be captured.

So, what happened?

The return of harsh reality, that's what.

As always Mrs. Kincade monitored our progress in succession. Orbiting outside the circle, she would stop, appraise, offer a few words of advice, encouragement, before moving on to the next student.

"Very nice," I heard her say to Mrs. Lowell, the Reverend's wife. Then "Ah. Yes. Much better" to Jim Fry, who, along with Jimmy Jr., ran Fry & Son Hardware. The remark brought a proud smile that arced ear-to-ear across Jim's bearded, bifocaled face. Beaming, he was. Like he'd just sold a gallon of weatherseal to Noah himself.

I could hardly wait for Mrs. Kincade to get to me. I was pumped, Pollyanna, primed for a much-needed dose of approval . . . . But as she passed behind me all I got was a rosy waft of her perfume. For some reason the woman seemed intent not to acknowledge my labor of love.

Only after several more laps around the room was she finally compelled to stop. I could feel her breath. A heavy, discouraging sigh on the back of my neck.

"Good Lord," she said.

Turning, I saw that her high brow was deeply furrowed, her nose wrinkled. As if she'd just caught a big whiff of something foul.

"I'm having a little trouble with her eyes," I replied, ever the optimist.

A condition which proved not in the least infectious.

Mrs. Kincade shook her head. Her pageboy hairdo swayed in a way that suggested I'd just uttered the understatement of all time.

"To be totally honest with you, Woody—" Her tone had an ominous ring, a doctor about to deliver a grim diagnosis. "—I believe the trouble lies with *your* eyes."

My eyes?

"But I have perfect twenty-twenty vision."

She nodded. Laid a sympathetic hand on my shoulder.

"Then you must see that you don't belong in this class."

It was a staggering blow. Another crack ran through my heart. The others must have heard it; I could feel their stares, boring into me. Still I couldn't bring myself to face them. Instead, I turned back to the easel. And that's when it hit me: Mrs. Kincade was right. My painting—grotesquely proportioned, in nonliving color—screamed ineptitude. Oh, it was a true portrait, all right. Only not of the fair Sally Jo.

No. What it was was a true portrait of my own futility.

Again . . . a complete, and miserable, failure.

"It was twenty years ago today," the leggy *Entertainment Tonight* blonde reported, "that Ford Sinclair—one of the most versatile artists of the 20th Century—slipped into the shadows of a baffling seclusion . . ."

It also happened to be my birthday.

" . . . In his wake Sinclair left a life marked by phenomenal accomplishment. An acclaimed pianist and composer, a Pulitzer Prize-winning playwright, a best-selling novelist, a painter who's works have adorned the walls of the world's most prestigious galleries. An Academy Award-winning filmmaker. Truly a modern Renaissance Man.

"Yet the question remains: Where is Ford Sinclair?"

"Woody," my mother called from downstairs.

I clicked off the TV.

"Kelly Ann's here."

Kelly Ann Price. My steady since the tenth grade. Six months officially engaged. To be married in exactly seventy-one days, sixteen hours and nine minutes. And counting . . . .

She was there in the kitchen with Mom and my dad, Wood, as he was affectionately known.

"Happy birthday, dear Wooooody," they sang. "Happy twentieth birthday to you!"

Kelly Ann bubbled. "Make a wish 'n blow, Woody."

Of what single young ladies there were in Bird in Hand Kelly Ann Price was considered a grand prize. With her long shiny brown hair, a cute little freckled nose, she was the thing any red-blooded country boy in his right mind dreams about.

Plus, her daddy owned one of the largest feed mills in the county.

"Quite a catch" as I was often reminded.

I closed my eyes, made the wish, and blew out all the candles on the chocolate cake Mom had baked from scratch. *Hoorah!* A round of applause from the people who loved me. Then Mom said, "Before we sit down Woody should open his presents."

"Mine first." Kelly Ann jabbed me with a small, rectangular box wrapped in fine white paper, topped with a silver bow.

I took the offering, it was cushy under the paper, a jewelry case of some sort, I gathered, and gave it a little shake.

"You'll never guess what it is. Now go on, open it."

I carefully slid off the bow. Then removed the wrap. It was a case, all right, and a nice one. And when I cracked it open out came the warm shimmer of gold.

"Oh, my," Mom cooed.

"It's solid," Kelly Ann assured us. "Twenty-four carat."

I didn't know what to say. I just stared at the piece. An elegant chain, adorned with a gold charm . . . shaped like a cow.

"Must've cost a pretty penny," Wood chimed in.

"There's an inscription on the back."

I had no choice but to turn it over.

"What does it say?"

I hesitated. Kelly Ann gave me a nudge. "Read it out loud."

I swallowed hard. "It says . . ."

It caught in my throat.

"Well?"

"It says 'Udder-ly yours. Love K.A.'"

"U*dd*erly. With two Ds. Get it?"

The pun was painfully hard to miss.

I nodded. "We get it."

"Here—let me put it on you."

I forced what I could of a smile as Kelly Ann fastened the chain around my neck.

"It's beautiful," said my mother.

Was she kidding? It was a golden calf, for Godsake!

"I just thought it was so . . . *you*."

"Yeah, well, they say it's the thought that counts."

"Really, Woody, don't you just love it?"

I lied of course.

"I do, Kel. Really. Thank you."

A polite peck on the cheek was all I could muster.

"And these are from me." Mom slid two more boxes, identically wrapped, in front of me. She always bought me clothes. This time a heavy red and white flannel shirt and a pair of bibbed blue-denim overalls. They wouldn't land me on the cover of *G.Q.*, but they didn't rub me the wrong way, either. I could put them on, take them off, no strings attached; for that I was sincerely grateful.

"Thanks, Mom."

Had the gift-giving stopped there I would have considered myself lucky. Sure, the gold cow had come as an unpleasant surprise, but it was dressy enough to put away for special occasions, the rarer the better, and then it could be hidden under my shirt.

So, up to that point I'd gotten off relatively easy. As it turned out, however, the worst was yet to come.

"I wonder what your father has for you."

I looked over at Dad. He grinned, then reached for the pocket of his Carhartt jacket hanging from a hook next to the back screen door. He pulled out a single sheet of heavy paper rolled into a scroll, tied with a festive red ribbon.

He passed it to me, baton-like. "Happy birthday, son."

The paper had a parched feel. I sensed a history behind it. Something . . . ghostly.

With all eyes on me, I reluctantly removed the ribbon. A twinge of impending doom as I unrolled the document; fixed a blank stare at the notarized formality of the boldfaced text.

"Well?" Kelly Ann pressed. "Don't keep us in suspense. What is it?"

"It's a d-deed," I stammered, feeling for the first time the full downward press of gravity. "The deed for the farm."

"I had his name added to it," Dad explained. "Like my father did when I turned twenty." He slapped a proud hand down on my shoulder. "Now it's official, son. Someday it'll all be yours."

I bit down on my lip to keep from screaming.

It was not what I had wished for.

It was all official now: the farm, my June wedding date, and the general consensus that I couldn't paint, act, or play the trumpet worth a damn.

In no mood for cake, I snuck off to the barn to brood in private.

For as long as I could remember the hayloft was where I went in search of answers. But on that day, as I sat on a dry bale, looking out at the setting sun, I felt more confused than ever.

It just wasn't fair.

I mean there I was—willing to trade my right arm for the ability to create a work of art with my left. While, somewhere, there was Ford Sinclair, who had what it took and so much more, and chose to turn his back on it all.

What a waste. No, it went beyond waste; it was a blasphemy. His God-given gifts, perhaps the most generous a man could receive, left to wither inexplicably on the vine. Was he crazy? I could fathom no other reason for it.

"Woody?" It was Kelly Ann. "I know you're in here."

It figured. Even when it came to hiding Sinclair put me to shame.

"Up in the loft," I answered.

Braving the ladder, she entered my place of refuge, and considered me through chiding eyes. "Kind of rude, don't you think—sneaking away like that?"

I nodded in agreement. "Sorry."

She sat down beside me. "Is there something bothering you?"

I didn't know where to start. Besides, she'd heard it all before;

and was either incapable of (or simply not interested in) understanding.

"No," I said. "Everything's just fine. Peachy keen."

"I know what'll make it even better." She nuzzled up to me. "A proper birthday kiss."

She pressed her soft lips to mine. Her tongue more playful than usual. I welcomed the passion, the distraction—a palliative if not a panacea.

She spoke between the kisses. "Someday we'll have a son. And I'll bake the cake. And you'll do what your father did tonight."

"What if he doesn't want it?" I panted.

"Who?"

"My son. What if he wants something else?"

"Like what?"

"He could be a scientist." I rubbed her flat belly through the thin cotton of her blouse. "Or build skyscrapers." (Freud would've had a field day with that one, given the erection rising out of my lap.)

My hand crept down toward her chest . . .

"Woody—"

I cupped a high, ripe breast.

"Woody, slow down."

"You can do it, Kel. You can be my inspiration, my muse."

"I said stop!" She pushed me away, nearly off the bale. "We agreed—not until we're married."

She had me there. The deal was no heavy stuff before our honeymoon, in Niagara Falls, Canada, where her father had a cousin in the hotel business.

I slumped. Buckling under the albatross-like weight of my prolonged virginity.

"It's only ten weeks away," she reminded me. "In the meantime you'll just have to control yourself."

That struck a nerve. Control? "Don't you see—I have no control! Over anything! My life, it's like one big puppet show!"

"I swear," she shrugged, "sometimes I have no idea what you're talking about."

"That's because you have no idea what if feels like to have a herd of cattle jammed down your throat."

"Woody, please, it's your special day. Now don't spoil it with one of your moods."

"Kel, I love my father. But I don't want to be my father."

"Then just who do you want to be?"

"Michelangelo. Ford Sinclair. I wanna have my name on something more important than the deed for a patch of dirt in Bird in Hand, Pennsylvania!"

From the way she looked at me, I might as well have been speaking Greek. "It's getting late," she said, then got to be her feet. "*Be* a gentleman and walk me to my car."

She climbed down the ladder.

"Are you coming?"

I exhaled, deflating.

Happy birthday to me.

CHAPTER TWO

"As Henry Miller said: 'Writing, like life, is a voyage of discovery.'"

Walking the aisles between our desks, Mr. Coho—a high school English teacher moonlighting as our creative writing instructor—was handing back the assignments we'd handed in the previous Wednesday night to be graded. "And as I was reading your stories over the weekend," he continued, "it struck me that many of you have well embarked on that voyage."

He paused to clear his throat.

"Then again, it was also quite evident that some of you have yet to leave the dock."

He laid my manuscript facedown on the little wooden desktop in front of me. I'd written a fictional short about a hardboiled private detective on the trail of a master jewel thief. For two exhausting weeks I'd slaved over it—typing away late into the night on the portable I'd picked-up at a flea-market until my fingertips were bruised black and blue, stopping only to pour another cup of strong coffee or consult my thesaurus for just the right word.

It was twenty-five double-spaced pages long, triple checked for spelling. A clean, crisp copy.

I flipped it over. The title page read "Hot Ice" by W.W. Washborn. Black on white. Except now there was a jarring jolt of red at the very top: Mr. Coho's critique, underlined by an emphatic slash—

UNINSPIRED! was all it said.

I didn't need the thesaurus to provide me with a synonymous conclusion. *LOSER!* popped immediately into my head. Which I hung, teary-eyed, in defeat.

W.W. WashOUT.

I stayed in my seat when the class ended. Waited until the others had filed out of the room before I approached Mr. C. for an explanation. He didn't mince words. My story, he said, lacked credibility. It was filled with pulpy cliques and my characters were paper-thin, one-dimensional. He called it a poor imitation of Dashiell Hammett and Raymond Chandler. Not my own, therefore not believable. His advice:

"Forget about the cloak and dagger stuff, Woody. Write about what you know."

What I knew? It would've seemed a less implausible suggestion had he told me to fashion a silk purse out of a cow's teat. Other than life on a diary farm in the middle of *dullsville* I didn't know a damn thing. I'd never flown in an airplane, or sailed on a boat. Had never gotten drunk or been in a real fight. The closest I'd ever come to dying was—at age nine—when I chucked a rock at a hornet's nest, and got stung a dozen times. Painful, yes, but a stupid kid covered with itchy welts and pink calamine lotion seemed hardly the fodder of great literature.

What I knew would've fit on a pastoral postcard, with room to spare.

I drove the long way home in a pouring rain. It was nearly eleven o'clock when I eased open the back door and sloshed into the kitchen. Careful not to wake my folks, I tip-toed up the stairs to my bedroom; where I sat, dripping, at my desk in front of the typewriter, and thought seriously about throwing the machine out the window.

But the rain was pelting the glass, and besides, the old Royal wasn't to blame anyhow. It was all me. The fault rested entirely on my shoulders.

I just sat there in the dark. Drenched. Drained. Demoralized.

Feeling too sorry for myself to even move. Until a *BOOM!* of thunder caused me to flinch. The dreary night sky cracked in two by a catalytic megabolt of sly white lightning.

By morning the storm had passed and the promise of a sunny spring day brightened the horizon. As usual we were up with the first rays of light. Dressed and at work in the barn even before breakfast.

Not until the milking machines had suckled every swollen teat dry did we clomp into the kitchen for our allotment of eggs and bacon. My mother was at the sink, scrubbing the frying pans while Dad sopped up his yolk with a hunk of homemade biscuit. Seated directly across from him, I hid from the daily routine— behind the amazing biography of Ford Sinclair: *Half a Life*.

"That weathervane's been up there since I was baby," Dad said between bites. "Nineteen fifty-six, I figure."

He was referring to the iron rooster atop the barn. It stood a good three feet tall, perched on an arrow that turned to point whichever way the wind was blowing. The vane was on Dad's mind only because it had been struck by lightning during the storm, and was now teetering precariously on the nearly fifty-foot high peak. Another strong gust and it was bound to come down, a gritty, beak-first slide off the steep, shingled roof.

"Fifty-six," I replied. "That was the year Ford Sinclair recorded his first jazz album."

It seemed a smooth enough segue. But Dad, true to form, wanted no part of it. "Since when do we read at the table? Put that book away."

"Sorry."

I closed the bio and set it aside. That would have been the end of it had Dad not felt compelled to share with us his irreverent take on my choice of reading material.

"Artists," he grumbled. "Bunch'a drunks, dopers and fruitcakes."

It was a jab I couldn't let go uncountered.

"And what kind of world would this be without them? Art is freedom, vision, beauty, imagination. The exploration the human spirit."

"It doesn't feed, doesn't shelter. We'd survive without it."

I tried an appeal to his financial sense.

"One hit song, or one great painting—it would bring in more money than a thousand head of cattle."

"How many times I gotta tell you, you don't sow a dairyman and reap an artist."

Too many times. Still I could not bring myself to believe it.

"If I just had someone to show me what it takes—"

"And if you had wings you could fly," Dad scoffed. "But a bird's a bird and a Washborn's a Washborn. You are what you are, got what you got. That's all there is to it."

"What about Mom? She was Amish until she met you."

"Your mother left the flock but she still lives off the land."

"What did Ford Sinclair's folks so?" Mom asked, drying her hands on her apron.

"They ran a traveling circus," I answered.

"Showmen!" Dad slapped down his folk. "Like father, like son." He pushed away from the table. "Now you can go bring in those bales while I get that rooster back on its feet."

Mom cautioned him, "Careful on that roof, Wood."

"Maybe I'll run off and join the circus," he teased. "Then my boy can be a clown."

Very funny. He thought so anyhow. His laugh lingered like the smell of bacon grease even after he'd gone out the back door. I turned to Mom. She was smiling, but not at my expense. A thin, tight smile; Her baby had a big boo boo, and all her kisses would not make it go away.

She understood. Better than I did, it seemed.

"Whatever you do, Woody—" her tone warm, instinctively maternal "—don't let go of your dreams."

I reached out and took her hand. It was much smaller than mine. Still, behind it, there was a much stronger sense of self. I held on, hoping that some of it would rub off.

"The problem is my dreams won't let go of me."

The thing about farm work, for better or worse, is that the wide-open space allows for some deep reflection. As I bounced along on the tractor, stopping every few yards to hop off and toss another hay bale on the wagon, I thought back to what my father had said: about me being a clown.

On the upside, Ford Sinclair had been a clown, literally, for the first ten years of his life. Little Omo the Clown, in grease paint under the Big Top. He was part of the midget act. They would drive around the center ring in a tiny car, a seemingly impossible number of them piling out to tickle the local funny-bones with broad slapstick and wacky tumbling routines.

Until Sinclair outgrew the act. In more ways than one.

On the downside, there was Woody the Clown. Mad with ambition and, sadly, without talent. My pie in the face.

That's what I was thinking on that unseasonably warm mid-May morning as I labored stoically in the field. Not a cloud in sky to suggest that my world was about to experience a change so sudden, so dramatic, it continues to elude my full comprehension even now.

Out of the blue. Indeed. The tri-polar mood swings of fate. One minute it's smiling on you, the next it's laughing at you. And then there are those moments—as if to refute all claims of predictability—when fate just grins. Pokerfaced. *Ambiguous.*

Had the hay been dry I would have stacked the bales four high. But they were soaked from the rain (my fault: I'd neglected to move them indoors before the storm hit, intent as I was on getting to my writing class on time) and too heavy to lift above my head. Three high was all I could manage. A concession I'm sure wasn't lost on my father, who was standing on the roof of the barn, returning the old iron rooster to its lofty perch.

I watched him from the distance. He straddled the peak, muscling the vane back into place. A noble silhouette against an endless backdrop of blue sky. Entirely within his element.

And I resented him for it. If only . . .

My train of thought was suddenly derailed by a premonition. A split-second before it happened, I saw the shingle come loose, slide out from under Dad's work boot. He flailed his arms in a desperate attempt to reclaim his balance, but to no avail, it was lost, he was going down. Unless—

He grabbed hold of the weathervane, a last-ditch effort. Only to have it break free in his hand. "Dad!" He went down, still clutching the rooster, a crazy tumble of flesh and iron. I bolted across the field. "Dad!"

They went off the roof together. A long thirty-foot drop before they landed in a heap on the soggy ground. "Dad!"

He was curled on his side facing away from me. I sank to my knees. Laid a trembling hand on his shoulder. "Dad?"

When he didn't move I eased him onto his back. That's when I saw it. The arrow. It was lodged deep into his belly. The tee-shirt around it soaked with blood.

"Oh God." A chill ran through my body. "Dad."

He looked up at me. Blood trickled out the corner of his mouth. He willed himself to speak, and then managed barely a whisper:

"You see, son . . . no wings."

I shivered. Waited for more. What? I didn't know. A soliloquy in extremis, perhaps. Or some resonant death-scene music. An apparent transcendence of soul. At the very least a rumble of acknowledgment from the heavens.

But there came no monologue. No swan song. No crescendo from above.

My father simply closed his eyes. Exhaled the last breath of his life.

CHAPTER THREE

"Wood Washborn was a *great* man," the Reverend Lowell eulogized from his pulpit beside the open casket, the satin-lined mahogany box where my father was laid out, in state; looking 'natural'—or so I was told by the steady stream of mourners who came to pay their final respects.

For three long days we had gathered at the funeral home. A montage of doleful faces that included Kelly Ann, with her family, my proposed in-laws, headed by Big Bill Price.

Also on hand were Mr. and Mrs. Arnold, our nearest neighbors, who farmed with their five boys up the road. Rob Dobson from the bank. Hank, our postman. Along with the dozen or so relatives on Dad's side who lived within driving distance.

Then, on the fourth day, it was Standing Room Only for the pre-burial service at the Church of the Good Shepherd. Where, from my point of view, Dad looked anything but natural.

His face was tightly drawn, cheeks sunken, rouged in some sad simulation of slumbering health. I couldn't remember the last time I'd seen him in a suit and tie, his "monkey duds" as he always called them. No, he'd never looked more un-natural. Like a mannequin, made of wax. Hollow. Dead.

"He was a great friend," the Reverend continued, "a great neighbor, a great farmer. And, most importantly, Wood Washborn was a great husband to his devoted Eliza."

I heard Mom sigh behind her black veil.

"As well as a great father to his son and namesake, Woodrow Wilson Washborn the Fourth."

Mom squeezed my hand. How she found the strength I don't know. The way she had wailed at the sight of his lifeless body on the ground, hysterically; and then the draining shock that followed the official pronouncement of death. After that she'd retreated inside herself, oblivious to all but her own grief.

The firmness of her grip was a good sign. She was pulling herself back out . . . .

From the church we went directly to the cemetery. Again the Reverend Lowell presided—reading dark passages from his Bible as my father's coffin was lowered into the ground, to an early grave on a plot of green lawn where three generations of Washborns had now been laid to rest.

It was, of course, an intrinsically solemn affair. Made all the more surreal by the presence of my maternal relations, who'd been notably absent from the earlier proceedings. A curious clan standing off by themselves—reticent, austere, anachronistic in their Amish-ness.

Although we lived only a few miles apart I barely knew them. My Grandfather Lapp: tall, angular, unflinching behind his long gray beard, dressed, like the other men, my uncles, in a simple black woolen suit, his wide-brimmed hat removed in acknowledgment of the deceased—a man he'd denounced with dogmatic resolve in life for the stealing of his only daughter.

Beside him stood Grandmother Lapp. Her face creased but still quite lovely, an older version of my mom, trimmed in a plain black bonnet . . . . Despite the years of humble subsistence there was a stubborn dignity about them. In horse-drawn carriages they joined the slow procession of motorcars as it followed the two-lane garden path back to the farm.

Lady friends of my mother had volunteered to remain at the house and ready a wake-styled buffet. It was laid out on the dining room table with paper plates and soft drinks, sobriety being the overriding theme of the day.

For my part, I played the consoled host. All the while wishing everyone would just go home. And if things weren't depressing enough, Grandpa Lapp decided the occasion was right for our first man-to-man chat. He pulled me aside, and with a heavy, calloused hand on my shoulder, he said, in a deep, Dutch-flavored voice, "Da sweat 'n blood of your father and forefathers have nourished dis land. Now it is your turn. To keep the past alive."

It was the most he had spoken to me at one time, the first time he'd ever stepped foot in our house. It was all too much.

"Excuse me, Grandfather. I'd better go check on Mom."

I beat a hasty retreat into the kitchen. There I was immediately wrapped in a weepy bear-hug by Miss Ada Pierce, the grandam of the local 4-H Club, to which my dad had belonged since he was a kid. "Oh, Woody," the old woman bawled. "I remember when little Wood won his first blue ribbon at the county fair. He was such a—sucha—sucha beeeuuutiful boy!"

I patted her bony back "I know, Miss Ada" and tried to extricate myself from her sobbing embrace. But she hung on; so I signaled to Kelly Ann, who came right over and cut in—

"Come on, Miss Ada," she said, gently prying the sweet old maid off me. "Let's go get you a nice cup of tea."

A cup, a pot, a thermos to go, whatever, I thought, just keep her away from my mother. Mom didn't need anymore hysterics. Speaking of Mom . . .

"She's out back," answered Mrs. Arnold, cinching a big green garbage bag full of dirty plates, "with my husband."

I crossed to the screen door and pushed it open to find Mom and Bo Arnold seated at the picnic table off the back porch. They looked up from what appeared to be a rather serious conversation.

"Everything all right out here, Mom?"

She nodded wearily.

"As right as can be expected under the circumstances."

"Gotta keep a stiff upper lip," said Mr. Arnold. "That's what your pa would want."

Indeed. Dad certainly wasn't one for flagrant displays of

emotion. If he had ever broke down and cried it wasn't in front
of me. I could image him at that very moment, watching us
from beyond the clouds, grumbling, *Enough with the moping
already! There's work to be done!*

"Well, as long as you're okay . . ."

"I will be," Mom assured me.

"Then I'd better go check on the stock."

"Don't you worry about those animals." Bo Arnold waved it
away. "My boys'll give 'em a snack and tuck 'em in."

Mom managed a little smile. "It's been an exhausting day.
Why don't you go upstairs and rest for a while."

"But—"

"I'll call if I need you. Now go on. You deserve a break."

"Are you sure?"

"Listen to your mother, Woody. She knows what's best."

I did as I was told.

In the solitude of my room I closed the door on the voices
downstairs. I put some early Sinclair—*Buster Live in Paris*—on
the record player, and then flopped onto the bed. The sweet jazz
a welcomed relief from the bitter wind that was blowing me
into the future.

Still, between the magical fusion of notes, the mundane vision
persisted: my sweat and blood, valued only as fertilizer for the
fields, keeping the past alive. I could see no way around it now. It
seemed my destiny to grow old on that paltry parcel of land. My
world confined to seventy-five all-too-square acres. Where my
hair would turn gray, my face fossilized by a perennial farmer's
weatherburn. With Kelly Ann, my levelheaded bride, baking
birthday cakes to mark the passing years.

Were these the ingredients that went into the making of a
great man?

I thought not.

Wood Washborn was a *good* man. An honorable man. A man
of quiet integrity. But "great?" Only in eulogy. In life he had

never aspired to, nor achieved, as I saw it, greatness. He was content, and it cost him his wings. Being good was good enough for Woodrow Wilson Washborn III.

The rest of us would just have to live with that.

Mom was right; I was exhausted. I fell asleep to "Buster's Island Dream." It must have given me a vicarious release, because on that sojourn through the Land of Nod I didn't dream. Time simply jumped ahead. A few fleeting hours of somnolent nothingness.

I was awakened by a faint knock at the door. My eyes opened to the soft red tones of sunset. All was quiet but for the gentle rapping. "Come in," I answered.

It was Mom. She poked her head into the room.

"Everybody's gone," she said.

"I'm sorry. I must've dozed off."

"Good for you." She stepped inside. "Last time we had that many people over was on our wedding day. Only back then your Grandpa Lapp wanted no part of it."

She'd been shunned. Ostracized by the Amish community for falling in love with the handsome "outsider" she met while selling homemade bread at the crossroads on the outskirts of town.

I envied her will—unbreakable even under the threat of severed ties. It had taken a lot of guts. The courage to brave the forbidden, the unknown.

"It must've been pretty scary for you. Leaving your home, your family, the culture you were raised in."

She sat on the bed beside me.

"Sometimes you just have to follow your heart."

"Yeah, well, easier said than done."

She looked me straight in the eye.

"Woody, I know how you feel about this farm."

"Mom, don't worry. You planted a Washborn, you got a Washborn. I'll make the best of it."

She studied me for a moment. Behind her eyes I could see the wheels turning, there was something on her mind, something she had to share but wasn't sure how to begin. She got up and crossed to the window, looking out across the grazed grass pastures that stretched like a plush green carpet to the horizon.

"I had an interesting talk with Bo Arnold," she said, choosing the words carefully. "He made us an offer."

Huh? "An offer for what?"

"The land, the house, livestock, everything. Two hundred and fifty thousand dollars."

Everything? The part about the money went over my head. If she'd said we'd been offered the moon it would've seemed no less conceivable. It was the implications of "everything" that defied my imagination.

"Uhhh . . . what did you tell him?"

"That it's a fair price." She turned to face me. "But I'd have to get your approval."

"You mean you'd sell?"

"Without your father we'd only be going through the motions." Again her gaze went out the window. The last rays of the sun painted her a sad shade of red. "This place deserves more than that."

"What about us? Where would we go?"

"I could get a little house in town. And with your share you could find something that better suits you."

I just sat there with my mouth open, stunned. She was serious—at a crossroads again, another decision to be made. Only this time she was leaving it up to me: Which way shall we go?

I hesitated.

"How long do we have to decide?"

She came over to me. Took my face in her hands.

"However long you need." She kissed my forehead then turned away. She was halfway out when I asked—

"If we decide to do it, how long would it take?"

She stopped, looked back over her shoulder.

"In this case I think it's easier done than said."

She closed the door behind her. Suddenly the room felt strange, as though I was seeing it—if not for the first time—from a new and dizzying perspective.

Wow.

Three weeks later it was a done deal. The Arnolds—using their nearly two hundred working acres as collateral—had secured a business loan from the bank for the sum of two hundred and fifty thousand dollars. Rob Dobson handled the paperwork, which had been signed and processed without a hitch. That made it official:

The Washborn legacy was now a thing of the past.

Chipper Arnold, the eldest of the five boys, was set to move into the house, along with his wife, Jude, who was six months pregnant with their third child, as soon as we could pack up and move out.

I had given Mom my answer the morning after the funeral. The decision was never really in doubt, but still I'd tossed and turned on it all night long; haunted, as I was, by a vision of my father rolling over in his grave. I felt guilty, ungrateful, that I'd opted too readily for betrayal. It weighed heavy on my conscience.

Mom was there to lessen the load. After all, she consoled, the farm would continue to be what it was intended to be: a family-run operation. It would be well cared for, the ethic behind it essentially unchanged. Furthermore, and most importantly, the Arnolds wanted it; and I did not. That alone, she assured me, was ample justification for going ahead with the sale.

As for her, at forty-three, she was still young enough to pick up the pieces and go on with her life. The first priority was to find somewhere else to live, and as luck would have it there was a pretty little two-bedroom cottage on the market. Just a short walk from downtown Bird in Hand, it was cozy, convenient, and solidly built. Rolling decisively with the punches, Mom bought it without waver, paying in full on the very same day that she landed a job as a hostess at the new Cracker Barrel due to open mid-summer. Despite the fact that her independence had been forced upon her, Eliza Washborn was not about to play the helpless widow. On the contrary, she accepted the challenge like the capable, resilient woman who had struck, and sustained, my father's ever-practical fancy.

I, on the other hand, was at something of a loss. My immediate future adrift in a fog of uncertainty. The obvious choices were: A) move in with Mom until the wedding, or, B) use my share of the money to buy the redwood ranch house Kelly Ann had already picked out for us. The problem was that both options seemed on line with a missed opportunity. A waste of the few weeks of freedom fate had allowed me. So, I procrastinated. Deciding to put off my decision for as long as possible.

There was one thing, however, I felt had to be done. On the morning of our last day, while Mom was still busy packing, I dragged out the big extension ladder and leaned it up against the side of the barn. I then climbed the wooden rungs with one hand as I carried the iron rooster in the other. The least I could do was finish the job my father had started: return the Washborn weathervane to its place of prominence.

I scaled the pitched roof to its peak. I sunk four large screws through the rough asphalt shingles and into the thick ridge beam below, until the angled iron base was securely fastened, and the venerable cock again stood tall. Free to follow the prevailing caprice of the wind.

I stepped back and watched it turn. With a squeak it revolved a full one hundred and eighty degrees to face the road. The bloodstained arrow pointed due south. In the direction of a long yellow moving van coming for what remained of our life on the farm.

"Daddy says you can start on the loading dock," said Kelly Ann. We were seated on the front porch swing, swaying slowly back and forth as the men from the moving company loaded our belongings into the truck. "With business booming like it is you'll get plenty of overtime."

They had it all figured out. I would join the Price family at the Feed & Seed. My job to haul burlap bags heavy with wholesale banality. From dawn to dusk. And if that wasn't enough to break both back and spirit, there was now the added promise of grueling overtime.

Kelly Ann went on, "Since we have the money we might as well buy the house flat out. There's no sense in paying interest on a mortgage."

My head dropped into my hands. "No, it makes no sense. Nothing makes sense. Least of all leaving my father's farm to work in your father's mill?"

"Woody, it's a good job, with good benefits and a good future."

"Good . . . but not great."

"You could do a lot worse. So don't look a gift horse in the mouth. Because when daddy retires in a few years—"

"What did you say?"

"He's planning to turn everything over to my brothers and me. Which means you and I will be in charge of running the office."

"No, you said 'don't look a gift horse in the mouth.'"

"It's an expression. Don't nitpick when someone's being generous."

Suddenly the fog in my head began to dissipate. It came as a revelation, my first, a vision so clearly defined I could see my reflection in its eyes. It was channeling me—transmitting the simple wisdom of yet another equine-inspired proverb.

"Kel, have you ever heard the one about getting it straight from the horse's mouth?"

"Yeah. What about it?"

"It makes a lot of sense too, don't you think?"

"But it has nothing to do with what we're talking about."

I turned to her. Lit by the glow of my grand awakening she never looked prettier.

"Kel, it has everything to do with what I'm talking about."

I kissed her like a G.I. on V-E Day. Then I swung to my feet and bolted into the house.

"MOM?"

"I'm in the kitchen."

I found her at the china cabinet, wrapping the heirloom gravy boat in newspaper. "Mom, it just came to me! I know what I have to do!"

"And what's that, dear?"

"I have to get it straight from the horse's mouth!"

She tilted her head. "Get what? From which horse?"

"Ford Sinclair. He knows the secret. What it takes to be an artist."

She was understandably perplexed.

"Even if he does. Isn't Ford Sinclair . . . hiding somewhere?"

"That's what I'm gonna do. I gonna go find him!"

I had her full attention now. But before she could respond Kelly Ann beat her to it—

"You can't be serious."

I turned to my fiancée framed in the archway.

"Kel, I'm desperate. I gotta at least try."

"What about the wedding, our plans?"

"Just once why can't I have a plan of my own?"

"Because it's too crazy to even consider. Tell 'im, Mrs. Washborn."

"It does sound rather farfetched."

"You see, your mother agrees with me."

"Then again," Mom added, "if you have to get something out of your system, it's best to do it while you're young."

"Three weeks, that's all I'm asking for."

"You can't just show up at the altar! There's the fittings, rehearsals. Three weeks is three weeks too long!"

"Okay, so we'll push the date back a few days."

"So you can indulge some pipe dream—no! I am not going to put my life on hold while you're off on a wild goose chase!"

"Please, Kel, this could be my only chance."

"In more ways than one. Because if you go don't expect me to wait!"

I looked to Mom for help. All she could do was shrug. The choice had to be mine, and mine alone. Whatever the consequences I would have to take the full responsibility.

Tugging at my leash, Kelly Ann delivered her ultimatum.

"Woody, enough is enough. Now it's either Ford Sinclair or me."

I took a moment to think it over. Weighing the pros and cons . . .

"So, who's it gonna be?" Kelly Ann pressed.

Her heaviness tipped the scales decidedly. In favor of the crazy, the farfetched, the mad and impetuous heart.

"I'm sorry, Kel. But I gotta go."

There came an unexpected silence. The room cooled as the emotion drained from Kelly Ann's face. Her eyes narrowed, the muscles in her jaw tightened. A look that said, *I'm not going to make a scene. Why should I? It will be, after all, your loss.*

I knew then it was over. The "good catch" was about to get away. And I had neither the right, nor the inclination, to stop her. I just stood there, watching without protest as she tugged the gold engagement band off her finger, and placed it on the countertop.

"When you get back," she said, "don't bother to call me."

She turned and left the room. I could still see her through the archway as she fell in behind the moving men. Following, of all things, a love seat out the front door.

A few days later I stopped by the Price house to face the music. Kelly Ann refused to see me, but her father gave me an earful. He called me a fool, a slacker, an ingrate, immature. He said my head was so far up my ass it was lost in the clouds. Good riddance to me!

I stood sheepishly on the front stoop and took the barrage, no rebuttal. When he ran out of invectives, I gave him the gold chain with the cow-shaped charm in the hope that Kelly Ann could return it, or at least trade it in for something that wasn't so . . . me.

I reimbursed him for the down payment on the hall he'd reserved for the wedding reception. He took the cash, told me I was a disgrace to the Washborn name. Then he slammed the door in my face.

It could have been worse, I suppose. Given the embarrassment I'd caused all involved, I justly deserved a good rump kicking. So it was with a sense of having gotten off relatively unscathed that I drove back to the quaint little cottage Mom now called home. Where I proceeded to pack for my quixotic journey into terra incognita.

CHAPTER FOUR

"Are you sure you want to do this?" Mom asked for the hundredth time as I carried my suitcase out to the truck.

"I'm sure I'll regret it if I don't." I tossed the bag onto the passenger seat.

The old pickup was tuned up, gassed up, ready to roll. I had a thousand dollars in cash and a shiny new credit card in my pocket. Whatever the cost, I was financially prepared for my flight of fancy. As for the mental and physical aspects of the odyssey, I could only hope to have what it would take.

Now free from all commitments, I had no reason to hurry back. I could extend my search indefinitely. Go wherever the trail led me. It was an equally liberating and daunting proposition.

Of course Mom was fraught with worry. Her babe was about to wander in the woods; ill-prepared, she feared, to face the wolves, the snakes, the Darwinian-wise predators just waiting for a country bumpkin to blunder into their reach.

"It's a wild world out there, Woody," she warned me, her eyes welling with tears. "Don't take any chances. If you have even the slightest doubt, please, just turn around and come home."

"I'll be careful, Mom. I promise."

"Is there anything I can say to change your mind?"

"No. There's nothing anybody can say. Although I'd appreciate it if you wished me luck."

She smiled obligingly. "I wish you everything you hope to find."

We hugged. She planted a teary kiss on my cheek, reluctant to let go. When she finally did it was a clean break. She pulled away and took a deep, resigned breath. "Now you'd better take off before I start blubbering."

"I love you, Mom."

"And I have faith in you," she said.

Faith . . . in me! It was exactly what I needed to hear. Even if she was a denomination of one.

I climbed into the driver's seat and turned the key, and the truck came to life—two hundred fuel injected horses under the hood, all chomping at the bit in anticipation of the hunt. *Tally ho!* With Ford Sinclair the fox.

I was invigorated, in control, in gear. I pulled out of the driveway and headed north. I honked the horn, a declaration. Two resonant blasts to signal the commencement of my expedition.

Sinclair was born a nomad—on the road with the Big Little Circus—and remained one for the entirety of his documented life. So I'd decided to conduct my search chronologically. To follow the paper trail and see what clues I could pick up along the way.

On the I-78, bound for New York City, where Sinclair, at age sixteen, first entered the public's consciousness, playing big time jazz in hot time Harlem, I tried to isolate the ingredients that had produced such a phenomenal talent.

I knew from the biography he'd come into the world aboard a bus parked on the side of a road, an interstate not unlike the one I was now traveling. The bus was part of a caravan that included the canvas-topped trucks used to transport and shelter the elephants, lions, horses, chimpanzees—highly-trained animal acts—symbolic of the exoticism and wonder that came with the circus.

The story went that Carmen Sinclair gave birth to the ten-pound bundle of genius on March 12, 1940. In the dead of night, just south of Richmond, Virginia, with Ford's Scottish immigrant father, Angus Sinclair, by her side. An acrobatic dwarf named Teeny Teena serving as midwife.

Also on hand for the blessed event: Tabu, the Tattooed Man, covered from the soles of his feet to the top of his bald head by a magnificently miniaturized reproduction of the ceiling of the Sistine Chapel, Michelangelo's masterpiece. The depiction of God touching Adam's finger, bringing him to life, indelibly inked onto Tabu's prominent forehead.

And there was Otis "Oats" Sleet. A black New Orleans Jazz cat, hired on to lead the three-piece Big Little Band, it was Sleet who would introduce little Buster to the piano he went on to charm so precociously.

Rounding out the happy ensemble, Alice Faye Sinclair. She was five years old when her baby brother arrived. "Whadda we gonna call him?" she had asked over the newborn's hungry cries.

"Seein' he was born in a bus," Oats suggested, "how bout Buster?"

"Buster Ford," Tabu chimed in. "Being it's a Ford bus and all."

"Ford," Carmen echoed, the infant suckling at her breast. "Ford Buster."

As legend has it, the name barely left Carmen's lips when there sounded the thunderous roar of a lion. Which was enough for Angus. Who, in his deep ringmaster's brogue, proceeded to announce—"Ladieees and Gentlemannn, the Big Little Circus is proud to present:

"FORD . . . BUSTER . . . SINCLAIRRR!"

It was mid-afternoon when I passed through the Holland Tunnel and came out on the island of Manhattan. I'd never seen anything like it. The streets clogged with yellow taxicabs, sidewalks thick with people of every size, shape, color. A regular rat race, as my father would've called it.

Still, despite the idea of a "melting pot," there was a very strong sense of individuality in the air. Like a moving mosaic made from distinctly singular components. The way they rubbed against each other, it seemed to generate a sort of static electricity that held it all together.

It quickened my pulse. To the blare of horns and sirens and crisscrossing voices I drove north in bumper-to-bumper traffic, along the concrete canyon known as the Avenue of the Americas. I passed Madison Square Garden and the Empire State Building, familiar landmarks where tourists gathered to marvel at the history and extravagance of human ingenuity.

I wasn't a tourist, however. I was young man on a mission. Resisting the urge to stop and take in the sights, I continued on to 43rd Street. Where I found what I was looking for. *The New York Times* building.

Now semi-retired, Arthur Brimm retained an office on the third floor. When the lady at the reception desk in the lobby called up to announce my arrival Mr. Brimm was at first reluctant to see me. Only after I dropped Sinclair's name was his curiosity sufficiently aroused.

I rode the elevator to the sixth floor. When I stepped out a tall, white-haired figure dressed in a dandy pale-blue suit and lavender bow tie waved me down the hall.

"Mr. Brimm?" I asked, approaching.

"Yes. And your name again?"

"Woodrow." I extended my hand. "Woodrow Washborn."

"Put your hand down, Woodrow. Microphobia."

"Microphobia?"

"Germs. This city's a breeding ground."

"Oh, right. Sorry." I kept my distance.

Stepping aside, the biographer gestured into his office.

"You can use my sink to scrub up."

I entered with my hands in the air and was immediately struck by the smell. Lysol, Clorox, ammonia—a sterilizing potpourri— ineffectually sweetened by some faint flowery deodorizer. It nearly knocked me back. My eyes watered as Brimm closed the door behind him.

"Use the hot water." He pointed to a little washroom beyond a wall of books. "Open a fresh bar of soap. When you're done wrap it in paper towels and drop it in the waste basket."

"Yes, sir."

After several minutes of meticulous antibacterial hygiene my hands passed inspection. I took a seat in front an immaculately neat desk. Seated behind it, Arthur Brimm looked every bit the dapper arts maven

"I've been singing the praises of Ford Sinclair since I joined the paper as a music critic back in '56," he said after I'd explained to him the reason for my visit. "But as I wrote in the book we've never had a conversation. Even back then Sinclair didn't give interviews."

I noticed a picture frame hanging prominently on the wall behind him. There was a piece of notepaper under the spotless glass. I pointed to it. "Is that it . . . the letter?"

"Certainly is." Brimm swiveled around to look at it. "Postmarked Mexico City." Very carefully, he took it down, then swiveled again to face me. "April 17, 1980. You read that the F.B.I. verified it."

"Yes, sir. It put to rest the rumors of foul play."

He handed it to me over the desk. Sure enough there it was: *To whom it may concern . . . Gone fishing . . . Sincerely, Ford Sinclair.*

I examined it closely. The crisp cursive suggested a steady hand, the author evidently free of hesitancy or doubt. I wondered what he was thinking when he wrote it. Had he realized the irrationality of what he was about to do?

Brimm seemed to read my mind. "I've always pictured a mischievous grin on his face as he was penning it."

Looking up to meet the old gentleman's gaze, I posed the pressing question. "And after all your research—you still have no idea where he might be?"

He shook his head lamentably. "Not a clue."

"But someone must know something."

He shrugged. "I interviewed his lawyers, accountants, family, friends, colleagues. They all claimed to be in the dark. And I've found no reason not to believe them."

He reached for the letter. Handing it back, I said, "Quite an honor, his last public statement addressed to you."

He smiled at that. "In the land of the blind the one-eyed man is king. And the two-eyed man . . . is Ford Sinclair."

As I watched him return the relic to its place of honor on the wall, it dawned on me that the man's appreciation of Sinclair went beyond the professional. He not only loved the art, he was in love with the artist. After more than forty years he was still carrying a star-struck, homo-romantic torch.

"So why do you think he did it?" I asked. "Take off, I mean?"

"I've asked that question a thousand times," Brimm replied, adjusting the frame until it hung perfectly straight. "Some believe he felt exploited. Others that he couldn't handle the pressure, the expectations. Then there are those who assume that he simply ran out of things to say."

"And you?"

"I don't know," he confessed. "Maybe he just got tired."

Burnout? Could it be as prosaic as that? I wondered.

"You wrote in the book that his parents are dead. What about his sister, is she still living?"

"Ah, yes, Alice Faye. Alive but not quite with us, I'm afraid."

He reached down, pulled open a bottom desk drawer, and took out a can of disinfectant. "She lives right here in the city." He got up from his chair and began spraying about the room. "She spends her days in Washington Square Park. Feeding the birds," he informed me, his head in a gray-white cloud of obsessive fumigation.

"A very strange girl, indeed."

Compared to the air in Brimm's office, the smog outside on the street proved downright refreshing. As I dodged my way along the sidewalk, with its multitude of invisible germs, I thought how easy it would be to get lost in the pedestrian shuffle. A person would have to go to some great length to stand out in such a crowd. Otherwise it would be like finding a needle in a haystack. A tough chore. Even if the needle shined with the brilliance of Ford Sinclair.

Tougher yet given that, despite his fame, Sinclair had managed to remain mostly behind the scenes, his face far less well known than his works. The shadow he'd cast, and a long one it was, seemed to come from an almost disembodied source. His contact with the public had been kept to an absolute minimum: those rare occasions, many years ago, when he'd taken the stage with his jazz band, or to act in one of his plays. He was young then, a teenager in the music halls of Europe. Just twenty-three when he last performed on Broadway.

After that he'd maintained an even lower profile. By the time he disappeared few people would have recognized him on the street. It was conceivable that he could have simply dissolved into the mix of some metropolitan stew.

Still, it seemed unlikely. The news of his disappearance was widely reported. His picture plastered in newspapers, on television. And when the letter surfaced it only served to further fire a collective curiosity. It stirred people's imaginations, became a quirky human-interest story. His extreme desire for anonymity had, in effect, made him more conspicuous

Was that his intention? A publicity stunt? If so, to what end? After all, he never returned to reap any benefit from the action.

I took notice of every passing middle-aged male face as I walked to the underground garage where I'd parked the pickup for ten dollars an hour. I saw a man who looked a lot like my father but nobody who even remotely resembled Sinclair.

Consulting my map of the city, I located Washington Square Park. It was downtown, in Greenwich Village. I went south on Broadway. Slow going in the rush hour traffic. Sometime later, I turned onto a narrow side-street, and proceeded to get lost in the jumble of old brick arteries that give The Village its quasi-quaint charm.

At one point I stopped to ask a friendly-looking blond lady

standing next to a lamppost in a short black leather dress and
high heels for directions to the park. She told me to just follow
her legs, then pulled up her dress and flashed me a matching
blond pubis. "Here's your park," she said, and let out a wickedly
witchy laugh as I sped away.

On my own, by trail and error, I finally happened upon an
open space with a patch of green. Washington Square. I drove
around it several times until I found a parking spot. There was
music in the air, reggae, coming from a grassy area where a circle
of dreadlocked black men were simultaneously dancing and
kicking around a soccer ball. They paid me no mind as I walked
passed them toward the paved center of the park, where a diverse
congregation of Manhattanites had taken refuge from the hustle
and bustle of the city. There were old men playing checkers,
shirtless boys on skateboards, women pushing baby strollers, bag
ladies and bum-types on scarred wooden benches basking in the
sunshine. Jugglers, sketch-artists, baby-boomers in sharp business
suits hunched over laptop computers. Food venders hawked
hotdogs, shish kabobs and flavored ices.

Yet no sight of the strange bird woman Arthur Brimm had
said I would find here on any given day.

Then I saw several pigeons fly just overhead. I followed them.
They flapped their way to a remote, tree-shaded corner of the
park, where they joined a great obfuscation of birds—flocked
around a lone figure standing under a wide-brimmed sunbonnet.

Approaching the swarm, I saw that it was in fact a woman.
An older woman, very thin, fragile-looking, wearing a long black
raincoat with white polka dots. She had birds perched on her
shoulders and one on her hat as she reached her hand into a sort
of haversack, then tossed seed to the feathered throng on the
ground.

"Miss Sinclair?" I asked from the perimeter.

She looked over at me. The hat was secured to her head by a
silky scarf tied under her chin. It framed a ghostly-pale, deeply
wrinkled face.

"Excuse me but are you Alice Faye—"

"Stay away!" The birds fluttered at the squawk of her voice. "You'll scare my babies!"

I realized then that the white spots on her coat weren't polka dots. They were bird droppings. Consistent with Brimm's allusion of strangeness.

"I was hoping we could talk," I persisted. "About your brother."

Her blue eyes got suddenly bright. "Fordie. Have you seen Fordie?"

"No, ma'am. At least not in person." I stepped closer. "I'd sure like to, though."

"That boy," she said, "always running off. If he doesn't come back soon he's gonna miss the show. Father said he could be Omo tonight. Omo the Clown."

"Tonight?"

"I get to shoot the cannon. Little Miss Liberty." She raised a clenched hand above her head, held the pose.

It threw me for a moment. Then I remembered, it was in the book. How it was Alice's job to fire a cannon that shot confetti into the air over the audience. A task she performed dressed like the Statue of Liberty, using the torch to light the fuse.

I was watching a ten-year-old girl in possession of a sixty-five-year-old body. It gave me a touch of the willies. "So . . . uh . . . have you heard from Fordie lately?" I knew from the bio that he'd established a trust fund to support her. "A phone call, or a letter maybe?"

Her hand dropped into the sack. "Pigeons are very smart, you know. They can deliver mail."

"Yes, ma'am, I've heard that."

"Here—"

The next thing I knew seed was raining down on me. Immediately the birds swarmed. I felt their tiny feet on my head, my shoulders. I froze.

"See—they love you too."

I stood like a cringing statue as their pointed beaks picked the seed out of my hair, off my clothes. "We were talking about Fordie, ma'am."

"They say he went fishing. But what do they know? I bet he's at the Gum Drop. Playin' Jam Boogie with Oats and the boys."

"The Gum Drop. In Harlem?"

She started to sing "Bop bop, jam boogie . . ." and dance, slowly, careful not frighten her flock " . . . bop bop, jam boogie . . ."

"Miss Sinclair—"

" . . . bop bop, jam boogie . . ."

"Alice, can we—"

" . . . bop bop, jam boogie . . ."

It was no use. She was already gone, deep into some private inner space, a world all her own. Far away and back in time.

Leaving her to bop bop with her "babies," I turned and shooed the pigeons off me. As I crossed the park toward the truck, my thoughts went in another direction, drawn to a basic principle of heredity, that siblings—a brother and sister—are genetically the same. I pondered the idea of a thin line between madness and genius. Are they merely opposite sides of the same coin? Flip "heads" and you get Alice Faye?

"Tails" and you get Ford Buster?

So far my search for answers had only led to more questions. Which I had to put on hold, while I pulled a warm gob of white bird crap out of my hair.

CHAPTER FIVE

The Gum Drop Club. In Sinclair's day it was the jumpin'est jazz joint going. Back in the 1950s. When the hippest of the hip, the beatest of the beats were drawn uptown to Harlem like nocturnal moths to a dirty dancing flame. They came to get down, get high, get off on the swinging sounds of Miles, Diz, Bird, Monk, the vanguard of a musical revolution.

On the corner Lenox Avenue and 127th Street, the club's marquee had flashed like a neon red beacon in the fog of homogenized popular music that politely defined the times. Above blackened windows it had blinked—GUM DROP—while the crowds gathered way past midnight waiting to get in. A desegregation of colors all dressed to the nines and feeling the heat that blew out the front door like cigarette smoke through a siren's pouty red lips every time it was opened. Kerouac, Brando, Bardot, Dali, Capote, just to drop the names of a few who came to the club to get their kicks. A sexy, slangy, jamming birth-of-the-cool flashpoint of counter-cultural innovation.

And now it stood in ruin.

The signboard long gone, windows boarded up. The weathered brick blighted by undecipherable graffiti. Standing on the sidewalk, I recalled what Brimm had proposed in regard to Sinclair; and wondered if it might apply to the Gum Drop as well—

Maybe it just got tired.

I tried to imagine those salad days. When it was be there or be square. When from out of nowhere this kid, baby-faced and road wise, arrived on the scene, at the piano, and proceeded to blow the room away. Buster! The summer of '56. Around the time my dad's dad was planting the weathervane rooster at the top of Mount Washbarn. Historical references. Unrelated except that fate had converged them within me.

Ghosts.

For nearly an hour I stood there, silently immersed in the past. Until the sun disappeared behind a tall building to the west and in the twilight I became increasingly aware that mine was the only white face in sight. Better beat it, I figured, before one of the locals mistook me for some punk out looking for trouble. I was just about to climb into the truck when a car pulled in behind me, and another white guy hopped out. He had on a flowered Hawaiian-type shirt, his long hair streaked with gray, pulled back in a ponytail that suggested an aging hippie. He shot me a glance— striking in that it insinuated some sort of fraternity—then he ducked into an alleyway that ran alongside what remained of the Gum Drop.

It was enough to stir my curiosity. Perhaps I wasn't the only one interested in the club's Sinclairian history. So I followed him. Sneaked a peek down the alley and spied as he walked through the scattered trash to a brick wall at the back. Where he turned and knocked twice on what sounded like a steel door. And after a moment it opened. Just enough to let him in before it was slammed shut again.

Evidently the place wasn't completely abandoned after all.

I paused. Should I or shouldn't I?

True to my vow to leave no stone unturned, I decided to investigate. I slipped into the alley. The courage of the ignorant. Upon reaching the door, I noticed there was a peephole—about the width of a pencil—drilled through the heavy steel.

I tried to peep in but there was something on the other side blocking my view. There was only one way to find out, firsthand, what was going on behind that door. I took a deep breath . . . and knocked.

"Whaddaya want?" The voice had a sharp edge to it. I could feel the man's eye sizing me up through the hole.

My first instinct was to turn tail, run away. Only something in my gut kept me there. Against better judgment, I planted my feet on shaky ground and answered with the only articulate thought that came to mind:

"I'm looking for Ford Sinclair."

"Who?"

"Ford Sinclair," I repeated. "I was told he might be here. With Otis Sleet."

Silence.

"Hello?"

No reply.

"You still there?"

The voice returned. "Who sent ya?"

"Alice Faye Sinclair," I answered.

More silence. Then the sound of deadbolts sliding, and when the door finally opened a coffee-colored man built like a NFL linebacker filled the gap.

He said, "Alright, get your ass in here." And when I hesitated he reached out a giant hand and jerked me inside. The next thing I knew the door was closed, double-locked, and I was standing before a long metal folding table. In front of it stood the hippie dude in his loud aloha top. Behind it, another man, a bit younger and a lot darker, a large gold crucifix dangling from a thick gold chain around his neck. Both men wary of my intentions. Understandable, considering there were three shiny silver scales on the table between them; each scale depressed by the weight of a skunky smelling, herbaceous-green brick.

It didn't take a Deadhead to recognize what the bricks were made of.

Still, as a way of breaking the ice, I presumed to ask.

"Is that . . . uh . . . marijuana?"

"Why?" asked the man behind the cross. "You lookin' to buy?"

"Oh, no. I don't . . . uh . . . never have. But thanks anyhow."

"So how is Allie Faye these days?"

I turned and met the gaze of an old black man standing in front of second closed door across the room. He had to be pushing ninety. His face a web of deep creases, hair white as thin cotton. But it was his eyes that hooked me. Bright, inquiring, spirited in a way that defied his age. Even more so when he smiled.

"She still doin' the bird thing?"

I nodded. "Yes, sir."

"Yeah, well, God bless 'er."

He studied me for a moment. Like he'd seen my kind before.

"What's your name, son?"

"Woodrow. Washborn."

"Washborn," he reflected. "I knew a Willie Washborn. Bourbon Street. Ran a honky-tonk."

"I'm from Pennsylvania. Bird in Hand."

"Never heard of it," he said. "But I reckon it beats Two in the Bush."

"It's a small town. About sixty miles from—"

"Ain't here to give us a geography lesson are ya, Woodrow?"

"No, sir."

"Good," he replied. "'Cuz I ain't gettin' any younger,"

"The reason I'm here, sir, is because I'm trying to find Alice's brother. Ford Sinclair."

That drew a laugh. Old bones rattling under a baggy baby-blue seersucker suit.

"I'm serious, sir. I'm prepared to follow any lead."

He said, "In that case you can do me a favor."

"A favor?"

"If'n you do catch up with that boy, you tell 'im his ol' pal Oats is still kickin'."

"Oats?" My heart skipped a beat. "You mean . . . *you*? You're Otis Sleet?"

He shrugged. "At least what's left of 'im."

My jaw dropped. Suddenly Alice Faye wasn't so far out of it after all. Lurching forward, I offered my unscrubbed hand to the man who had helped launch the starship Sinclair.

"This is an honor, Mister Sleet. A great honor."

We shook on it.

"So tell me," he asked, "what's your business with brother Buster?"

"Well, sir, it's . . . uh . . . it's about art. You see I'm an aspiring artist myself."

He squinted at me. "You mean you're dying?"

"No, sir. Not EXpiring. ASpiring."

"Oh, right. I getcha. Ya wanna be but ya ain't."

"The thing is I'm having a hard time getting started."

"And ya reckon findin' Buster's gonna somehow grease the skids."

"Frankly, I'm hoping he's contagious. Because I'd sure love to catch whatever it is he's got."

Otis Sleet laughed again. "Wouldn't we all," he said.

"I realize it's a long shot. But the fact that I'm standing here talking to you proves anything's possible. I mean I only came to look at the place. It never occurred to me that you'd actually be here."

"Maybe Allie Faye's got them birds keepin' tabs on me."

"Like you said, sir, *God bless her*."

"As for Buster now—hell I ain't heard from the cat 'n better than thirty years. Last we met up was his momma's funeral. Atlanta. Christmas time as I recall. His daddy passed on the winter before."

"Anything you can tell me, I'd really appreciate it. If you're hungry we could talk over dinner. My treat. Just name the place."

He smiled. "That's mighty generous of ya, Woodrow. Only a man don't live on bread alone." He turned, opened the door behind him. "Step inside," he said. "Let's us feed the *soul* for a spell."

By the light of several kerosene lanterns, I counted a half dozen more old men, black and white, seated around an ancient upright piano. Each man with an instrument of his own: two acoustic guitars, a standup bass, a small drum kit, saxophone, and one tarnished trumpet.

A sort of clandestine, antechamber orchestra.

After closing the door, Oats Sleet introduced me.

"Folks, this here's Woodrow Anything's Possible Washborn."

"Please," I said, "just call me Woody."

"Youngblood's got a jones for Mist'a Ford Sinclair."

"I hear that." The bassman started to pluck impressively on his fat strings. The low, melodious tones of a familiar tune.

"Nickles 'n Dimes," I said. "Off *Buster's Island Dream*. Jim Garrison bass, Chet Baker trumpet, and Junior Taps on drums."

Gong! the drummer smacked a cymbal.

"Fuck that namin' me last shit!"

I looked to Oats. He winked at me. I turned back to the drums.

"You're Junior Taps?"

"Well I sure as hell ain't Ringo Starr."

That brought a giggle from a dark corner of the room. I shifted and saw a girl sitting there. A very pretty girl about my age. Bare legs reflecting the soft lamplight like finely polished mahogany.

"Sit yaself down, son," Oats said, his gaunt frame sounding a rheumatic creak as he lowered it onto a stool behind the piano. "I'll tell ya li'l story."

He must have had a million of them. I would have gladly sat through them all. I took an empty chair between the two horns, my ears wide open as the venerable old music man in the slack blue suit tickled the ivory. His long, nimble fingers a lesson in rhapsodic improvisation.

"The Great Dee-pression . . ." he began, his voice a melange of road gravel and raw honey. "I was fresh off a Georgia chain-gang/Hard time for doin' too much'a noth-ang . . .

"So Sleet is on the street At-lan-ta/Blowin' har-mon-i-ca for that loose change, dues change, change change change, no change in the cup, it's all up/Up up up in the air, over there, jus'a shiftin', driftin', comin' this'a way, hey there buddy whaddaya say . . ."

His hand swept across the keyboard, a neat glissando.

"He was this funny talkin' fella, fresh off the boat in a ragged

Scot-land coat/Had a prop-o-sition for po' handout Oats . . ."

He picked up the tempo—a funky cavalry to the rescue thing—for a few bars. Then he slowed it down again. A seamless transition into a very jazzy take on a tune straight out of Barnum & Bailey.

"Come join the circus Mist'a Angus propose, a dream in his eye, jus'a seed but it growed/Into the Big Little. Did ya hear what I say?"

"Big Little!" intoned the others in harmony.

"That's right," Sleet continued. "North in summer, south in winter, spring 'n fall in the middle . . ."

"Big Little!"

"Put up a tent, put on a show, pull up stakes 'n down the road/Saint Lou, Saint Paul, we hit 'em all, O-hi-o, hi-o, hi-o, hi-ohhhh 'n whadda we got here? a charmin' Carmen, oh, so nice, sugar 'n spice, I do, she cries, the blushin' bride, now the ringmaster's wife . . ."

"Big Little!"

"The gypsy life/One step ahead'a the blues, spreadin' that bigtop news/When from out of the stew a boy child came . . . the world his oyster . . ."

(arpeggio)

"Buster his name."

From there he went into Sinclair's instrumental homage: *Thinkin 'Bout Oats*. Written and recorded in Paris in the late-50s after Ford got word that Sleet had been stabbed by the husband of some floozy he was messing around with. John Coltrane had added a moody smooth saxophone to the record. But hearing Oats play it solo sent a chill of intimacy up my spine. I sat spellbound.

Until the saxman nudged me out of it.

"Ere ya go." Holding his breath, he offered me a thick, hand-rolled cigarette. The rising ribbon of smoke carried the pungent musky sweet scent of marijuana.

I waved it off. "Oh, no, thank you."

He exhaled—a white mushrooming cloud.

"Now now, brother," he said, "when in Rome," and smiled enticingly.

I looked around. All eyes were on me. Still playing, Oats smiled over the piano. I reconsidered the weed.

"Well . . . maybe just *one* puff."

Careful, like it might bite, I pinched the reefer from the saxman's hand. I wasn't exactly a total stranger to the stuff. I had friends back in Bird in Hand who got high, but I'd always opted to pass when the opportunity came my way. For one thing, my father would have blown his conservative stack if he'd ever found out. And certainly Kelly Ann wasn't one to experiment, or even tolerate anyone who did. Furthermore I'd never really felt the urge to partake, to alter my consciousness. It just wasn't in me.

Then again, by my own accord, I wasn't so much the old Woody anymore. Not to mention the fact that Dad and Kel were no longer active participants in my decision-making process.

Taking all that into account, I threw caution to the wind and accepted the joint. I put it to my lips, and proceeded to suck the unlawful smoke deep into my virgin lungs.

"Hold it," the saxman instructed.

I pressed my lips together. Felt a flush warm my cheeks. Only when it seemed my chest was about to explode did I let the smoke go. With a dry, tear-jerking cough fit that nearly rocked me off my chair.

Laughing, the saxman slapped me on the back.

"Don't worry, kid. Happens to the best of us."

By the time I caught my breath the room had taken on a different light. More intense, hotter. As if the lanterns had been turned up, the flames higher than before.

"Jus' relax, Woodrow," Oats advised me. "Go with it."

I closed my eyes and waited. Slowly, the warmth began to spread through my body. A lulling vibration rippled in my head. When the trumpet-man slipped the cigarette from my fingers I opened my eyes, and watched with a sense of communion as the offering was passed from one hand to the next.

Oats took a short drag. Contemplating the cherry-red tip, he exhaled. "I've never seen anything like it," he said. "One day Buster jus' climbed up on my lap. Barely five-year-old. Now don't ask me how or why or . . . all I know is the li'l shit took to that piana like a baby duck takin' to water. No thinkin', no ASpirin', no nothin' about it. Pure instinct, I reckon. A freaky act of nature."

"And when he turned sixteen you brought him here," I'd read.

"The circus was on its last leg," Oats confirmed. "It was time."

The joint came around again. I inhaled a second helping of the smoke. I was able to hold it in longer than the first. Hardly a cough. It left my head very pleasantly abuzz. A floating, tapped-in feeling as Oats recounted the night he'd sprung Sinclair on the Gum Drop. How he'd talked the owner—an ex-pimp with a fondness for hot diamonds and cool jazz—into giving Buster five minutes onstage while Lester Young and his band were off on a break.

Five minutes. That was all it took.

"Halfway through the first number the crowd was in his pocket, man. I remember Billie Holiday, the Lady herself, she come over to me, wantin' to hire 'im on the spot." Oats laughed. "And when ol Lester got an earful he told his pianaman to take the rest of the night off. So that five minutes turned into an hour with the band. Then a regular Friday gig, headlinin' mind ya."

"God, I wish I could'a been there." I swallowed the last toke from the roach.

"The next day the circus moved on without 'im. Fore I left I hooked 'im up with the combo. Mooch Wilson, the Pike brothers, Hank Jones, course Junior on drums."

"Fuck that naming him *last* shit!" I blurted.

"You tell 'em, kid." Taps did a rim shot and we all shared a laugh.

"Anyhow, that was that," Oats concluded. "The rest, as they say, is his-tor-ee."

"Tourin' through Europe," Junior Taps added, "that's when we really cooked. France, England, Italy, Germany. On the road for a good three years runnin'. Till we lost Jonesy to the needle. Wasn't long after that Buster just up 'n called it quits."

"You think that's why he stopped playing?" I asked.

Taps shook his head. "I think he used it as an excuse. The real reason," he shrugged, "only Buster knows."

"What about you, Woodrow—" asked Oats "—you play?"

"I wish," I answered. "Took some trumpet lessons back home but my teacher dropped me. He said I don't have what it takes."

"Yeah, well, ain't no teachers here. Oscar, lend the boy your horn."

"Oh, no," I begged off. "I'll just sit 'n listen."

"Save the lip for blowin'," Oscar said, and pushed the brass into my hands.

"Really, I can't. I'd only embarrass myself."

Oats ignored my objections. "Buster's Island Dream. On fo'."

"I'm telling you, I stink!"

He counted it off. "A one, a two, a one two three fo'—"

On cue the band struck up, sliding easily into the breezy ballad.

"Seriously, Oats, don't do this to me."

He grinned. "Sink or swim, Woodrow."

Apropos, as the water seemed way over my head.

"Jus' come in when you feel it."

When I feel it? What a lousy thing to say to someone under the musical equivalent of anesthesia. I scowled at Oats for putting me on the spot. For setting me up to look like a fool.

I deferred, grudgingly. "Okay. But don't say I didn't warn you."

The band played on; patiently waiting for me to take the bait, challenge my inhibitions. With nowhere to hide, I sat straight in the chair. Bracing for the humiliation, I took a couple of deep, dread-filled breaths. Then I put the trumpet reluctantly to my lips, and started to blow. So far off key it sounded like I was strangling a tone-deaf goose.

Mercifully, I stopped after a few sour notes.

"It's no use," I lamented.

The others were still in their groove. Not a snicker at my expense.

"I just don't have it."

Oats looked to the young woman in the corner.

He said, "Keisha, honey, come on over 'n talk 'im through it."

She—Keisha—got up from her seat. In high-topped red sneakers, she approached with a shyness that only furthered my doubts. How in the world was this girl, pretty as she was, going to help a lost cause like me?

She glided to a stop. So close I could've reached out and touched her. Under a wrinkled pink summer dress her hips began to sway. Her body moving easily with the round, sensual rhythm of *Buster's Island Dream*, she lifted her gaze to meet mine. And when at last her mouth opened out came one of the sweetest voices I had ever heard. An edgy soprano. Scat. Trumpet-like in a way that seemed inherently beyond me.

I sat mesmerized by the fluid movement, perfect pitch. Ella Fitzgerald and Salome rolled into one hypnotic, dreamy package. I forgot there was anyone else in the room, in the world.

"On your feet, Woodrow!" Oats called out.

I stood, a simple reflex.

"Now throw it back," Oats conducted. "Echo her voice."

At that Keisha repeated the first two notes of the refrain.

Intoxicated by it all, I tried to reproduce the sounds through the horn. I was still off, but surprisingly not so far off. And I was even closer yet on the second set of notes, two quick blasts, from the gut.

Then came the third pair; which I proceeded to blow with a mimetic exactitude that bordered on the miraculous. God and Otis Sleet as my witnesses.

By the time we got to the end of the phrase my feet were barely on the floor. Then Keisha took it from the top again, and halfway across the bridge I caught up with her, anticipating the tricky inflectional changes she added to test my newfound chops.

Finally, graciously, she backed away and let me fly on my own.

"You got it now, Woodman!" Oats shouted over the melody.

I played louder. Played without a thought in my head. No farm, no funeral, no broken engagements, not even Sinclair. Just me and the horn and a feeling of swinging euphoria. Maybe it was the smoke, maybe the girl, the place, or maybe the Muse sisters were just out slumming today. Whatever the reasons—how? why?—they didn't matter. It was enough that I had what it took. From somewhere inside me it was coming out, intact and in tune. Music!

The band stopped for my solo. And, baby, I let it wail. I went up high, bent down low, blowing a sultry island breeze across the gritty raised brow of hip-hoppy Harlem. I was weightless. *In flight.* Soaring so high I was oblivious to the commotion happening elsewhere in the building until Oscar slapped his hand over the mouth of the trumpet and effectively muted me.

"POLICE! FREEZE! HANDS IN THE AIR!"

Harsh voices on the other side of the door.

"Busted." Taps smacked a cymbal.

"Show's over," Oats announced. "Keisha honey, take Woody 'n make like mice."

She took my hand, "Follow me."

"Where?"

Oats nodded. "Best go with 'er, son."

"What about the rest of you?" I asked.

"Too old 'n too slow," Oats answered.

Keisha tugged at my arm. "This way." Leading me again. This time toward her dark corner of the room.

I looked back over my shoulder. "I felt it, Oats. I really felt it."

Otis Sleet smiled, thumb up. "I heard ya, Woodrow. We all heard ya."

Something heavy rammed against the door, the cops wanting in.

I turned and found Keisha down on all fours, squeezing through a hole where the walls came together. When she was gone I dropped to my knees and followed her . . . into the dark of a stairwell. Just as the door was rammed open behind me. Angry voices yelling "FREEZE! NOBODY MOVE!"

We scurried up the stairs, stirring up decades of dust. We climbed three floors—where many of the great Gum Drop musicians, including Sinclair, had lived and loved—and then Keisha pushed open a flimsy door and we were out on the rooftop. Under a waxing spotlight moon.

"Now what?" I asked, still riding the wave.

"Over here." She led me to a side ledge.

There was a long wooden plank, laid like a narrow bridge, spanning the alleyway to the roof of the building next door. A daunting ten feet across at least. When Keisha crawled out onto the board, it bowed treacherously under her weight.

"You sure it'll hold?"

She shushed me and pointed down.

Looking over the ledge, I saw a policeman posted in the alley. Had he thought to look up he would have certainly gotten an eyeful as Keisha was already halfway across, hard not to notice in her swaying pink dress.

But the cop kept his sights low. Keisha made it safely across. From the far rooftop she waved for me to join her. My fear sufficiently suppressed by the buzz—enhanced by pure adrenaline—I climbed up on the plank, and braved the crawl. The cop directly below me, I inched along, trusting the 2x12 to bend but not break. Otherwise arrest would have been the very least of my worries. The better than fifty foot fall to the hard brick alley floor promised an abruptly fatal conclusion to my first day away from home.

Still the board held. Undetected, I hopped to the tar beside Keisha.

"We did it!" I crowed. "The Great Escape!"

She hustled me along. "C'mon, let's get inside."

We ran for the stairwell. We got there just in the nick of time. I could hear voices on the Gum Drop. The cops arriving a New York second too late to catch any sight of us.

"It never fails," Keisha said as we hurried down the steps.

"Is there a back way out of this building?" I asked.

"Don't need one," she answered. "I live here."

A minute later we were standing in the front room of her modest third floor apartment. All in all, a rather slick getaway.

CHAPTER SIX

From the window we watched as the cops herded Oats and the others, their hands cuffed behind their backs, into a pair of paddy wagons double-parked alongside my truck.

"What's gonna happen to them?" I asked Keisha.

"Oats and the guys ain't part of the dealing," she told me. "They'll just have to pay a fine for trespassing. It's not the first time, probably won't be the last."

When the wagons sped off, sirens blaring, she moved away from the window. "You better hangout for a while, till things cool down."

I turned and surveyed the small flat. The furnishings were old and worn but it was neatly kept.

"Do you live here alone?"

"No," she answered, "with my older sister. She's in Jersey singing with a blues band. Won't be home till tomorrow."

"Speaking of bands," I asked, "I wasn't dreaming was I? I mean it really happened, right? Me, Otis Sleet, Junior Taps— making music together."

"You were fine, Woody," she assured me. "No dream."

"I felt so . . . loose. Maybe I should buy some of that reefer."

"It wasn't the weed," she said. "It was you. You just needed a little push, that's all." She went into the kitchen. "How 'bout something to drink? We got soda or juice."

"Whatever you're having'll be great."

She returned with two cans of root beer. We sat on opposite ends of a saggy sofa and sipped in silence while I tried to collect my thoughts. What at day: the drive, Brimm, Alice Faye, Oats, and now there I was laying low with a beautiful young songbird.

"Keisha. I don't think I've ever heard that name before."

"It's African," she said. "I forget what it means."

"So . . . how old are you?"

"Nineteen. Well, almost. I'm a Leo."

"I'm Aries," I said. "Turned twenty in April."

"That explains it then."

"Explains what?"

"Aries are usually thoughtful, sensitive, trusting."

"By trusting you mean naïve."

She smiled. "Let's just say they tend to put more faith in others than they do in themselves."

"Maybe we're less likely to be disappointed that way."

"Maybe. Or maybe not." She shrugged then took a sip and changed the subject. "Is this your first time in the city?"

"In any city," I said. "I was supposed to go on a field trip to Philadelphia when I was a kid—to see the Liberty Bell and stuff—but I got stung by a bunch of hornets and had to stay home."

"What do you do there? Where you're from, I mean."

"Until a few days ago I lived on a farm. We had dairy cows."

"That sounds pretty cool. Out in the country. Peaceful, I bet."

"Among other things. Anyhow, we sold it all."

"And now you're into Ford Sinclair."

"Yes. I'm hoping to find him."

She tilted her lovely head, hair close-cropped and shiny.

"To hear Oats tell it you're gonna need a lotta luck."

"Yeah, well—" I smiled "—so far, so good. But, hey, I already know about me. What about you? What do you do when you're not next door singing with Oats and the guys?"

"Not much." She frowned. "Mostly I wait tables at a jazz club in the Village. But tonight's my night off."

Another stroke of luck. "In that case, after all you've done for me, there must be something I can do for you."

Her almond eyes narrowed. "And just what do you have in mind?"

Half an hour later Keisha emerged from her bedroom in a snug blue and gold sarong-styled dress. It belonged to her sister, she confessed; but from the way it hugged her girlish curves—leaving her shoulders and those long legs bare and silky smooth to the eye—I couldn't image it looking better on any other body. She gave it wattage. The kind of exotic illumination you see in slick fashion magazines. She smelled great, too, like a perfumed page in those same magazines.

She wrapped a loose-knit blue shawl about her shoulders, and together we went down the stairs, out into the warm night air. To my relief there were no cops left on the scene. Rather than have me give up a good parking spot, Keisha hailed a yellow cab, my first ride in a taxi, and it took us downtown to Times Square. Where we occupied a corner booth in a fancy steakhouse with pictures of legendary stage and screen stars lining the walls.

Under the photogenic gazes of Elizabeth Taylor and Richard Burton, we talked, and talked, very much at ease, like we'd known each other all our lives, about music and art, and what we hoped the future held for us.

Keisha had the clearer vision. She saw herself in front of a large orchestra, singing love songs in the footsteps of her heroes, divas such as Aretha Franklin and Whitney Houston.

"They started out singing in the church choir," she said, brightly. "Just like me."

As for my own lofty ambitions, there was only one thing left to say. "I've never been hungrier in my life."

Keisha agreed. "Hungry to learn, to experience, to be heard."

"To eat," I replied. "Because right now I believe I'm experiencing what they call the *munchies*."

She laughed. "That's one of the reasons I don't smoke. The pigging out afterward."

"Me," I said, incredulous, "of all people! Woodrow Wilson Washborn the Fourth, on Broadway, with a trumpet jazzed, shared-a-high-with-Oats Sleet appetite!

"And if that don't beat all," I added, " . . . with you."

"Not to mention a fifty dollar steak." Keisha smiled at the choice cut on my plate.

"Fifty, five hundred, heck," I said, "I would've paid five thousand dollars for this moment."

"I'm glad to hear that," she said, nibbling on a French fry. "Cuz if you clean your plate like a good boy I have another surprise for you."

"Where? What—what is it?"

She grinned slyly.

"If I tell you then it won't be a surprise any more."

I polished off the steak in record time.

Stuffed with the meat, I returned to the gravy:

"Now what were you saying about a surprise?"

"It's right around the block," Keisha teased. "If we skip dessert we should make it just in time."

I paid the check, left a handsome tip, and whisked her out the door.

Under the storied lights of Broadway we walked south. Despite my pestering, Keisha kept me in suspense as to our destination. Turning west on 41st Street, she said that she'd noticed an ad in the *New York Post* that morning, while she was checking her horoscope for the day. That she hadn't thought anything of it until she saw the newspaper on the bed when she went to her room to change for dinner.

"I figured you'd appreciate it," she said coyly.

We were about halfway down the block when I spotted a large sandwich board standing on the sidewalk ahead of us. Once we got within reading range the name Ford Sinclair jumped out at me. Beneath it, the title of a play: *The Messenger.* The last of four Sinclair wrote after he'd inexplicably quit the music scene.

A controversial one-man show, *The Messenger* had gone on to win a Pulitzer Prize for Drama. Sinclair had also directed and starred in it: a so-reviewed "gripping performance" that earned him a Tony Award for Best Actor. Which, characteristically, he never showed to accept.

In the present, however, the curtain was only minutes away from rising again. A lower rent, late show, off-Broadway revival.

"So whaddaya think?" Keisha asked. "Up for a little after dinner theater?"

Was I? I could've kissed her. Instead, I made a beeline for the ticket window. I got us the two best seats in the house. Front and center.

The show had already been running for several weeks but there was still a respectable crowd on hand. An audience for the work of a man who claimed he did not work for an audience. When the lights went down, we settled in our seats, with high expectations . . .

And, not surprisingly, we weren't disappointed.

It was a poetic and provocative piece. A street corner prophet is arrested, put on trail, and absurdly sentenced to death for speaking out against the hypocrisy and inhumanity of a paranoid, self-righteous society. It spoke to fear, ignorance, intolerance, oppression, and, finally, state execution.

At the end the prophet is strapped into an electric chair on the otherwise bare stage. Tall, dark shadows—his accusers—loom over him. The toll of an amplified, disembodied voice:

"Prisoner 6-66, you have been found guilty of capital crimes against the State. Specifically, the conception, gestation, and public articulation of ideas and principles judged to be seditious and immoral by a high court of law."

"Thank you all!" exclaimed the condemned man, addressing the audience. "For I could not have done it without you!"

The actor looked to be about forty; nearly twice as old as Sinclair when he played the role. I pictured young Ford in the hot seat. The fire of defiance burning in his eyes.

The voice continued impassively. "You have three seconds to recant your transgressions and appeal to this body for mercy."

To which the prisoner responded, "The suppression of ideas is by far the most criminal act of sedition!"

"Three . . ." the voice began to count down.

"Morality at its very lowest towers well above your highest court!"

"Two . . ."

The man looked upward in mocking supplication.

"Fuck them, Father," he petitioned. "For they *know* what they do."

"One . . ."

"Hail the messenger!" the prophet cried.

"Power on," ordered the voice.

With that the sparks began to fly—accompanied by a sizzling sound effect that drowned out the electrified agony as both stage and house lights flickered violently, and smoke spewed from the chair to envelope the frying, dying man.

It was cruel, unusual, powerful stuff. Keisha gripped my arm, repulsed by the brutality but unable to look away. Finally, after the prolonged and deliberately punishing crescendo, all went to black. The last crackle of sparks giving way to a drained silence. When the house lights came up nobody moved or spoke. Our senses effectively shaken, we could only stare at the dead man on stage.

The collective digestion of unsweetened, gut-wrenching Art.

"He wrote it after his friend Lenny Bruce got arrested for using profanity in his comedy act," I told Keisha as we exited the theater.

"They didn't kill Lenny, did they?" she asked, still clutching my arm.

"No. At least not officially. They were content to crush his spirit and leave him for dead."

As we headed back toward Broadway, Keisha pondered the enigma of Sinclair. "The more I learn about him, the harder he is to figure out. I mean there's still plenty of injustice in the world.

It's just strange that he could go so long without calling any more attention to it."

"It's strange, all right." I checked my watch; already past midnight. "It's getting late," I said. "I'd better see you home."

She agreed, and at the corner whistled for a taxi. The cabby wasn't exactly thrilled about going to Harlem at that hour, but he deferred to my promise of a worthwhile tip and we got in for the ride.

With the driver sealed-off by a thick pane of smudged Plexiglas Keisha and I discussed the unwavering courage of Sinclair's work. How in all his plays—*Ring of Fire, Visions of Paradise, Taboos,* and of course *The Messenger*—he'd not only challenged authority but also the darker sides of human nature itself.

"That's what separates the great from the good," I told her. "Having the guts to call it the way it is, let the chips fall where they will."

Keisha smiled at my enthusiasm. She laid her hand over mine and it made the digital red mileage meter on the dashboard click ahead too fast. I was not looking forward to saying goodnight to her.

Standing on her front stoop there a sudden awkwardness between us. The possibility that we would never see each other again as real as it was sad. After all, it was only an improbable gust of fate that had carried us to where we were. Unlikely to be recaptured.

"That was one of the best dinners I've ever had," Keisha said. "And the play was terrific, gave me goose-bumps."

"It was certainly a wonderful surprise. I can't thank you enough."

She titled her head to the side. "So, where do you go from here?"

"South in the morning," I answered. "Sinclair's got an ex-wife and daughter in Florida."

"What about tonight?" she asked.

"It's been a long day. I'll just check into a hotel."

"A hotel—at this hour?"

"Nothing swanky. A bed, a shower."

"Seems to me like a waste of gas and money. Driving around, paying a hundred dollars or more just to sleep." She shrugged her bare shoulders. "I mean when you're more than welcome to come upstairs."

"Upstairs?"

"Like I said, my sister won't be back till tomorrow."

"Yeah, but . . . you've done enough good deeds for one day."

Her eyes squinted. Her tone deepened to impersonate the "voice" from the play. "You have three seconds to recant and accept the invitation."

"Seriously, Keisha, I don't want to impose."

"Three . . ."

"'Cause you are in no way obligated."

"Two . . ."

"The last thing I wanna do is take any advantage."

"One . . ."

And with that the sparks began to fly.

I followed her up the stairs to her flat. Inside, the easy rapport we'd shared all evening was trumped by a heady, self-conscious, distinctly non-platonic tension. I tried to relieve it by proposing to sleep on the sofa.

Keisha frowned. "That's not *exactly* what I had in mind."

She went to her bedroom. Leaving the door open, suggestively, she lit a fat, scented candle on the nightstand beside her pillow. I stepped into the doorway. Her room was done in a soft orchid color, trimmed in pastel green. Like a fragrant flower grown through a crack in the big city concrete.

"Exactly what did you have in mind?" I asked timidly.

She looked at me like the answer was written on my face, and she a mirror reflecting it back at me. In case it wasn't altogether legible from the distance, she came toward me until it read perfectly clear. *Kiss me, you fool!*

I froze. Immobilized but for a warm surge between my legs.

A mix of panic and lust, it jolted me into a kind of throbbing paralysis. Picture a wide-eyed mannequin . . . with a very animated boner.

Fighting the lump in my throat, I managed to utter a few remindful words: "Keisha, we might never see each other again."

She nodded, well aware.

"Then we better make the most of right now."

That said she did as she'd done from the moment we met; she took the lead. Leaning in, she pressed her lips to mine. Her mouth opened. Her tongue began to flick, coaxing me out of my stupor.

I mumbled, "Keisha, there's something I have to tell you."

"Oats says making love is like making music," she whispered. "Harmony, melody, and rhythm."

"The thing is . . . uh . . . you know how today was my first time making music."

"And you were amazing," she replied.

"Yeah, well, uh . . . the thing is . . . uh . . . tonight would be my first time making . . ."

"It's okay, Woody," she assured me. "Just come in when you feel it."

She rose tippy-toed and kissed me harder, deeper, exhaling a breath of sweet heat that infused every cell in my being. My inhibitions melted, boiled, evaporated in a steam of irrepressible passion. I slid my arms around her waist and pulled her in. My erection pressed full against her pubis. Her high breasts brassiere-less against my chest. There was no more room for doubt between us. We were entwined in a swirl of stardust. Bewitched.

Keisha pulled away, stepped back. Reaching over her shoulders, she loosened the little knot that was holding her dress and like the unveiling of a divine work of art the sarong spilled to the floor in a blue and gold puddle at her feet.

Slowly, I ran my eyes up those lean brown legs, over the gentle swell of her thighs, to a silky puff of sheer white panty where it all came together. She stood perfectly still, statuesque, allowing me to drink it all in. The crescent of her hips, flat of her belly, nipples in full bloom on dark areolas. It was more than a dream come true; even in the wilds of my subconscious I hadn't dared a vision so fantastic.

I gazed on her face. So delicately lined. Her swollen lips radiating an innocence in estrus that made the moment seem only natural, that there was no need to hurry. That we had time, instinct, everything on our side. I undid the buttons of my shirt and let it drop to the floor. Then, unbuckling my belt, I slid my Dockers and BVDs down around my ankles. I felt no sense of Bird in Hand modesty as Keisha contemplated the full length of my nakedness.

In kind, she too rendered herself completely vulnerable—shedding the panties to reveal the fleece-covered mound of her sex. The curly black hair like a slender arrowhead pointing down between the columns of her legs. *Mons veneris!* The first I'd experienced since birth. I opened my arms and she came to me. Skin on skin. Fingers in tender caress, exploring, stoking the fires of amorous youth. My nostrils flared at her rising scent, a succulent musk that permeated my brain. I ran my hand along the arc of her bottom. Then I swept her, literally, off her feet. My intent to carry her to the bed and place her gently. A smooth, Don Juanian move. Except that my pants were still around my ankles.

I tripped. With small, frantic, shackled steps we went bumbling across the room, out of control, in the direction of romantic disaster. We could have easily crashed into the candle stand, set the whole building ablaze; or even gone out the window and plummeted, in a rather compromising position, to the far concrete ground.

But we did neither. For reasons unknown, good fortune again intervened on my behalf. A dynamic display of kind luck that veered our course, and flopped us onto the downy patchwork quilt spread thick over Keisha's cushy, clean-sheeted mattress. A socially clumsy yet mercifully soft landing.

"Are you all right?" I asked, heaped on top of her.

She thought about it for a few seconds, as if she wasn't sure, then let out a sudden burst of laughter. At least she wasn't hurt. And I had to admit, all embarrassment aside, it was pretty funny. So I cracked up with her. We cackled like two little kids tickling the other's fancy . . . . Until we found ourselves—through a philter of silly tears—in each other's eyes, and the laughter faded.

In its place the slurpy, soulful seriousness of smacking lips.

With dawn creeping in through a rip in the window shade, I cradled Keisha in my arms while she sang to me in a low, cuddling voice. "Mamma may have/And papa may have/But God bless the child that got his own/That got his own . . ."

Billie Holiday. Only better.

"Harmony, melody and rhythm," I cooed, blissful in the afterglow.

"Oats said it right," Her head nested on my chest. "Making love is like making music."

"In a way I suppose it's like dying, too."

She looked up at me. "Dying?"

"Yeah. I mean you hear about it, read about it, see pictures of it. But you really can't comprehend it until it happens to you."

"'Cept you only die once." She slid her warm hand under the quilt, between my legs. "And we just proved that you can make love over 'n over again."

"Unless it's true about reincarnation. That we do die and come back over 'n over again."

"Is that what you believe?"

I sighed. "Me, I don't know what to believe. Maybe that's why everything came so easy for Sinclair. By some luck of the draw he inherited an artistic soul."

"Tell me more about him." Her fingers stroking me gently.

"Well . . ." I could feel the blood returning to my loins "after he conquered the theater world he bought a boat and sailed off to write books. Spent three years island hopping through the Caribbean. Wrote three novels. *Windward, Castaway* and *Noble Savage*. All best-sellers."

"Then what?"

"Then one day he blew into Biscayne Bay in Florida. Where he dropped anchor and married this rich girl. A Palm Beach debutante named Olivia Sutton."

"Was she pretty?"

"From the pictures I've seen, very pretty. Anyhow, the plan is to pay her a visit. Find out if she's gotten any new information. If she'll even talk to me, that is."

"Even if she won't," Keisha said, "it's gotta beat hanging around this neighborhood."

I had to disagree.

"Now that I find hard to believe . . ."

Aroused again by her touch, I rolled her onto her back. Again, I slipped easily inside her.

" . . . Cuz Harlem's been *heaven* on earth to me."

CHAPTER SEVEN

I t was a bittersweet morning.

On the sidewalk in the early sunshine I kissed Keisha goodbye. We'd taken a shower together. She'd fixed me a breakfast of eggs and grape-jammed bagels. I was clean, full, a man in the biblical sense, and very sorry to leave her.

But she had great songs yet to sing. And I still had a long way to go.

And I was destined to go it alone.

"I'll be rooting for you, Woody," Keisha said through the passenger side window, her fingers crossed for me as the truck's engine idled.

"Tell Oats, if I ever get the chance, I'll be sure to do him that favor," I said, "and let Sinclair know he's still kickin'."

Keisha nodded—an investment of faith.

Driving off, I kept one eye on the rearview mirror. I could see her waving, growing fainter, and finally dissolve into a beautiful memory. A lilting serenade that will forever echo in my head . . . .

I followed the Hudson River to the Lincoln Tunnel. Having tunneled into The Apple, I now tunneled out—onto the New Jersey Turnpike, which took me to the southbound I-95. According to my *Rand McNally Road Atlas* it was an almost straight one thousand mile shot along the Atlantic coast to the Florida border. Then another three hundred or so miles to a place called Palm Beach, and the next long passed phase of Ford Sinclair's life.

By the age of twenty-seven Sinclair had already proved himself a prolifically productive force. The list of creative accomplishments to his credit included five phenomenal jazz albums, four dynamic stage plays, three heavyweight novels, and one child. A daughter, named Mara.

The boy wonder was now a family man.

Evidently it didn't suit him very well.

I drove on. With so many faces pressed against my windshield—Sinclair, Keisha, Oats, Mr. Crino my music teacher, Kelly Ann, my father—I hardly noticed the passing of Maryland, Virginia, the Carolinas. Only when the sun went down was I reminded that I hadn't slept in more than thirty-six hours.

I found a Motel 6 just off the interstate and turned in for the night. I went out like a light the second my head hit the foamy pillow.

I didn't dream.

"Georgia-a-a, Georgia-a-a, the whole day through, that ol' sweet song keeps Georgia on my m-i-i-i-nd . . ." I sang it from Savannah to Harrietts Bluff.

Crossing over the Florida state line, I started to really feel the heat. It was pushing ninety degrees, humid as a tropical greenhouse in Hades. The pickup didn't have air-conditioning so the windows were rolled down, the hot wind blowing briny over my already sweat-salted skin.

It only got hotter as the I-95 continued past Daytona Beach, New Smyrna Beach, Vero Beach. Miles later, I saw a sign announcing West Palm Beach and veered off onto the exit ramp. It funneled me into the late afternoon traffic on Palm Beach Lakes Boulevard.

From Arthur Brimm I'd gotten an address for Casa de Sol— the Sutton estate on North Ocean Boulevard in Palm Beach: a colonized sandbar separated from lower rent West Palm by a narrow blue waterway—where Olivia Sutton Sinclair Woolbright resided with her second husband, Carlton Woolbright, of the cruise ship building Woolbrights.

I crossed a bridge to the bar then rolled north on Ocean. It was like climbing the rungs of an increasingly gilded ladder. The money getting bigger, older as the blood got bluer. A coral-colored reef of palatial homes fronted a fine white ribbon of sandy beach. Palm trees swayed above private piers adorned with sleek speedboats and gleaming, cost-unconscious yachts.

It only got fatter the further I went.

Nearing the end of the peninsula, I came to a long wrought iron fence. It led me to a high gate set between two thick white marble columns. Both columns bore the same chiseled inscription: *CASA de SOL*.

I turned into the driveway. Well beyond the gate stood a grand Mediterranean-styled mansion, a great shimmer of bone-white stone, capped by a multitude of reddish clay tiles.

The opulence was dizzying.

I knew from the Sinclair bio that the Sutton wealth was a product of the liquor trade. Harry Sutton had started as a bootlegger during Prohibition. With the repeal of the booze ban he'd brought the business above ground, establishing distilleries and bottling companies worldwide. A legitimate tycoon, he'd passed away in the early-70s, leaving everything to his only child, the heiress Olivia.

I noticed a speaker set into the side of the column on my left. I inched forward, reached out, and pushed a shiny silver button. Almost immediately a man's tinny voice answered. "Yes?"

"Hello." I asked, "Is this the Woolbright residence?"

"It is," the voice confirmed.

"My name is Woody Washborn. I'm here to see Mrs. Woolbright."

"Woody who?"

"Washborn," I repeated. "Woodrow Washborn."

"Is Mrs. Woolbright expecting you?"

"No, sir, she's not. But—"

"I'm sorry. Solicitors are not permitted on the premises."

"Oh, no. Excuse me. I'm not here to sell anything."

"Then why are you here?"

"It has to do with her first husband. Ford Sinclair."

"One moment, please."

The speaker went silent. I looked to the house. There was no sign of movement. I waited, and after a moment the voice returned. "Mr. Washborn."

"Yessir?"

"You may proceed directly to the front door."

The gates opened, swinging back with a motorized hum. I thought, Well, that was easy enough, and wheeled slowly onto the property, following the long flower-lined driveway between manicured expanses of rich green lawn until I reached the shade of a pillared portico that extended out over the mansion's main entrance. A beefy-looking fellow in a tailed black service tuxedo was standing by to receive me.

"Mr. Washborn?" he asked formally as I climbed out of the pickup.

"Yes, sir." Feeling somewhat underdressed, I flashed on the suit and tie I'd worn for my father's funeral packed in my suitcase. But it was too late to make a change; the lady was waiting.

"Mrs. Woolbright will see you in the parlor."

I stepped inside a cool, cavernous foyer. A large crystal chandelier rained diamonds of light onto the impeccably polished black and white tiled floor.

The butler gestured, "This way, please." His gait erect, dutiful, he led me past a grand marble staircase, and down a wide hallway bathed in a rainbow of light coming through a tall stained-glass window at the far end. Halfway down the hall he stopped in front of a set of high French doors. He rapped twice, and a woman's voice answered through the slats:

"Show him in, Russell."

With that I was ushered into the parlor. A veritable treasure trove of antiques gave it a museum-like elegance. The past preserved at no spared expense. "Mr. Washborn, ma'am," the butler announced.

The "ma'am" in question being a rather striking, blond coifed woman in a chic cream-colored blouse and matching Capri slacks—standing very heiress-like with a long-stemmed yellow rose in one hand and a pair of shiny silver garden snips in the other.

"Ah, Woodrow," she said, hospitably, "welcome to Casa de Sol."

"Thank you, ma'am," I nodded.

"Can we get you something to drink?" She motioned to the butler. "A glass of wine perhaps?"

"Oh, no. I'm fine, thank you," I said to them both.

"Then that will be all, Russell," she said with a slight flick of her wrist.

Dismissed, Russell gave a little bow and backed out of the room. He closed the doors in front of him.

"You'll have to excuse this mess." Olivia pointed with the snips to a pile of stem clippings next to a large egg-shaped gray clay vase holding more roses on the oversized coffee table at her knees. "I was just arranging a few flowers."

"That's a very pretty yellow, ma'am. Really brightens up the room."

"Yes, it does."

She set the snips down on the table. A big ice-blue wedding ring diamond sparkled on her finger as she carefully fed the dethorned rose into the bouquet. She was in her mid-fifties, I figured, and she wore the years well. Her face had a perennial loveliness about it. A notable absence of wrinkles suggested not only a fair-skinned aversion to the sun but also many visits to the spa, and, I suspected, the occasional trip to a first-rate nip and tuck man. The only real gravitation of age was a subtle looseness about her neck. A splendid strand of pearls, however, provided for a very effective distraction.

All in all, Olivia Sutton Sinclair Woolbright possessed the slender, determined good looks of the meticulously maintained.

No significant stretch of my imagination was required to picture the young beauty who had claimed Sinclair from the sea. The roses bunched just right, Olivia lifted her attention back to me.

"So, tell me," she asked, "How is your father?"

Huh? "My father?"

"I haven't heard from him in ages."

"Heard from him?"

"Dear Wash. Always the gentleman."

"Wash?"

"I very much enjoyed his company."

"His company?"

Her green eyes narrowed, hands akimbo on her hips.

"Woodrow, why are you repeating everything I say?"

"Why? Uh . . . well . . . uh . . ."

"Well, what?"

"Mrs. Woolbright, my father is dead."

Her mouth dropped open, curiously saddened by the news.

"Oh, Woodrow, I'm so sorry. I had no idea. Good heavens, when did it happen?"

"Just a few weeks ago, but—"

"Forgive me. If I'd known I would have sent—"

"Mrs. Woolbright," I interrupted, "excuse me. It seems there's been some misunderstanding. Because unless you've spent time in Bird in Hand, Pennsylvania there's no way you could've known. You see my father was—"

"Walter Washborn. *Washborn Press.* The house that published Ford."

I shook my head. "No, ma'am. Wood Washborn. Washborn Dairy Farm."

You could've heard a pin drop. Puzzled, the lady crossed her arms, gave me a stern look. "Young man, I believe an explanation is in order."

"Yes, ma'am. You see, the thing is, the reason I'm here—"

"MOTHER!" The voice came from out in the hall.

Suddenly the French doors were flung open, and in rushed a

younger woman. Thirty-something, I guessed. Her pretty face
was alarmed to a flush. "Mother, call the police, he's crazy!"

"What?" I yelped.

"He climbed over the fence!"

"No, no," I protested. "Mrs. Woolbright, I swear, someone
opened the gate. Ask Russell."

"MARA!" A man's voice. Frantic, he came barging into the
room. Dark, handsome, disheveled, "Mara," he cried, "I no leabe
teel we a talk!"

"I have nothing more to say to you!"

"You eez steel my wive!" the man exclaimed.

"A mistake soon to be rectified!" the woman shot back.

I raised my hand. "I can see I've come at a bad time."

The man sneered at me. "En who da hell a you?"

"Woody," I answered awkwardly, "Washborn."

He snapped back to his wife. "You got a boy-a-toy, eez dat
eet?"

"And what if I do?" she volleyed. "You think you're the only
one who can screw around?"

"Mara, you muss beliebe me—I no a touch er!"

"But you damn well wanted to!"

"Too much rum," he pleaded. "All talk. I no inten anymore."

"Well I intend," Mara announced. "I intend to divorce your
Cuban Casanova ass!"

"For dis?" He aimed a loaded finger at me. "You leabe me
por dis, dis . . . *geegolo*?"

"At least he appreciates me," Mara countered. "Tell him,
Wally."

"It's Woody. And I really should be going."

I made a move toward the door but Mara grabbed hold of
my arm, foiling my escape. She said, "For your information,
Wally is a gentleman. He is sensitive to my needs." She hugged
my arm, provocatively. "And I mean *all* my needs."

I could see steam rising from the man's swarthy head. Latino
blood reaching a boil, his voice vibrated in my direction:

"I show a you, you . . . wive-stealer!"

He charged—pounced—knocked me back, down to the hardwood floor between the big coffee table and a heavy Queen somebody sofa. His hands clamped around my throat, strangling me. His mad handsome face twisted by jealous rage. "Diablo!" he spat. "I keel you!"

"Carlos!" Olivia tried in vain to pull him off me. "Carlos, let the boy go!"

"See how senseeteeve he eez dead!"

I saw the dark of his eyes shift to the tabletop; to the shiny silver gardening sheers. Cobra-fast, he snatched them up. The curved, four-inch blades glistened in the light as he raised them above his head. Cocked to strike in a feverish fit of homicidal passion. It was do or die time. So I did. I forced my hand free of the couch and latched desperately onto his wrist as it came stabbing down. The lethal-looking clippers momentarily held in check.

"Carlos, stop!" Mara screamed.

"Russell!" Olivia Sutton Sinclair Woolbright called out.

Sinclair. It was his life not mine which passed before my eyes. Flashes of grainy snapshots—rapid-fire and fuzzy around the edges—like a subliminal slideshow. Fleeting glimpses of Omo the boy clown, Buster at the piano, Ford frying in his electric chair, Sinclair the nautical novelist steering his own unpredictable course.

With a jolt the images came to a stop. Freeze-frame. In focus so that it all became very clear to me. Olivia. "Mara." "Mother." *Mara*! Of course. I was about to be murdered by the irate husband of Ford Sinclair's only daughter.

Weakened from the lack of oxygen, my arm started to fold; the grim, gleaming, stainless steel blades inching insanely toward my fast beating heart. I was about to blackout, to bleed in a very bad way, when, through the dimming of my senses, I heard a sudden shattering sound. I felt the shards of something 'cool hitting my face. I didn't know what was happening, but whatever it was it effectively zapped the strength from Carlos' body. He went limp. The snips dropped from his hand and slid harmlessly off my chest to the floor. Followed by Carlos. He collapsed in a heap. Belly-flopped full and flat on top of me.

Gasping for air, I recognized Olivia's commanding tone.

"Russell, I want Mr. Garcia removed from the grounds."

"Yes, ma'am."

In one clean jerk the weight was hoisted up, off me, and I could breathe again. Could see the brawny butler standing at my feet. He was holding the semiconscious Carlos like a hay bale about to be tossed. "Shall I call for the police, ma'am?" he asked.

Olivia deferred to her daughter, the wife. "Mara?"

"It would serve him right," Mara Sinclair Garcia answered.

Carlos sobbed weakly. "Mara, I a love you."

"Only I'd rather not air my dirty laundry in public."

"I agree. Russell," Olivia instructed, "put him in the Rolls and have Ricardo drive him home."

"Mara, I a love you," Carlos wept again as the butler toted him out of the room.

Rid of her crazed son-in-law, Olivia leaned over me.

"Are you all right, Woodrow?"

"I think so."

Sitting up, I winced at the ache in my neck. "Ouch!"

"Here—" Mara took me gently by the arm "—let me help you."

She eased me onto the sofa. I could definitely see the Sinclair in her now. The same piercing blue eyes, straight Gaelic nose, squared jaw. A pretty chip off the paternal block.

"What happened?" I asked, trying to rub out the kink. "What stopped him?"

"Mother," Mara said. "She broke the vase over his head."

I looked to Olivia. She frowned. "It was Colombian," she said, and together we panned to the devastated artifact in pieces on the floor. The yellow roses bent and scattered amongst the wreckage of gray clay.

"I'm sorry," I said, assuming some circumstantial share of the blame.

"Don't give it another thought," Mara consoled me. "It was just an old pot. Isn't that right, mother?"

Olivia forced a smile. "Yes. Over two hundred years old, in fact."

"The important thing is you're still in one piece," Mara said.

"Need we phone for a doctor?" Olivia asked.

"Oh, no," I declined. "I'm sure it's just a strain."

"In that case," Olivia proposed, "I think we can settle this unfortunate incident out of court."

"Settle?"

"So what did I miss?" Mara put in. "Why are you here anyways?"

"It has something to do with your father," Olivia shrugged.

"The thing is I'm . . . uh . . . I'm trying to find him."

"Ha!" Mara laughed. "Then you really are in the wrong place at the wrong time."

A less than encouraging response.

"I take it that means you haven't heard from him lately."

"Let's put it this way," Mara replied, "If ignorance is bliss, then we are absolutely euphoric where the phantom Ford is concerned."

"In other words, Woodrow," Olivia summed up, "we can't help you. Now, about your neck—what sort of restitution would be fair? Financially speaking, of course."

I considered the question for a moment. My answer, "Mrs. Woolbright, I hope you won't take this the wrong way. But, uh . . . even with all your money I couldn't buy what I'm after."

Her eyes narrowed, quizzically. "Exactly what are you after?"

"To be honest with you ma'am, I'm not exactly sure," I confessed. "All I know is it's something only your ex-husband's got to give. And since you can't help there, well, I'll settle for getting out of here alive."

I tried to stand but Mara's hand on my shoulder kept me on the sofa.

"Hold on, Woody. Mother, we can't let him leave like this."

Olivia sighed, grudging agreement. "Do you promise not to sue?"

I raised my right hand.

"I swear on my father's grave, Mrs. Woolbright."

This time her smile had a genuine arc.

"Then I think you will find that we can be quite hospitable."

CHAPTER EIGHT

I was invited to join the ladies for dinner in the formal dining room at Casa de Sol. It would be just the three of us as the man of the house, Carlton Woolbright, was away on ship building business up north.

Furthermore, I was welcomed to stay the night in the guest cottage at the back of the property. In the meantime, Mara insisted I use her old bedroom to wash and dress appropriately for the evening. I didn't want to put her out but she was adamant about it for some unexplained reason. So, with Carlos left to the chauffeur, Russell showed me the way: up the grand staircase to a second-floor suite of rooms that clearly reflected the many privileges of Mara's childhood. It was all very soft, frilly, the giant stuffed animals and girlish indulgences that went along with being born to a Gold Coast manor.

Left alone with my suitcase, I wondered why Mara had been so keen on allowing me access to such a private and personal place. Was she simply showing off, impressing upon me the enviable trappings of a rich kid? I thought not. Why would she bother when the wealth was surely obvious in every room of the house? No. There had to be another reason. A more accommodating motive behind it, I suspected. Perhaps there was something of relevance she wanted me to see. At least that's how I rationalized taking a good look around.

I was in a young socialite's sitting room. Big overstuffed

couches and chairs, plush carpeting, TV, telephone, a neat retro-deco Werlitzer jukebox lit up in a corner. Along one wall there was a library lined with leather-bound copies of children's classics. On closer inspection it appeared that the books, little cracked, if at all, were mostly for show.

Leaving Alice to her own Wonderland, I stepped into an adjacent room, where I immediately felt the fix of several hundred unblinking eyes on me. Dead eyes. Dolls' eyes. A legion of lifelike, lifeless faces; everything from Raggedy Anns to Barbies to the most exquisite porcelains and intricate Japanese woodcarvings standing silent and watchful over the princessdom. They gave me a touch of the creeps. I backed away from their vacant stares, and moved on—into a powder puff white bedroom trimmed in needlepoint lace.

A light was left on. A fine night table lamp next to the canopied bed. Its shade, bell-shaped, gave off a pinkish aura. I was drawn to it. Little pink ballerinas hand-painted on the Tiffany glass glowed in the escaping light. Projected, they danced on the white wall, white bedspread, white carpet. My attention fell to the shiny base. There was something written on the brass. A fluid, indelibly engraved inscription. It read

For Mara. Love, Daddy.

Was this what she wanted me to see?

The lamp wasn't alone on the table. Beside it stood three framed photographs. Keepsake portraits of a little girl, Mara, captured with the man she now called the "phantom."

In one photo she was a toddler standing like a circus acrobat in a pink tutu on her daddy's shoulders. In another a pigtailed tomboy in dusty dungarees astride a saddled appaloosa, Sinclair handing her the reins. Thirdly, a baby picture. Mara then a year old or so—a chubby cherub taking her first steps while the proud papa waited with open arms to receive her.

Precious Kodak moments.

Yet . . . when considered in chronological order there was an underlying uneasiness about the photos. A sense of growing estrangement. The smiles got fainter with the years, as if these were rare occasions, and getting rarer. Shying away from the camera, it seemed Sinclair was sequentially inching out of the finely crafted framework of his daughter's life. I found the implications rather troubling. This was, after all, no mere biographical footnote or creative phase to be explored in passing. This was a child, of flesh and blood and fragile heart, that Sinclair had left in his wake.

Saddened by the sudden reality of Mara's loss, I found the bathroom and splashed my face with cold water. Slipping on my suit jacket, I felt the necktie stuffed in a side pocket. When I pulled it out something fell to the carpet—a card. I picked it up. On one side the color-copied image of the Good Shepherd. On the other, a somber memorial: *In loving memory of Wood Washborn.*

The card went back in the pocket.

The tie around my neck.

A Windsor knot.

The way my father had taught me.

Russell was waiting for me at the bottom of the stairs. "The ladies are in the dining room, sir," he said, then led me down another hallway and through a double leave of heavy oak doors which parted to reveal a long banquet-sized table, elegantly set at the far end for three.

Off to one side of the room, in front of a swanky silver wine wagon, stood my two hosts. Both looked quite lovely in contrasting cocktail dresses. The mother in basic black; daughter a winsome light floral print.

"You're just in time, Woodrow." Olivia smiled. "We were about to choose an aperitif."

"Do you prefer French or Italian?" Mara asked.

French or Italian? If I had a nickel for every time I'd been asked that question I would have been worth, well . . . a nickel.

"Whatever you think is appropriate," I answered evasively.

"Since we're having seafood," Olivia decided, "let's go with a nice white Bordeaux." She opened the wagon's cooler compartment and removed a chilled bottle of the wine. Which she then delegated to Russell who was ready with a corkscrew.

"Have a seat, Woody." Mara motioned to a high-backed chair at the head of the table.

"Ladies first," I said, standing on manners.

Once they were seated, across from each other, I sat with Mara to my left, Olivia my right. Centered on the table in front of us were two thin white candles in burnished sterling holders. The flames cast undulations of golden light over the antique Waterford crystal and bone china that distinguished our place settings. Yes, indeed. In the case of one moonshiny good ol' boy bootlegger crime had certainly paid. And very handsomely, at that.

After he'd filled our wineglasses with the Bordeaux, Russell was dispatched to the kitchen with instructions for the dinner staff—we would take the first course shortly. In the meantime we sipped the cool dry white and chatted pleasantly. Mostly about me. At the ladies request, I gave them a synopsis of my life in Bird in Hand: the daily grind of dairy farming, my desire to be an artist, the tragically freak circumstances of my father's death, and the subsequent termination of my engagement to Kelly Ann.

I was pre-empted for a moment when a maid appeared with a silver service tray carrying the start of our meal. Then, over a crisp green salad topped with strips of lobster, I told of my adventures in New York. How I'd gotten their address from Arthur Brimm (who's request for an interview they'd flatly refused). How I'd fed the birds with Alice Faye, and jammed with Oats Sleet (neither of whom Olivia nor Mara had ever met). How I'd gone to the theater to see Sinclair's *The Messenger* (which they both had only read). I left out the parts about smoking reefer and running from the cops and how I'd lost my virginity to Keisha. Still, they seemed genuinely entertained by my experiences. I'd pretty much brought them up to speed by the time the entrée arrived.

It was an exotic presentation: strips of tuna cooked cold in lime juice, I was told, served over a bed of fresh vegetables, in a cool coconut sauce. "Poisson cru" Olivia called it, adding with a gracious nod that it was "Ford's favorite dish."

"We haven't had it since mother married Carlton," Mara said. "He doesn't like to be reminded of my father."

"But seeing that Carl's away," Olivia put in, "I thought you'd enjoy the nostalgia."

I did, of course. And since she'd put it on the table, I used it to probe further the depths of an ex-wife's reflection. "It says in Brimm's book that you first met Sinclair at Tennessee Williams' birthday party on Key West."

Olivia crinkled her nose, refutably.

"That's the official version," she said. "Actually it was a few days earlier." She sat back in her chair, returning in her mind to a place enshrined in the gallery of her youth. "You see, I had this friend," she continued, "Chip Moran. He'd just gotten a new speedboat and wanted to show it off. So he took my cousin Judith and me for ride down the coast to Key Biscayne, where his family owned a yacht club. They sold it years ago. Anyhow, the plan was to have lunch at the club then come straight back." A naughty glint sparked in her eyes. "Only it didn't quite work out that way."

She paused for a few seconds, as if losing herself in a picture.

"There was an old sailboat," she went on, "anchored just inside the bay. This fifty-foot, seaworn-looking thing. It seemed so . . . unpretentious, so out of place. Being the curious young snobs that we were we had to cruise by—to see what sort of riffraff was aboard.

"We were just close enough to make out the name— *Endeavor*—written in black paint along the bow when we spotted someone climbing the mast, without even a rope, like a native climbs a coconut tree. We didn't want to be too conspicuous, so Chip eased off the throttle. Keeping our distance as Jude spied through a pair of binoculars. Her breath suddenly taken away.

"'Wow!' she gushed.

"'Wow what?' I asked.

"'It's a guy. A wild-looking guy.'

"Of course Chip being Chip, he said, 'Just so he keeps that tub out of the marina.'

"But Jude was seeing it differently. She said 'It could be a dingy for all I care. He is an absolute dreamboat.'

"'Here that, Olivia? Miss Priss is swooning over Captain Tramp.'

"'Let me see.'

"I had to practically wrestle the binoculars away from her. By the time I had him in my sights he was in the crow's nest, with his back to us. No shirt on, just a pair of cutoff shorts. His hair well past his shoulders. Mind you, this was before hippies. I'd never seen a man with hair so long. Bleached a golden blond by the sun."

She paused again, basking in the warm glow.

"I watched as he untangled his flag," she continued. "It was white, with a deep sea-blue dolphin hand-painted on either side.

"Chip said, 'I'm surprised it's not the Jolly Roger.'

"Finally he turned around to face us. He had this scruffy beard, but still, he was perfect, beautiful. His body all bronze and lean. Simply gorgeous on that high pedestal. His arms stretching out . . . like a wild angel.

"'He's gonna jump,' Jude said.

"Chip, jealous, bet against him. 'A hundred dollars says he belly flops.'

"'You're on,' I said.

"He looked so free and fearless up there. Not much older than we were, yet as different as anything could be. His face to the sun. Not even a glance down as he launched himself into the air. The way he soared, I thought he was actually going to fly. Until at last he reached the top of his arc, and started down. The most graceful swan dive I've ever seen. Barely a splash as he knifed into the water.

"When he surfaced Jude started to clap. 'Bravo! Bravo!'

"Chip, having lost the bet, thought otherwise. 'Show-off.'

"Ah, but what a show. My heart was racing. I dropped the glasses, and climbed onto the side of the boat.

"'Olivia, what the hell are you doing?' Chip asked.

"It was a silly question. When the answer was right there—swimming back to the *Endeavor*. "'I'm falling in love,' I said . . . . And then, with all my clothes on, I dove in and swam after him."

She emerged from the reverie and turned to me. "I would have sailed away with him that very day." A little laughed creased the corners of her mouth. "Of course daddy was furious. His pride and joy, his princess, under the spell of this bohemian pirate. He forbade me to ever again step foot on the *Endeavor*. But," she shrugged, "as fate would have it, I didn't have to. Because a few days later Ford showed-up at Tennessee's party."

"And two weeks later you were married," I remembered from the bio.

"And eight months later Mara was born." With the inference being a premarital conception, Olivia smiled at her daughter.

I was unsure how to respond to it. I couldn't help but wonder if Sinclair had entered gladly into the whirlwind marriage. Or had he simply conceded to propriety—done the "honorable thing?"

It was a question I saw no point in pursuing. Instead, I shifted my attention back to the fish. Poisson cru. So much more than just a free meal, it gave me a culinary insight into the long ago appetites of the elusive "wild angel." I savored it. Allowing the conversation a thoughtful lull, we dined politely while beads of white wax ran like teardrops along the length of the candles; my thoughts nibbling on the fodder of an ill-fated love story. Compelling, yes, but seemingly of no help to me in terms of finding the man who had abandoned the *Endeavor* for the terra firma of Palm Beach high society.

Mara broke the silence.

"Do you know about the tree sculpture?" she asked.

I swallowed. "Tree sculpture?"

"To mark my birth," she said, "Daddy carved an old sycamore in the backyard."

"No. I didn't know that."

"It's called *Mara's Moon*."

"You mean . . . it's still there?"

It stood a good fifteen feet high. The tree's trunk fashioned into the figure of a young woman, one arm branching out, upward to a flat hand, open so that it appeared from where we were standing on the lawn to be holding aloft the fullness of a pale-yellow moon.

Mara's Moon.

"We've been offered over a million dollars for it," Olivia told me.

"As far as I'm concerned it's priceless," Mara said, her appraisal curiously inflated by an unconditional, emotional attachment.

All sentimental value aside, the sculpture remained a singular work of art. It depicted the smooth, naked body of a nymph. Her fine, Grace-like face, looking out over the dark ocean behind us, emoted an inquisitive innocence . . .

As though God Himself had whittled from the tree a prototype of Eve.

Considering the meticulous effort that had obviously gone into it, a warm thought came to my mind. "He must have loved you very much," I said to the muse who'd inspired its creation.

"At the time at least," Mara replied. "I haven't gotten so much as a birthday card from him in twenty years."

"What about before he disappeared—did he keep in contact?"

"When I was little he came around on occasion. After that it was just a phone call every now and then. Less and less as I got older."

"I lost him barely a year into the marriage," Olivia offered. "To Jack Buzbee of all people."

"Jack Buzbee," I recalled, "the painter."

"Once the two of them got together that was it. There was no room in the sandbox for a wife and baby."

"I'm sorry," I said sincerely. "That must've hurt."

"Oh, I went through the full gamut of emotions," Olivia confided. "Hurt, anger, denial, depression." She laughed, at herself.

"Until I realized it was inevitable. That you can't hold a tempest in a teacup."

"So you let him go."

"I surrendered, Woodrow. To a force of nature."

"No hard feelings?"

"Does that surprise you?" Mara asked.

"In all honesty, yes. It does."

"Tell me, Woody," the daughter questioned: "Now that you know, about his self-indulgences, his irresponsibility, do you think any less of my tree?"

I looked up at the sculpture again. I searched for a flaw, a wrong stroke of the chisel. Still, I could not find even one. The moon rested like a fairytale in the fair maiden's outstretched hand.

"No," I had to confess. "It's just . . . wonderful."

"Genius, Woody. It is, and will always be, its own excuse. Self-indulgence, irresponsibility, insanity even—as long as the art moves us we will make allowances for the artist."

"We'll even make a few for an aspiring artist," Olivia put in. "Like allowing him to digest a lovely evening in the privacy of our guest house." She motioned to a quaint stone cottage beyond the swimming pool. "I'm sure you'll find everything you need."

I thanked them profusely. They'd been very kind and generous to me.

"Just remember," Olivia said, half-joking: "No lawsuit."

I half smiled. "Lawsuit over what, ma'am?"

"In that case—" again Mara surprised me, this time with a quick peck on my cheek "—Sweet dreams, Woody."

I watched as mother and daughter walked, arm in arm, back to the grand house. Then I turned to the cottage. Lamp light beckoned through the front windows. Soft yellow squares hovering in the darkness.

*   *   *

The guesthouse was cool inside, climate controlled for my comfort. And there on the front room sofa sat my suitcase. Good ol' Russell, he was really on the ball. Ahead of the ball, in fact, for he'd placed the bag, intentionally, I suspected, where I couldn't help but notice the framed charcoal drawing hanging on the wall directly above it. A sketch, and very skillfully done, of a sailboat. The *Endeavor*. Adrift and seemingly abandoned on wavy black strokes of ocean.

A ghost ship.

At the bottom right the now familiar signature. *Ford Sinclair*.

I studied the vessel for a long while, wondering what had become of it. Sold? Junked? Sunk? I made a mental note to ask Olivia about it in the morning. Then I went snooping about to see what other remnants of Sinclair the cottage might hold. In the kitchen I found a note stuck to the refrigerator door. "Mr. Washborn—Please help yourself to a snack." Russell again, I gathered. The fridge was plentifully stocked with bottles of wine (French and Italian), soft drinks, sparkling mineral waters, assorted cheeses, crackers and fresh fruit. I helped myself to a Snapple lemonade then retired to the bedroom. There I was immediately drawn to an arrangement of red, white and yellow roses in a glass vase on a handsome Victorian-styled writing desk.

Beside the bouquet, again strategically placed, stood a matching set of leather-bound books. They bore the inlaid gold titles of the three Sinclair novels: *Windward*, *Castaway*, and *Noble Savage*. All first-edition copies.

Noble Savage in hand, I kicked off my shoes, removed my suit jacket and tie, and stretched out on the bed. Opening the book I noted the copyright (1965 by Ford Sinclair) and the name of the publisher, Washborn Press. The next thing that caught my eye was something that wasn't there—a dedication page.

Evidently the author had no one he wished to thank.

I flipped to Chapter One. The tale began

> They had him washed, groomed, costumed in silks to be put on display. Yet, in spite of all efforts to tame, he bared his fangs in the black of night, when propriety closed its colorless eyes.
>
> And unleashed a silent roar . . .

I plowed through five prose-poetic chapters. Until the swirling events of the day caught up with me and, to the ambient lullaby of the surf nearby, I fell fast to sleep.

CHAPTER NINE

I was startled awake by a *THUMP!* against the wall just above my head. I sat up. My neck had stiffened some and it took me a moment to remember where I was. The fog clearing—Palm Beach, Casa de Sol, guesthouse—when there came another *THUMP!* This time from nearer the end of the wall.

Something was clomping around outside.

I left the bed and tiptoed to a window to investigate. Peering out between the curtains, I spied a moonshadowy figure hauling what appeared to be a long ladder across the dark lawn toward the pool area.

I checked my watch. 3:15 a.m.

A burglar? I scanned for a phone; then decided against it. I didn't want to cause a major scene if it happened to be Russell on some late-night maintenance mission. Heck, for all I knew the very rich possessed certain eccentricities that required climbing to greater heights at odd hours.

I watched the figure, expecting it turning left toward the main house but that wasn't the way it went. Instead, it passed by the pool and kept going, straight ahead, disappearing into the night.

I pondered what to do. Should I stay put, shrug it off as none of my business, and probably nothing to be concerned about? Or should I go out there, venture blindly into a possibly dangerous situation?

The smart move, I decided, was to make no move at all.

With that in mind, I proceeded to venture blindly.

I crept low. The grass was soft, dewy under my anxious footsteps. The Junior Taps drumrolling of heart drowned out, I hoped, by the incessant lapping of the sea. When I spotted the figure again it was over by the tree sculpture. The ladder leaned up against the tall silhouette of *Mara's Moon*.

Unaware of my presence, it started to climb.

I snuck closer. I could now see that it was a man, but too thin to be Russell. Within earshot, I heard him muttering to himself, sobbing in Spanish as he reached the statue's extended arm.

"Mara," he lamented.

I recognized the voice.

"Carlos?"

Startled, he turned, looked down.

"Who eeze eet?" he wanted to know. "Who dare?"

"Carlos, it's me." I stepped forward where he could see me. "Woody Washborn."

"Ay," he sneered, "so eet eez . . . da geegilo."

"Carlos, I'm not a gig—"

"Go way! Lee me lone!"

He climbed out onto the branch. I saw he had a rope in his hand.

"Carlos, what are you doing?"

"I weel proof my love." He hitched the rope to the limb.

"Carlos, please, you're gonna fall."

"No, geegilo, I no fall." He sat up, facing the ocean. "I hang myself," he declared. "From da seembol of my Mara's birth."

I saw that the other end of the rope was noosed around his neck.

"Carlos, don't be ridiculous, you're not gonna hang yourself. Now come on down and we'll talk about it."

"Too late talk!" He cinched the noose tight to his throat. "Ooly death can relief my suffer!"

"Carlos, this isn't gonna solve anything."

"Dios divino," he prayed, eyes to heaven, "to you a hand I comeet my soel."

"Help!" I yelled toward the house.

"Shut up!" he warned me. "Or chee weel watch me die!"

"Just stay right there. I'm coming up."

"You can no stop me!"

"Hey, if you wanna end your life that's your business." Not wanting to spook him I took the rungs slowly. "But seeing as I'm the only witness, I don't wanna miss any last words you might have."

"Chee refuse to forgeeve," he wept, poised to push off. "Dis way chee weel never forgeet."

"A quitter," I asked, nearing the bough, "is that how you wanna be remembered?"

"Nough a you! Come no closer!"

"Okay." I stopped, just out of reach. "I can hear you fine from here."

"You muss tell er, geegilo," he sobbed. "Tell my love it was her name last on my leeps. Mara!"

And with that he dropped from the perch.

What happened next happened so fast I had only a vague notion of it. Based on the evidence, however, I must have leapt from the ladder and grabbed hold of the branch with my left hand, while at the same time clamping my right hand around Carlos' wrist. My wingspan fully extended before the love-crazed Cuban reached the end of his rope.

His near dead weight nearly jerked my arms out of their sockets. Still, I hung on. Stretched between man and tree when I heard a terrible *CRACK!* from above. The sickening snap of dismembered sycamore. Then the sculptured arm came down, ripped from its body (aaah! la the *Venus de Milo*) by some three hundred pounds of desecrating humanity.

We crashed to the ground in absurd succession. Carlos first, then me on top of him, and lastly, but certainly not lightly, the severed seven foot long limb that had held aloft Mara's very own moon.

"Oh, no," I whimpered, sandwiched between very bad and much worse. "It's broken. We broke it!"

Carlos moaned. "I chould be dead."

"We are dead!" I cried. "When they see this they'll hang us both."

"To hell wit eet!" Carlos scoffed, wriggling out from under the heap. "Dare eez no art ware dare eez no heart."

On my knees, I surveyed the damage. It was extensive, gruesome. The tree torn and splintered. Carlos slipped from the noose and got to his feet. He said, "Dey can use da wood to beeld my coffeen," then headed off toward the shoreline.

"Carlos! Carlos, maybe we can fix it!"

I went after him. He wasn't going to leave me there to face the grim music alone. I chased him along a dark stretch of beach. To a private dock where a twenty-some foot cabin cruiser was moored, bobbing with the incoming tide.

Carlos was already on board. Cutting the lines with a knife.

"Carlos, you can't just run away from this!"

"I bean cast out," he said. "Now I cast off."

"Cast off for where?"

"Go, geeligo! Go craw back to my wive her bed!"

"Carlos, I'm not sleeping with Mara!"

"Take everyting! Jus leabe me my honor!"

The boat free of the dock, he hurried into the cabin.

"Carlos!"

The engine roared to life.

"Carlos!"

The craft pulling away, I ran to the end of the dock. In his madness there was no telling what he might do. The hanging fiasco wasn't a bluff; he would have gone through with it had I not intervened. No doubt he was intent on committing suicide. The question was what more could I do to prevent him from finishing the job?

The answer was ominously clear. If I let him go there would be nothing anyone could do to stop him.

"Shit!" I said. Then I made the leap.

I grabbed onto the starboard side railing, and held on, my feet dragging through the water, as the cruiser sped toward the open sea.

*   *   *

We were approximately two hundred yards from shore before I managed to pull myself over the ledge and flop onto the deck. Exhausted, I laid there for a moment, half-soaked, until a queasy sense of assumed responsibility dragged me to my feet. I sloshed into the cabin to find the calamitous captain at the helm.

"Carlos."

He spun around, surprised and ungrateful to see me.

"Geeligo," he sneered, the blade (a scuba driver's knife) still in his hand, "you are a fool."

"So, I've been told," I nodded. "But at least I believe. I believe in me and I believe in you."

"An Mara, chee beliebe," he growled. "Chee beliebe I em a stink!"

"Better a stink than a coward." I told him, "You want something bad enough, you fight for it."

"I wanna die!" He raised the knife, challengingly. "I fight for dat!"

"Carlos, I know how you feel. Believe me, I've been told over and over again that I stink. That I have no chance of ever getting what I want most. But no matter what anybody says, I'm not giving up. I'm willing to do whatever it takes to have what it takes. And if you really want Mara back you're gonna have to do the same—prove to her that you don't stink. That no matter what she says you're not giving up. It's not like you haven't charmed her before. I mean you had her yesterday, you can get her again tomorrow."

"Dare eez no tomodo!"

"Then do it tonight, right now! Turn this boat around and go tell her how it's gonna be!"

He reached behind him, cut the engine.

"Carlos, that's not around, that's off."

He came toward me, knife first, backing me out of the cabin and under the stars. "The ladder, Carlos, you can climb up to her bedroom window."

"Chee made eet said—finito!"

He rushed past me, keeping the sharp serrated steel between us, and went to the stern. There was a thick nylon rope coiled on the deck. He crouched, snatched up a loose end, and went about knotting the rope around his ankle. I appealed to his theological leanings:

"You said 'Dios'—that's Spanish for God, right?"

"Keep way, geeligo—doan may me ca chu!"

"Not only is suicide against the law, it's a sin," I reminded him. "So if you're thinking you'll go to heaven, think again."

"You wanna save me my sin . . ." The rope secured to his leg, he stood straight, tossed the knife to the deck at my feet "Den keel me. Put me out my meesery!"

"Carlos, give me a break here. Who do I look like—Dr. Kevorkian? I'm not gonna kill anybody."

He reached down, snatched up a four-pronged grapnel anchor. It was tied to the other end of the rope. "Den to a hell I go."

"Carlos, no!"

"Mara . . ."

I lunged for him; too late. He threw himself backward, anchor and all, overboard—*SPLASH!* "Carloooooos" I screamed at the ocean. At fading ripples of dreadful displacement. He was gone. Sinking. Falling to sleep deep with the fishes.

As it was, I had little chance of even finding him down there in that briny blackness. Frantic, I scanned the deck for an idea. Near the starboard wall I spotted an open cargo bag. A scuba mask peeked out at me. I grabbed it, ransacked the bag, tossing aside wetsuits and flippers, until I found a big flashlight-sized diving lamp. I switched it on, it worked, a halogen cone of blazing white.

I tugged the mask over my eyes, nose. I grabbed the knife off the deck then aimed the beam at the spot where Carlos had gone under. Inflating my lungs with salty air, I stepped up onto the ledge. "Dios Divino" went my prayer before I jumped, defiantly, into the dark chill abyss.

Submerged in a sudden silence, weightlessness, panic

percolated in my throat. I swallowed it, trying to orient myself to the hydrodynamic suppression of my senses. The lamp light, translucent, surreal, pushed back the black maybe five feet, maybe more, maybe less, hard to tell, it was all more or less the same in every direction: a swirling gray galaxy of tiny, piscatorial stars shooting every which way at the flick of a tail fin. I could feel the humbling crush of infinite galaxies beyond the eerie light. The primordial domain of cold-blooded man-eaters. But there was no time to think about any of that now. At the moment my universe was far narrower in scope; revolving solely around Ford Sinclair's suicidal son-in-law. Like it or not, Carlos, here I come. With the lamp in one hand and the knife in the other it wasn't easy swimming. Still, the popping in my ears told me I was getting deeper. Perhaps twenty feet down when—like an apparition materializing in the gloom—I saw him. His arms up-stretched. Eyes bulging. Cheeks bloated as they held on to his last breath of air.

He was floating in place. The rope extended taut into the darkness below. Evidently the anchor had sunk to rest on some obscure continental slope, shelf, whatever. Awash in the pale light, Carlos' face expressed a sort of moribund rapture. What else could it be but a divine beam coming to transport his spiritual self to the Great Beyond?

Imagine the disappointment when he realized it was no angel dispatched to repossess his eternal soul; that in fact his irradiant deliverer was none other than the meddlesome "geegilo." He exhaled just to spite me, the bubbles rising from his lips. I thought, Nice try, amigo, only you underestimated the staying power of this hardheaded country boy. I swam past him, to the vertical stretch of nylon holding him down. Luckily the knife proved as sharp as it looked. A few furious strokes sawed the rope in two. And up he went, skyward, like a helium balloon set free. A short streamer of nylon tailed behind him; I grabbed it and went along for the ride, kicking my feet to lessen the drag. A buoyant ascent through the darkness.

We broke the surface to a starry burst of twinkling applause, and not a second too soon. I gasped for air, greedy, water-treading breaths with one arm hooked tenaciously around Carlos' chest. No way was I going to let him go now. Come hell or higher water this work was irrevocably in progress.

Semiconscious, Carlos vomited the sea from his body. If there was any fight left him it was well diluted. He surrendered without a struggle as I hauled him back to the boat.

We flopped onto the deck. Sopped. Spent. Adrift. Rocking to the wavy biorhythms of the ocean, several minutes passed without a word between us. It was Carlos who broke the silence. His voice raspy, wistful, "I em remind of unudder boat," he began. "Much smaller den dis."

He paused to cough a last spume of seawater out of his lungs.

"Eet was da boat we take to leabe Cooba. Bary old, many leak. En da motor, no good, eet break doan. We adreef, jus like dis. Tree night en two day. Teel da U.S.A Coasaguard dey come to da resacue."

"When was that?"

"Fi year ago. Forta July. Dey take us to Miami. Say dey gonna sen us back to Habana."

"But they didn't."

"No. Da Coobanos here—dey make protest. So da immigracione say okay, we stay. Be free."

"Free is good."

"Si, but I know nobody een dis country. En I pay da man wit da boat all a my money."

"So what did you do?"

"I dance," he said. "Get job to teach salsa, mambo, rumba. Estudio Arturo Morree."

"Arthur Murray. Yeah, I've heard the name."

"One day we go beeg dance at fine country club. To instruction da meembers how to do." He sniffed back a fresh gurgle of tears. "Dats how I meet my Mara. My beeuuteefoe Mara . . ."

"Easy, Carlos. Let's not get all worked up again."

"I can no help eet. I a love er, geegilo."

"Then why did you go and get fresh with another woman?"

"I got a drunk. Eet may me loco. Eet no ever happen ageen!"

"Okay, okay, I believe you. Just stay calm. Look on the bright side."

"Wha bright? Dare eez no bright."

"The bright is that Mara wouldn't be so jealous if she wasn't still very much in love with you."

He perked up.

"Chee steel a love me?"

"One thing's for sure—you'll never find out at the end of a rope."

"But I muss proof to er."

"So do what other guys in the dog house do. Send her flowers, candy, write her a romantic poem."

"Dat no be enuff. Chee too much mad."

"It seems to me she's got a soft spot for sentimental things. I mean take her father for example. Sinclair walked out on her, and still she found it her heart to forgive him." That reminded me of the emotionally "priceless" and now armless tree sculpture; but this was hardly the time to dwell on the negative.

"Si," Carlos agreed. "Chee steel a love er pa-pa bary bary much."

"You gotta give her another chance, man. It's the only smart bet."

"Smart bet?"

"If you take the gamble and she takes you back, then you win, right?"

"Right."

"And if you take the gamble and she doesn't take you back, well, what do you have to lose?"

"Nada. Chee eez my everyting."

"But if you don't take the gamble and she would've taken you back, then you'll be an even bigger loser than you are now. And if that's the case then she's better off without you."

He pondered my point for a soggy moment.

"A pome, you say?"

I smiled, as best I could.

"She wouldn't be the first woman to melt over a mushy poet."

"But I a dance," he sighed. "No a writer of sweet tings."

"Just put what you're feeling on paper. Bleed ink."

"You muss help me, geegilo. Help me bleed a pome."

"Carlos, if I could I would. But—"

"Come!" He picked himself off the deck. "We fine wha we need een da cabeen!"

I followed him to the bridge. He rummaged through a cabinet under the steering wheel and came up with a ballpoint pen and a captain's logbook. He flipped the book open to a blank page then scribbled on the paper until the ink began to flow, red. "Perfecto," he said. "Rojo. Like a *blood*." In a fever he jerked off his waterlogged Polo top and sat at a small table attached to the cabin wall. "Seet, geegilo, we muss hurry."

I figured what the heck, it beat another dark dip in the drink.

Likewise I stripped out of my dripping wet white funeral shirt and sloshed onto the seat across from him. I waited supportively for the fair Erato—sister Muse of love poetry—to embrace the mad cause as Carlos tapped the pen against the edge of the table. Drumming a little samba beat, he stared, possessed by a pathos of great purpose, at the blank paper . . . . Then the tapping began to slow in tempo. When it petered out all together Carlos looked up at me, like he didn't have a clue. "How I begeen?" he asked.

"Just write what you feel," I told me. "What you know."

"All I know eez I feel like a keeling myself."

"Yeah, well, you might wanna ease into that. Start with something a bit less Edgar Allan Poe."

"Who Poe? I can no tink a less!"

"The main thing is not to panic. Relax. Stay focused. Concentrate on what's happening at this very moment. Where are you right now?"

"I em here. Adreef een da boat."

"Adrift," I waxed. "Cast adrift . . . on . . . uh . . . on the ocean of your tears."

"Si," he said excitedly. "Ocean a tear, dat eez me!"

"So what are you waiting for, write it down."

"No. You." He slid the open log across the table. "Go a faster eef you write."

He had me there. "Okay. But just the first draft. Then you'll have to copy it over. It's got to be in your handwriting."

"Si," he agreed, "I do later," and slapped the pen into my hand. "Now go. Mas."

I took it for what it was, a challenge. A challenge I couldn't walk away from without walking on water. Thus, feeling merely mortal, I put pen to paper, what we had so far: "Cast adrift on the ocean of my tears . . ."

"Si, si!"

Si, indeed. Because it was then that a most amazing thing happened. All of a sudden I saw the world from a distance. Shrunk to the size of a desktop globe, it spun ever so slowly. A reprieve from the chronic dizziness. I could actually see the great forest beyond the tree line of my own limited experience.

The disembodied, unobstructed view of a *ghostwriter*.

My head cleared. Above the white noise of my short, egocentric life the words came to me. Airborne. Precise. Like transmissions to a satellite.

"The heartbreaking waves cry out your name . . ."

"Mara!" Carlos cried. "Mara!"

CHAPTER TEN

When the sun came up I approached the big house in a change of dry clothes with my suitcase and the logbook in hand. I found Russell in the kitchen having his breakfast. He asked if I would like mine served out by the pool, such a beautiful morning. "No, thank you," I said. I didn't mention the giant arm—the sculptured sycamore limb—now laying ripped from its finely chiseled body out there on the back lawn. I had more pressing business to attend.

"Is Mara up yet?"

"No, sir," answered the butler. "Not for another few hours, I'm sure."

It couldn't wait that long. When I told him I had to see her, right away, he raised a bushy eyebrow at the idea of awakening the sleeping beauty prematurely. What he didn't know, what I thought it best not to tell him, was that I had been entrusted to deliver a literary kiss from her very own Prince Charming.

"Seriously, Russell, I need speak to her. It's very important."

He gave me a look that said, It better be; then hurried off to fetch her.

A few minutes later I heard footsteps again, and into the kitchen walked Olivia. In her black silk pajamas she looked, even at that early hour, like the hundreds of millions of dollars she had. "Woody, what's going on?" she wanted to know. "Why did you send Russell to wake Mara?"

I held up the logbook. "It's all in here, Mrs. Woolbright."

Soon Russell returned. Mara followed in a thick white bathrobe. Still half asleep, she said, "Woody, this isn't a farm. We don't milk cows at dawn."

"Mara, I've got something for you." I opened the book, the page marked with a black lock of Carlos' hair (his idea). "Something you need to read."

"What is it?"

"Something someone put his life on the line to write."

I handed it to her, the red ink woven into a valentine. Intrigued, she gazed intently at the poem Carlos had carefully copied over. Her lips moving in silence as she read: Cast adrift . . .

I watched her face. It began to soften. Blush to a warm pink. With a sigh she turned the page, reading faster, her icy-blue Sinclair eyes melting to shiny pools of tears that fell onto the paper like the first sprinkle of a new spring. Bull's eye! We had her. Carlos' passion put to my words. I felt a sudden surge of exhilaration. Poetic validation. Move over, Monsieur de Bergerac. There was a new agent d'amour in town.

At the end, a simple: Love, Carlos.

Mara looked up at me. "Where is he?" she asked, swept away.

"Outside," I told her. "On the front lawn."

She raced from the room, taking the book with her. Stoned by it all, I turned to Olivia. She was re-examining me in the shifted light of events.

"Woodrow, why do I suspect you had something more to do with this?" she asked.

"Oh, it's beyond me, ma'am." I shrugged. "I'm just the messenger."

How the ladies of Casa de Sol took the news about the damage done to *Mara's Moon* I don't know. I left that bit of mad monkey business to Carlos, who, grateful for my literary labors on his behalf, had assured me that he would take full responsibility for the sculpture's amputated arm.

"So, where will you go from here?" Olivia asked when I told her I had to be on my way.

"Key West," I answered. "See if I can get a lead on your ex-husband from Jack Buzbee."

Olivia cringed dissuasively. "Woodrow, that is not a good idea." She warned me, "The only thing you'll get from Jack Buzbee is grief."

She made no attempt to mask her contempt for the man. I sensed a transference of blame, as if she needed to believe that Sinclair's desertion was in no way a reflection of her own (or perhaps, more importantly, his own) faults. Making Buzbee the convenient fall guy for her loss.

In light of her hard feelings, I was reluctant to remind her that the two men had, by all accounts, been the closest of friends for a considerable time.

"Even Ford had his reservations about Jack," she replied. "He called him a walking contradiction. Equal parts creator and destroyer."

"But that was thirty years ago. He must've mellowed some by now."

"Men like Jack Buzbee don't mellow with age," she said. "They only get more rotten."

"Even so, I don't have much else to go on. He's a risk I'm just gonna have to take."

Once she saw there was no talking me out of it, she gave me a bit of information I could follow up on. She remembered—like the fresh dig of an old sliver embedded deep in some bleak corner of her brain—the address of the house on Key West where Sinclair had lived with Buzbee after he'd left her. Borrowing a pen from Russell, she wrote it down on a monogrammed sheet of pastel-blue stationary. When I thanked her she waved it off, saying she seriously doubted she'd done me a favor. Then she walked me to the front door, which Russell opened on my truck still parked in the driveway. A circular driveway around an island of rich green lawn, where Mara and Carlos were seated, locked in a resuscitative embrace, oblivious to all but their own tear-drenched kisses.

I didn't interrupt them to say goodbye.

"Remember what I said, Woodrow," Olivia reiterated, "be very careful with Jack Buzbee."

"Yes, ma'am."

As she shook my hand goodbye, Olivia Sutton Sinclair Woolbright appraised my face for the last time. "You know, Woodrow, it just occurred to me," she said: "There something in your eyes, exactly what I'm not quite sure." She smiled. "But I do believe I can see a little of the young Ford in you."

Was she just being kind? Probably. Still, sincere or otherwise, it was a swell compliment. I looked out at his daughter, wrapped in the rekindled romance of Carlos' arms, and then turned back to her mother.

"It seems there's some of him in all of us, ma'am."

Circling the flower-trimmed island of lawn in the pickup, I recalled what Mara had said last night under the sycamore moon: about her father and genius and acceptance without condition. A gracious sentiment, I thought, but how generous would she be with her forgiveness when she surveyed the busted statue that bore her name?

I could only hope that love, like art, would provide its own excuse.

The gate opened automatically to let me out. As it closed behind me I drove into the blinding sunshine. A short while later I was back on the I-95 continuing south. It promised another hot and sticky day ahead of me.

Beyond that I had no idea what to expect.

It took about an hour to get to Miami. There I segued onto Highway A1A for the one hundred and fifty mile or so drive to Key West.

On the bridge leaving the mainland a huge black cloud rolled in off the ocean and it started to rain. Through a full-fledged downpour, I island hopped the deep blue gaps between Key Largo and Big Pine Key—a reefy bracelet of lush greens flanked by the

Atlantic to the east and the Gulf of Mexico to the west. On a clear day I imagined a laid-back succession of maritime paradises. In that hard falling rain, though, there was a gray vulnerability about it all. A sense of being at the mercy of rising tides.

At Big Pine the cloudburst stopped as suddenly as it had started, like someone turned off a faucet, and the sky quickly brightened again. From there it was muggy smooth sailing to my port-of-call, Key West.

I stayed on a main drag to the extreme heart of the island. Under the lazy sway of palm trees it boasted quaint little souvenir shops and tempting tourist traps. Along with the many reverent reminders of the key's famous favorite adopted son, the late great Ernest Hemingway. There were actually grown men walking around looking Halloweenishly Hemingwayesque with their white beards and barrel chests and novelistic notions of romantic adventure. Library card bullfighters from Buffalo. Armchair big game hunters from Little Rock. Pilgrims come to raise a toast to *The Old Man and the Sea*.

I could pretty much pick out the locals. They moved like they had either somewhere or nowhere else to be. The lightweight business suits on lunch break, sun-baked sea dogs loading up on supplies, heat frazzled mothers herding small blond children toward shiny minivans. Diehard beach bums combing inland for handouts. At a red light a hotrod muscled in beside me. With the swarthy young driver bobbing his ducktailed head to a pulsating Calypso beat, I fished from my pocket the address Olivia had given me. When the light turned green, I pulled over to a space at the curb where a man with a real pegged leg—dressed in the puffy white shirt and silver hopped earring of a pirate—was playing a guitar, singing like Jimmy Buffett:

"I'm a son of a son, son of a son of a sailor/Son of a gun, haul the last ton, one step ahead of the jailer . . ."

I waited until he'd finished the song then cut in to ask for directions. He told me he took requests for a dollar. I handed him a buck out the passenger-side window and requested some assistance in finding Caroline Street.

"No sweat, mate." He pointed the way. "Just take a right here on Duval, go past Eaton, the next cross-street is Caroline. Can't miss it."

As I pulled away he broke into a Neil Diamond song, belting it out: "Sweet Caroline, ba da da da, good times never seemed so good . . ." I turned onto Duval. The voice grew fainter, faded entirely from earshot and several blocks later I crossed Eaton, the next intersection Caroline. "Ba da da da" I sang, cruising slowly to note the house numbers in passing.

The homes themselves were good-sized, well tended, painted the vibrant colors of endless summer. I could smell citrus in the balmy breeze, mingled with the heady sizzle of backyard barbecue. I'd gone a few blocks when, just up ahead on my left, I spotted one lot that stood out from the rest. Conspicuous by shadow and apparently years of neglect. Through a wild tangle of dark trees and high weeds, I could vaguely discern the undertones of a house, on the brink, as it was, of being swallowed completely by what amounted to a most unneighborly patch of fenced-in jungle.

There was no number to be seen. The front door only dimly visible. Given the sequential order of things, however, I deduced that it had to be the place I was looking for. The question was, Did anybody still live in the house? It looked abandoned. Not to be put off, I parked in front, and followed what there was of a footpath to a peeling black door. No number anywhere. No light coming through a picture window obscured by overgrown hedges. All in all, it exuded a gloomy sense of desertion.

I knocked. Waited. Unanswered, I knocked again, harder.

"He ain't home."

I spun around. Didn't see anyone.

"Hello?"

"He ain't home."

I looked up. There was a kid, maybe ten-years-old, sitting in a tree some ten feet above me. He had curly red hair and freckles, like Huckleberry Finn in baggy blue jeans and bare feet.

"Do you mean Mister Buzbee?" I asked him.

"He ain't home."

So I'd heard. "By any chance do you know when he'll be back?"

The kid mugged, shrewd-like. "Tell ya where he's at for a quarter."

A trend seemed to be developing; information wasn't free. I tugged a shiny new quarter from my pocket and flipped it into the air, the kid snatched it impressively. He gave it a good going over to make sure it was real. Then he grinned, and gave me the lowdown.

"I don't cry for anybody. And I say bullshit to anybody who says they'll cry for me. Funerals—pure narcissism veiled in black. Nobody mourns the dead. We only cry for ourselves; for our own maggots' lunch mortality."

He threw back what was left of a tumbler of whiskey then slammed the glass down on the scarred Irish Pub bartop. "All pity is self pity" he went on. "So fuck family, fuck friends, fuck the whole bullshit charade!"

"Excuse me," I said.

He swiveled around on his stool. His face was leathery like an old beat-up shoe. A dribble of the brown booze ran down the stubble that grayed his chin. "And fuck you too," he told me. "And you—" he swiveled back to the bartender "—you short-pouring mick, fill it up this time."

The bartender had some beef behind his shamrock-green apron. He looked to be about fifty, a strong twenty years younger the rawboned hell-raiser dispensing the grief. Had he a mind to he could've literally, justifiably, thrown the older man out of the joint. But he didn't. Instead, he took it in stride. Like he'd taken it before.

He said, "I gotta see some green first, Jack."

"The green's around my gills. Put it on my tab."

"I could wallpaper this place with your tab. No more till you square up."

"So, Shylock wants his pound of flesh. How typical," Jack Buzbee grumbled, plucking from the breast pocket of his paint splattered dingy white T-shirt a thick charcoal pencil, which he used to scribble on a clean cocktail napkin. Having initialed it, J.B., he pushed the napkin across the bar. "There," he said, "an original Buzbee. Worth more than you and this shithole put together."

"Only it's not green" the bartender stood firm.

"You're a fucking *philistine!*" Buzbee declared.

"His drink is on me," I interjected.

Buzbee swung around again.

"What are you, a fucking parrot? Get the hell off my shoulder!"

I stepped to his side.

"Give him whatever he wants," I told the bartender.

"Make it a double," Buzbee growled.

Pouring, the barman looked over at me. "What about you?"

"He'll have what I'm having," Buzbee answered.

I nodded, laid a twenty-dollar bill on the bar and watched the whiskey flow. Straight. Neat. As it neared the brim, my attention shifted to the square of generic white paper that lay scribbled on, signed, unaccepted. "If nobody wants this napkin," I asked, "Can I have it?"

"It's not a napkin anymore," the artist grumbled, "it's a Buzbee. And back us up with the change," he barked at the barman.

The tender gave me a curious look. It seemed to ask: Are you one? The sucker who was born on that day?

I nodded again. If the shoe fit.

The twenty went into the till and nothing came out. The booze already to Buzbee's lips when I raised a provocative toast— "To Ford Sinclair"—and gauged the old painter's reaction. Buzbee paused. He brooded into his whiskey for a distant moment. Then, without reply, he downed the drink. Only a slight, grizzled grimace on his face as the Old Fitzgerald hit the spot, a sore spot, it seemed, deep in his gut.

Having no experience with hard liquor, I followed Buzbee's

lead and took a big swig. It felt like a mouthful of bumblebees.
Swallowed, they stung all the way down, swarming hot in my
belly. I gagged. Teary-eyed.

"I figured as much," Buzbee scoffed. "Still feeding off mama's
tit." He handed me a napkin. "Enough already, mop it up, boy."

I dried my face. Wiped my running nose. My breath barely
caught when I realized, too late, that it was the napkin Buzbee
had scribbled on. The charcoal soaked, smeared, ruined, I turned
to him. Why?

"I would've framed it," I said.

His wetted lips curled into a crooked grin.

"Then you're even *dumber* than you look."

John Paul Buzbee. Described by Arthur Brimm in *Ford Sinclair:
Half a Life* as " . . . a once promising expressionist diminished by
uncompromising inner demons."

His early background is sketchy. Born somewhere in the mid-
west during the Depression, he arrived in Chicago a young man
with a hobo chip on his shoulder and a stolen paintbrush in his
hand. His talent was said to be clearly evident; but a chronic
intolerance for any suggestion of authority quickly put him at
odds with the established art circles of the time. When a little
career-minded ass kissing was in order, Jack Buzbee was prone to
bite instead.

From Chicago to New York to cities across Europe he'd
scrapped and scraped by—selling his art for a pittance of its true
value to wealthy patrons he would soon alienate—before finally
washing ashore on Key West in the early-1960s.

A few years later he had company, a cohort of sorts: Sinclair.
The ex-jazz kid, ex-playwright, ex-young literary lion blew into
town for what was supposed to be a short weekend away from
the domestic obligations of Palm Beach. A short weekend, it
turned out, that lasted for nearly three years.

Jack Buzbee drank unresponsively as I told him why I'd come
and who I'd found along the way. When my story came to him

he lit a fresh unfiltered Camel cigarette off the one he'd just smoked and got up from his stool. The back-up whiskey in hand, he lumbered to a far corner of the room where he sat at a table, facing the wall, to drink alone.

I looked to the big Irishman for a few wise words of bartenderly advice. He told me I had charcoal on my nose then walked off to share the laugh with the only other patron he had—a bleary-eyed regular, I gathered, under a floppy fishing cap stuck with dangling angler's hooks that swayed as he chuckled into his beer mug at my expense.

Very funny. Wiping the sooty black "yolk" from my face, I glanced over at Buzbee. He clearly wanted nothing more to do with any of it. Like we were all fools he could no longer bear to suffer.

So I waited. And *waited*. For over an hour, pretending to sip at my glass of bees, I allowed the artist his distance, while at the same time making it conspicuously apparent that I would not be so easily gotten rid of. Until at last his thirst got the better of him and he had to acknowledge me again.

"Woodburn!" he barked. "Another drink over here."

The bartender poured it. I paid and delivered it. Setting the full tumbler on the table, I turned to go back to my stool—

"Where the fuck you going?" Buzbee snapped. "Sit your ass down!"

I took the chair against the wall, directly across from him. He chain-lit a Camel, blew the smoke in my face. "Sinclair was a damned romantic," he snarled. "Always rummaging through the madness looking for something sacred. He saw more than was there. He painted what should've been there, what was missing from the picture. And people being what they are, they responded to that. It made them feel noble to be on his side."

"So what do you think made him, uh, you know, abandon them?"

"Abandon shit!" he scoffed. "They *chased* him away."

"What do you mean, chased him? Seems to me they couldn't get enough of him."

"Exactly. The work, the art, it wasn't enough. They wanted

the man, a piece of the artist. I saw it—they were climbing over each other to suck his dick. They drained him. Just like they drained Hemingway. Hell, I tied one on with Ernie not long before he blew his brains out. The poor bastard, they'd squeezed him dry. Drop by bloody drop." He took a pull off his whiskey, winced it down. "But Ford, he was on to them. He saw that they'd laid the same trap for him. So, rather than swallow a bullet like Papa, he flew the coop."

"When was the last time you talked to him?"

"Fall of '73. By then he'd gotten bit by the movie bug, plague-spreading little shit fly that it is. I told him to his face: Only thing a camera's good for is tourists and peepshows."

"You have to admit, though, he made some powerful films."

Buzbee paused, picked up his drink.

"How old are you?" he asked.

I told him, twenty.

"Yeah well . . ."

He knocked back what was left of his whiskey then slammed the glass to the table.

" . . . I can *still* kick your ass."

He was waiting for me outside.

"C'mon, Woodburn! Let's see what you're fucking made of!"

Leaving the low air-conditioned light of the pub, I squinted against the late-afternoon sunshine.

"So," Buzbee sneered, "you've got some balls on you after all." Flicking yet another spent cigarette onto the sidewalk, he came toward me. "The courage of the ignorant." He snatched the unopened bottle of Old Fitz the bartender had illegally sold me at a ridiculously inflated price from my hand, and then headed off, with only the slight hitch of a stagger, down the street.

I hesitated. He looked, smelled—

"Woodburn!"

—and sounded like trouble.

Still, I followed him.

CHAPTER ELEVEN

"We first met right here—on this very beach," Buzbee recalled as we left our footprints in the sand. "I remember it clearer than yesterday. I was into a watercolor, a washy little seascape I could always hawk for rent money in town . . . when along comes this smooth-looking rascal, all got up in loose white silk, letting the tide lap over a pair of fancy-ass Italian loafers, custom-made, had to run five hundred dollars or more, and he's wading through the surf like they were dime-store flip-flops, working on a bottle of fifty-year-old Rothchild Cabernet. Which I found out later he'd swiped from his fat cat father-in-law at the time.

"Anyhow, I didn't know who he was to look at him. But he damn well knew me. Said he'd caught some West End gallery show I did in London while he was over there doing one of his stage plays. 'Course when he told me Ford Sinclair it rang the bells. I'd heard his music, seen his books around, and the marriage to Olivia made all the papers. But there was never anything to suggest he was a painter. At that point he was just getting serious about it. It wasn't until we'd knocked off the bottle, and a few more back in his hotel room, that he finally decided to cut the Sutton strings and paint fulltime. The next day he went and bought the house on Caroline, and we moved in together. Three years of burning the candle at both ends, playing hard and working harder.

"We must've painted each other a dozen times. Mostly here on this very shore, face to face, mano a mano, dueling portraits at ten paces. A different school every time—classic, expression, impression, cubist, you name it—always stretching ourselves, pushing one another, busting the other's balls . . .

"'You're looking a little tired, Buzz. Need a break?'

"'Break my ass. Sinclair, I can out paint you, out drink you, and out fuck you on my worst day. And that ain't today.'

"'Don't get me wrong now. You've held up pretty damn well. For a middleweight, that is.'

"'Keep talking, Romeo. I'm gonna send you back to your rich Palm Beach bitch with your whipped tail between your legs.'

"'Problem is, You just don't have the muscle to go toe-to-toe with a heavyweight. Same way your boy Van Gogh didn't have punch enough to slug it out with a man the likes of Gauguin.'

"'You wanna go toe-to-toe with me? Then fuck this horse-hair shit!' I chucked my brush at him. 'Let's throw some real muscle around. Add some blood to the palette.'

"'Ah, what the hell. We're losing the light anyhow.'

"So we'd go at it. Beat the living tar out of each other. End up flopping around in the water like a couple of spent fish. That was the Ford Sinclair I knew. Only man on this earth worth the breath to call my friend."

Buzbee plopped down to the sand. He looked far off over the gulf. We'd covered a long stretch of beach and it had tired him, emphysemically. As he lit another cigarette, I sat beside him. Watching the waves roll in, I could almost see the two of them, an odd couple of eccentric artists, their easels standing by as they battled like kindred alpha-males over some aesthetic inner territory in the waning daylight.

He took a long pull off the whiskey bottle, then passed it to me. I forced down what I could without gagging before passing it back. It became a kind of solemn routine between us, a sloshing duet under the caw of circling seagulls.

After a lull of quiet contemplation, I questioned him:

"So what did Sinclair mean about Van Gogh, and Gauguin?"

"Ah," he grunted, recalling fondly, "it was a sort of running debate between us. Me—I'm a sucker for Vincent. While Ford, his hard-on bent toward Paul."

"Why? What did he see in Gauguin?"

"I'd say it had more to do with the subject matter than the technique. All that exotic schoolboy adventure shit." That said, Buzbee labored to his feet. When he started walking again I jumped up and hurried to his side—

"Adventure shit?"

—and paid the price.

"For chrissake, Woodburn, we're talking Gauguin, you idiot! The island paintings. Oceania. Sinclair had a fascination for the primitive. You can see it in his own work."

"What do you think of it?" I persisted. "Ford's work, I mean."

"If I didn't think he had what it took I wouldn't've given a rat's asshole when he turned away from it. Was a damn fool thing to do, and I told him so, straight to his face: Nothing compares to laying paint. You can't tell a story in one word, or one note of music, or one frame of celluloid. But with a Titian, or a Botticelli, or a Van Gogh, Gauguin—it's all there, all at once, the beginning middle and end. *Instant gratifuckation!*"

"I'd give anything to have what it takes."

Buzbee stopped in his tracks. He looked at me like my skin was transparent, like he could see inside me; his bloodshot eyes conveying the wounded wisdom of a man who had learned too many lessons the hard way, and considered himself in no way the better for it.

"Only one thing you got anybody could ever want."

He pushed the bottle into my chest.

"So go hang a For Sale sign on your soul."

We walked for hours. Drinking, stopping to sit just long enough for Buzbee to catch his breath, which he saved by not saying another word, my questions seeming to fall on deaf ears. Like I wasn't even there, even born yet.

From his silence I suspected a conjuration of private ghosts. That he was again sharing the beach, the booze, the brawls and the brushstrokes with only Sinclair. Treasured memories he dared not air for fear they would be finally lost to the scattering wind.

With the bottle wholly drained, the sun half sunk behind the watery red horizon, we turned about-face and walked the way we'd come. On an empty stomach the whiskey had gone straight to my head. When I suggested we could both use something to eat, my treat of course, to help soak up the drink, Buzbee shot me a look—as if he was starving. His hand trembling, he tightened the cap back onto the exhausted bottle. Then he threw it, with all the leverage his abused body could muster, into the deepening darkness of the sea.

"Maybe someday someone will get the message," he said. A wizened shadow of doubt in his twilight gray eyes as he slogged onward along the ever-shifting shoreline.

By the time we got back to the pub it was dusk. I figured we were going inside again for yet another round on me, but Buzbee had other ideas. "You bring a vehicle?" he wanted to know.

"Yes, sir." I motioned to the truck parked at the curb. "That white pickup right there."

He tugged on the passenger-side door handle. Finding it locked, he turned to me, his lips stretched by a sardonic smirk. "Think you've got something worth stealing do you, Woodburn?"

"My suitcase," I said.

"Open the goddamn door!"

I let him in, then circled around and slid behind the wheel. I'd left the Sinclair biography on the seat; Buzbee now had it in hand, eyeing the face of his old bloodbrother on the front cover. "*Half a Life*." He laughed, dismissively. "Whaddaya do—sleep with it under your pillow?"

"Have you read it?"

"Arthur Brimm, my ass!"

"You're in there. A full three chapters."

"I'd rather read my own obituary. So start this piece of shit up."

"Where to?" I asked over the rev of the engine.

"My place." Despite his objections, he cracked open the book. "I assume you know the way."

I knew it in daylight. Sober. But night was falling around us now, and I was under a strange influence. I had to rely on a purely instinctive sense of direction. With no help from Buzbee, who, by the light of a dangling cigarette, sat quietly reading. About himself, I suspected. The unauthorized echoes of once upon a time . . . .

I turned onto a road that looked vaguely familiar, the streetlights radiating a misty yellow. Confident that we would soon arrive at the weed strangled house on Caroline, I broke the silence to brave a request. "If you don't mind," I broached carefully, "I'd really love to see some of your paintings."

"Well I do mind," Buzbee grouched. His attention then suddenly drawn to something up ahead, he ordered me to pull over.

"Over where?"

"Right here!" He grabbed the wheel. Jerked from my control, the truck veered precariously to the right. We jumped the curb. A mailbox dead ahead. I stomped on the brake peddle, whiplash, and we came to a screechy halt just inches short of driving drunk into a federal case.

"Are you crazy?" I yelled at him. "We could've killed somebody!"

He threw open the door and leapt from the truck.

"Mr. Buzbee?"

He staggered across the sidewalk.

"Mr. Buzbee, where are you going?"

He bounded up the steps to a small church. His sudden spryness surprised me. He seemed to be feeding on, drawing energy from the chaos that swirled around him like a whirlwind.

"Mr. Buzbee, it's after-hours, it's closed."

He tugged at the double front doors. Finding both locked, he threw his shoulder against them. The blow repelled him nearly off his feet. I scanned the street. All was otherwise quiet, still, free (at least for the moment) of any potential witnesses. I stepped to the pavement, pleaded over the hood. "Mr. Buzbee, please, get back in the truck."

"I'm feeling it, Woodburn," he bellowed, "the Spirit!"

He kicked at the doors. Hearing the breath rush out of the bedeviled deadbolt, I declared, "I'm not gonna be part of this!"

"You're already part of it!" Buzbee announced for all the world to hear. "Like it or not we're all part of it!" He kicked again, and again, like an old gray mule, until the church doors began to give under the blasphemous barrage. Then he backed up, as far as the landing would allow, and called out in a loud, excommunicated voice:

"He created us in His own image! What does that tell us, Woodburn?"

"We can talk about it in the truck," I begged him.

"It tells us one of two things," he proposed irreverently. "Either it's lousy self-portrait, or He's every bit as ugly as I am!"

"Mr. Buzbee—"

"C'mon, Woodburn! Let's see if the so-called *artist* is in residence!"

With that he lowered his shoulder and charged. Full speed ahead, he rammed the whole of his weight, mind, his being against the barring of salvation's doors. And to my instilled Christian horror the bolt was defeated, ripped from its lock, the doors splintering open as Buzbee's misguided momentum carried him, profanely, inside.

I lifted a guilty gaze toward heaven. "Forgive us our trespasses," I petitioned. Then, cringing under the notion of wrathful omniscience, I hurried up the steps after him . . . . On my tiptoes, I entered the church, the vestibule, and peered through the holy dimness, in search of the holy terror.

"Mr. Buzbee?"

I found only racks of glowing red votive candles. The still, cloistered air heavy with frankincense and myrrh, I could hear, coming from deeper in, the echo of footsteps on hardwood. Following the sound, I crossed over a threshold, into the cavernous darkness of the nave.

"Mr. Buzbee?" I tried to whisper.

At the flick of a Bic an orange-blue flame gave him away. On the rise in front of the pulpit, he lit a sacrilegious Camel. Then three long white candles in a tall bronze holder standing beside the altar.

"Let there be light," he said.

"Mr. Buzbee, we gotta get outta here. This isn't right."

"Churches and museums," his sermon began, "they make them so goddamned dreary. How, I ask you—how can we celebrate life in a mausoleum? Where's the joy, Woodburn?"

I glanced about at the statuary silhouettes of saints. Graven figures forever frozen in their solemnity. And there on the walls the *Stations of the Cross*: the crucifixion playing out in all its sequential cruelty.

"They should be FUNhouses of worship!" Buzbee carried on. "The faithful swapping revelations over barrels of sacramental wine. In vino veritas. I want some truth, Woodburn! I wanna feel the energy! Butcher the fatted calf, strike up the band! And not some holy horse shit hymn! Make it snappy, Woodburn! Cuz I wanna dance! I wanna jitterbug on the bloody altar!" he declared, and climbed up onto the consecrated white marble.

"Mr. Buzbee, get down!"

He stood tall on the altar.

"I wanna swing with the angels. Cakewalk on water." He grabbed at his crotch. "I wanna jerk off to Raphael's *Madonna*!"

"For God's sake, man, show some respect."

"Let the dead bury the dead!" he cried. "The masters worked their miracles for the living. Christ took the cross to lighten our load. Michelangelo's ceiling, Rembrandt's *Prodigal Son*—they were created to breathe some life into the party. And what do we do . . . we lock them up in houses of gloom. The celebration of suffering, Woodburn, that's the sacrilege."

He sagged. The rant had taken what little he had left out of him.

"Mr. Buzbee, please, let me take you home."

"There was a time when even I had faith." He kicked off his

shoes. "My feet were off the ground, walking on air . . . until I let those miserable bastards pull me down. 'You gotta suffer for your art,' they demanded.

"So I stripped," he said, "*stripped* for the whip," and ripped off his shirt. "But even that wasn't enough for them. They wanted more, more, more, always more. The fucking pigs were at the pastry cart!" He yanked down his paint stained pants to the knees. "Well they can lick my stale old dick."

I stood dumbstruck as he stood fully exposed upon the altar.

"You know what happens when you're left naked in the cold too long, Woodburn?" He put out his hands. They quivered in the wavering candlelight. "You shake so bad you can't even draw a straight line anymore."

He hung his head. Spread his arms. Assumed a crucified pose against the large wooden cross fixed symbolically on the high wall behind him. The mad martyr tableau accompanied by the plaintive wail of police sirens arriving on the scene.

We shared a tiny jail cell that seemed more hell than limbo.

Hard stainless steel benches ran cold along two opposing gray block walls. An open stainless steel toilet faced the thick gray iron bars on the door that was slammed behind us after we'd been fingerprinted, and photographed, and stripped of our belts and shoelaces so we wouldn't hang ourselves before they could bring the full weight of Key West justice down on our all too guilty heads.

With Buzbee stretched-out on one of the benches, reposed in spiteful apathy, I knelt on the gray concrete floor and spewed a hot broth of regurgitated brown whiskey into the seatless metal toilet bowl. Thinking, if my father could see me now . . . .

Heaved finally dry, I slumped onto the bench opposite Buzbee. I moaned a foul breath. "So whaddaya think they'll do to us?"

"There is no us," Buzbee snorted. "There's you, and there's me." Then he rolled away to face the wall.

Waiting for whatever was going to happen next, I lost all perception of time. I guessed that maybe two hours had passed since we arrived at the jail, hauled in in handcuffs by the two uniformed officers who'd answered the call. They'd entered the church with their guns drawn. Thank God Buzbee went quietly. Like a storm that had finally blown itself out.

I started counting the seconds in my head. Keeping track of the minutes on my fingers, the hours with my toes, I clocked seven hours, nineteen minutes and forty-one "mississippis" before an officer I remembered from the "booking" desk stepped up to the bars and doled out an unexpected nugget of good news: The pastor of the church was willing to not press charges against us, provided we paid for our trespasses. Five hundred dollars. That included new doors, installation, and a repentant donation to the parish's poor box. I jumped at the deal. Hanging my hungover head in shame, I handed over to the kindly priest the assessed simony of cash, while Buzbee griped to the "property" officer for the return of his confiscated cigarettes.

If not completely absolved of our sins, we were at last released into the morning sunshine. Nearly nine o'clock by my handcuff-resistant wristwatch, we proceeded to a back parking lot where I had to shell out another eighty dollars in towing charges to retrieve the truck. As we drove away from our nightmarish run-in with the law, Buzbee smoked without saying a word, apologetic or otherwise, and that, perhaps more than anything, rubbed me the wrong way.

"Seeing I just bought your freedom, it wouldn't kill you to thank me."

He took a long drag off his cigarette. When he exhaled even the smokiest suggestion of gratitude deliberately out the window I decided it was time to give up this ghost, bring him home and move on. He didn't know, or much care where Sinclair might be. He was living his own mystery, searching for what he'd lost of himself at the bottom of a whiskey bottle; on the sacrificial altar of a sleeping church; in the putrid bowels of a jailhouse.

He didn't have to tell me the way back to his weed-weary

place on Caroline Street. I found it directly. Stopped at the curb in front, I turned to bid the impossible old rogue goodbye.

"Well, Mr. Buzbee, this looks like it. I won't bother you anymore."

"Shut the damn truck down!" he grumbled getting out.

As he hobbled for the haunt of overgrown shadows that enshrouded the house, I hesitated to follow. What was the point of prolonging our entanglement? My welcome to his world had been born thin, and worn to a single thread already stretched well beyond its limit . . . . Yet, for reasons I could not understand, and dared not to question, the thread refused to finally snap. All I knew was that somehow, in some unlikely way, we were still hanging by it.

I fell in behind him. From above there came a rustling of leaves.

"Get out of my tree!" Buzbee barked.

I looked up, saw that it was the kid again, the same barefoot redheaded ringer for Huck Finn who'd sold Buzbee out to me for a shiny new quarter. Given what the result had cost me, I had half a mind to ask the little scamp for my two bits back.

"Sits up there all day like a damn monkey." Buzbee huffed as he stepped to the front door. Which, unlike my truck, had been left unlocked.

I followed him inside. Into a large, unfurnished room under a very high ceiling. An atelier of a sort. Stretched canvasses, enlivened by great strokes and spectrums of paint, covered nearly every inch of wall space. The hardwood floor an abstract history of drips and splatters.

"Shut the fucking door!" Buzbee requested with his usual civility.

Closing the world out, I breathed in the paint, the piquant oils, and ran my eyes over the vibrant gallery of captured faces and seascapes and curvaceous women posed in the nude. It struck me that many of the paintings, most of them, in fact, appeared unfinished, abandoned at a neck, or an elbow, or on the edge of some lost horizon. They suggested a dusty sense of surrender. As if the artist had long ago given up on them, or, and even sadder, on himself.

Then, hanging at the center of a load-bearing wall, flanked by a portrait of Buzbee from a younger time, I saw a watercolor face that saucered my gaze: the iconic image of Ford Sinclair. I could only marvel at the brushwork, the saturation. "This portrait of Sinclair," I called to Buzbee in another room, "Did you paint it?"

"My fucking name's on it," his voice came back.

Indeed, it was. His signature splashed black in the lower right hand corner. I then turned my attention to the adjacent rendering of Buzbee. It too was signed, but in white, with a cursive flourish by now instantly recognizable to me—*Sinclair!*

My mouth agape, I stood in awe of the artistry. It was technically impressionistic. An emotional orchestration of small, colorful strokes, which, when viewed in their entirety, blended into a single, simply exquisite interpretation of the brooding Jack Buzbee: his cold stare pose brilliantly tempered by the sympathetic hand of its re-creator. A perfect example, I thought, of Sinclair having rummaged through the madness . . . to find what was sacred in his paradoxical pal Buzz.

Hearing the return of footsteps on the hardwood, I looked to Buzbee coming out of what I assumed was the kitchen— given that he had a can of beer for breakfast in his fist—and said, "There's some really great work here. I'm sure a lot of dealers would be more than interested."

"What the hell do you know about it?" He took a long swallow of the bargain brand brew. Belched. "Comic books, Woodburn. Cartoons. Subway punk graffiti. Jack Pollack's old shit-stained under-shorts. That's all they're interested in these days. Seduction has fallen out of fashion. We're dancing the limbo now, how low can you go."

"I read in the newspaper that one of Sinclair's *Everglade* paintings sold for five million dollars at Sotheby's."

"And a damn fine piece it is, only that's not what they paid for. They bought the hype, the sensation of his disappearance."

He grabbed an easel standing in a corner, dragged it to the middle of the room. "If Ford was still on the scene those pretentious pricks wouldn't have sense enough to give half a hoot about him." Taking in hand a clean, stretched canvas, he placed it squarely on the easel. "He sold them a mystery. Otherwise he'd be just another rotting exhibition of their collective ignorance . . . like me."

He snatched a crusty old palette off a wooden stool. When he began to squirt dollops of paint onto it, I felt a promising flutter in my chest. "Are you gonna start something now?"

He didn't answer.

"Do you mind if I stay and watch for a while? I'll be very quiet, not a sound. You won't even know I'm here."

"Grab a brush," he snarled.

Better yet. "Yes, sir." I leapt at the chance to assist the artist in some small but immensely rewarding way. I would hand him his tools—an honor, an education. I made a beeline to a cluttered workbench; on it stood a Folgers coffee can full with different sized brushes soaking in mineral spirits.

"A big brush or a little brush?" I asked eagerly.

"Whatever it's going to take?" Buzbee answered vaguely.

"Take to do what?"

"To ream out those hayseed inhibitions you got packed up your ass."

I shrugged. "If you'd just tell me what you need—"

"I told you to grab a damn brush!"

"Okay!" I grabbed one at random. "Here—here's a damn brush!"

He glared at me. For the first time I thought he might actually take a swing at me. But he didn't. Instead, he said, "Now haul your sorry self over to that canvas and start painting."

I flinched. "Me?"

He shoved the palette into my gut.

"You're going to paint a portrait, Woodburn. My portrait."

"Oh, no." I backed away. "Uh-uh, not me. I'm not falling for that."

"You didn't fall, boy, you jumped. And this here is rock bottom."

I envisioned a *splat!*

"Mr. Buzbee, I'm sorry to disappoint you, but I am not gonna prove my incompetence for your amusement."

"Woodburn, there's nothing you could or couldn't do that would amuse me."

"I'm telling you, I tried, I took a class, I made a complete mess of Sally Jo Fergu—"

"Spare me the life story!"

"Mr. Buzbee, there is no way you're going to bully me—"

"You need some inspiration, is that it?" He smiled. "Well you're in luck, Woodburn. I've got just the muse for you."

He turned to a still-life, a half done unmade bed captured at dawn, at the front of a stack of paintings leaning against a wall. Pulling the stack forward, he reached behind them . . .

"Whatever it is, it won't help," I insisted.

. . . and when his arm came out there was the sawed-off shiny blue-blackness of a double-barreled shotgun in his hand. "Then at the very least it'll put you out of your misery." He aimed the gaping 12-gauge muzzles point blank at my chest.

I froze, shocked, every hair on my body stood at attention.

"Mr. Buzbee, this is not funny."

"A true artist creates because he'll *die* if he doesn't," he replied, his forefinger itching against the twin triggers. "So how does it feel, Woodburn?"

"It feels like you've made your point." A cold bead of sweat rolled down between my shoulder blades. "So you can put that gun away."

"You're losing the light." He grinned. "And I'm losing patience."

"Please, Mr. Buzbee, tell me that thing isn't loaded."

"Buckshot, Woodburn. Lay you out like the Devil's own decoupage."

"You're not gonna shoot me." Clinging to a last semblance of reason, "You may be crazy, but you're not insane. And this is pure madness."

"A madman sells!" Buzbee declared bitterly. "Take Hitler for example. Before the holocaust he couldn't give his paintings away. But once he got some blood on his hands, well, his art sold like hotcakes at your damned Sotheby's. Now I'm thinking it could be the same with me. A bit of morbid curiosity and my work will be worth something again. Hell, if I pull these triggers chances are they'll even make a movie about me. The tortured has-been who blew away the rosy-cheeked farm boy because he refused to paint his picture. Be a shrewd career move, if I must say so myself."

Tilting his head back, he looked down his nose at me.

"So what's it gonna be, Woodburn? Are you gonna give me new life?

"Or save your own?"

CHAPTER TWELVE

I was hard-pressed to believe Jack Buzbee capable of cold-blooded murder. Then again I couldn't quite put him above it, either. If the last twenty hours proved anything, it was that he had enough loose screws to be dangerous. He might've had just the right mix of booze, bitterness and bad luck in his system to finally explode, and shoot me dead on the spot.

So, reluctantly, I surrendered to the threat, and started painting.

With Buzbee seated still and silent on the wooden stool—the shotgun resting ominously on his lap—I dabbed at the canvas. Tentative, trembling strokes. It was difficult to focus beyond the gun. I had to somehow incorporate it into the process. After several shaky starts, I decided to use those conspicuous blue-black barrels as a sort of crosshair, the sawed-off centerline of the portrait. Everything else would ripple out from there.

I worked slowly. Laboriously, I painted myself tighter and tighter into a corner. It left me only two ways to go: either up (to meet the challenge) or down (six feet to an early grave). Unless! if I prolonged the matter, kept it hanging desperately in the air, maybe, just maybe, Buzbee might at last succumb to the liquor and nod off. Pass out. Allow me a merciful moment to sneak away from the madness.

Deliberate as I was, however, the opportunity for escape refused to present itself. He remained wide-awake, alert, his finger seemingly glued to the triggers as the morning bled into afternoon.

"The light keeps changing," I complained.

"Deal with it," he growled—my problem, not his.

A shadow crept across his face. It only darkened his mood. He was losing patience, and getting thirstier, no doubt, by the minute. Yet he held the pose. A contest of endurance, it seemed, in which he had something more at stake than I did. A game with only one rule: no excuses allowed.

I pressed on. And although the inspiration was suspect, the perspiration it extracted streamed all too evident. It soaked my shirt like a fire hose. "I can never get the eyes right," I sighed after many failed attempts to capture the living menace in Buzbee's otherwise dead cold stare.

"Fuck the eyes!" he said without blinking "The eyes lie. Get behind the eyes, to the truth, Woodburn."

I painted. Repainted. Again and again trying different sized brushes, tilting my head from side to side, forward then back, blending, re-blending subtle variations of glowering browns . . . . Until, hours into it, and almost by accident, the oils began to smolder—like a chemical reaction—when they came in contact with the canvas. Then a spark flew out of it. And another. The eyes suddenly, miraculously, aflame. They burned hotter with every stroke, every stoke of the fire crackling cantankerous inside that scar-hardened shell of a man.

Did I do that? I could hardly believe it. I stepped back from the heat. Exhausted. Exhilarated. Unfamiliar with this newfound sense of myself, I muttered in amazement. "I think I'm done."

"You think?" Buzbee barked.

"I mean—"

"You mean nothing! Now yes or no? Is the damn thing done or not?"

I paused. Reconsidered the portrait. Returning to my original conclusion, I said, "Yes. The damn thing is done."

"Well it's about fuckin' time."

His body stiff, cracking, Buzbee got up from the stool. "Now let's see if the game was worth the candle." Shotgun in hand, he limped around to face the easel. I looked on breathlessly as he absorbed the image, his image, through a keen and critical eye.

"Well?" I pressed him.

He sniffed. "Ain't exactly jumping off the canvas."

"Why?" I wanted to know.

"First of all, your chiaroscuro—flat, no depth to it. And obviously you don't know impasto from your asshole."

I sagged.

"But . . ."

But? It straightened me up.

" . . . faint as it may be: I'll be damned if it doesn't have a pulse."

"A pulse? What do you mean a pulse?"

He turned the gun on me.

"I mean it doesn't stink."

Coming from Jack Buzbee it was high praise, indeed. I would've jumped for joy, if not for the explosion that followed. Both barrels *booming!* I *d*ropped to the floor. Deaf, dumb, dying, I feared. He shot me! echoed through my head. Me—an innocent. A complaisant country boy dreamer who never hurt anybody. Except, of course, for Kelly Ann and her family. And, to a greater degree, my father, who'd had to suffer a moody malcontent living under his roof. Was this my belated punishment for having indulged my dreams? Was I now reaping the ironic karma I had sown? Was Jack Buzbee simply the ultimate instrument of Bird in Hand revenge? Curled in a tight, quivering ball, I waited for the pain to flood the holes in my body. Eyes slammed shut, I couldn't bring myself to look. I envisioned blood and guts spilled on the paint-splattered hardwood. I figured the buckshot must've severed my spine because all I could feel was the sting of burned black powder in my nostrils.

Then, through the ringing in my ears, I heard Buzbee's voice.

"On your feet, Woodburn."

On my feet?

I wiggled my toes. Still, no pain.

I cracked open my eyes. No blood or guts to be seen.

I looked up at Buzbee. The shotgun, smoking in his hands, was pointed away from me. I followed its aim, downward, to the floor across the room, where the legs of the easel lay singed and fractured; what was left of the canvas slumped lifelessly against a blast-riddled wall. The face gone, obliterated.

It finally registered. He'd turned the barrels on the portrait, his portrait, before pulling the triggers. Confused, I staggered to my feet. Stepping in front of the gun, I crossed to the savaged fruit of my labor. My one and only work of art annihilated even before the paint could dry. I wanted to cry. Some strange, shaken sector of my consciousness wishing he'd killed me instead, I faced the assassin. Staring into those brooding brown eyes, through which I'd glimpsed an ugly version of truth, I saw not a flicker of remorse.

"Why?" I asked him.

His answer: "You did it 'cause you had to. And if you have to you'll do it again."

The art lesson over, Jack Buzbee dropped the shotgun, and limped away, down a dim hallway toward an open bedroom door at the end of the line. "Sinclair's long gone," he grumbled over his shoulder. Beyond the threshold, he turned to me. "Now get the fuck outta my house."

The door slammed shut between us.

Outside the house on Caroline Street, I found the tree abandoned (the kid scared off by the blast, I assumed) and followed the path to the pickup parked at the curb. Behind the wheel, I idled for a moment to reflect. However questionable Jack Buzbee's teaching methods may have been, I'd learned something in there: that the Muses had a dark side, their natures prone to unpredictable and potentially deadly shifts in temperament. That what they inspire they can destroy on a whim.

A hard lesson, indeed.

I drove on.

Sleep tugged at me. Still I felt a need to extricate myself

from the Keys, from the lingering fallout of Palm Beach, from the state of Florida altogether. I crossed the border into Alabama sometime around two the next morning. There I finally pulled into a rest stop. Laid out in the cab, I nodded off only briefly, Buzbee's words "Sinclair's long gone" replaying in my brain.

Long gone. But when did he start to go? I pondered. Was he en route from the beginning? Blessed to reach the highest peak and cursed to keep moving? Only two ways to proceed once you get to the top: either head back down . . . or take flight.

In the light of dawn I was roused by the rumble of eighteen-wheelers. I brushed my teeth, washed my face in the public restroom there. I bought a cup of coffee and package of powdered doughnuts from the vending machines, then ducked into a phone booth to call my mom, collect.

"Yes, I'll except the charges." Her voice warm, worried, far away.

I told her "Really, Mom, I'm fine. I just wanted to let you know I'm bound for Los Angeles."

"California? What's in California?"

"There's a couple of people I need to talk to."

"Are you eating right?" she asked.

I looked at the stale doughnuts.

"Yes, Mom, I'm eating."

"How about the truck, is it running okay?"

"It's running great. Not a sputter."

"So you haven't had any trouble, at all?"

The drug raid at the Gum Drop, my dealings with Carlos, everything about Jack Buzbee, passed through my mind.

"No, Mom, no trouble at all." What else could I say? Except that there was no need for her to worry, and that I loved her from the bottom of my heart. That said, I hung up and studied my map. Interstate 10 appeared to be the straightest route west. It would take me through the cotton fields of Mississippi, the swamps of Louisiana, the long dusty plains of Texas. I drove for nearly twenty-four hours straight. Stopping only for gas and quick bites, I reached southern New Mexico at around two o'clock in the afternoon. It was there, on a bleak, rust-red stretch of open desert, that things took a fateful turn toward the surreal.

It started when the red ENGINE light flashed on. I was running hot. Stupidly, in my haste, I hadn't thought to pack more water than the liter bottle I bought to drink at a filling station some two hundred dry miles ago. The temperature outside was close to triple-digits now. With nothing but shadeless wasteland as far as the eye could see, I had little choice but to press on, and pray there was another station not too far up ahead.

As my luck would have it, there wasn't.

The truck lost power. It started to cough. Buck. Spew steam like a giant teapot. I pulled over to the side of the road. *Damn!* I slapped the dashboard. I got out, and when I lifted the hood a geyser of released steam knocked me back. *Double-damn!*

Okay. Take it easy. It's not the end of the world, I told myself—when in fact it looked like the uninhabitable surface of another planet, Mars, I thought, red and desolate—sooner or later a car will come along. I'll just hitch a ride to the next service place. It sounded good, anyway. Only the first prospect came along later rather than sooner, and getting the driver to stop posed more of a problem than I'd anticipated. He had his family with him, a minivan clan under a rooftop luggage box, the windows rolled-up tight to seal in the conditioner-cooled air. At least I assumed they were a family. I can't say for sure because instead of slowing down at my wave, the wheelman warily hit the gas to pass me by. The kids' noses pressed against the rear glass, their eyes wide with spooked wonder: Was I that psycho *stranger* they promised never to talk to? I must've fit the general description, seeing how three more cars came along, and sped up to leave me in their dust as well.

When it got late in the day I had to finally concede that a lift couldn't be counted on. Not exactly thrilled by the idea of having to spend the night alone out there in the dark, I decided to take a walk, go in search of some help I could pay to get me rolling again.

So I set off on foot. Away from the security of the truck, the land grew even more intimidating. A parched flat nothingness interrupted vertically by scattered spikes of tall cacti and distant mesas, unchanged for thousands of years. It was easy to imagine half-naked Indians spying me through brave-sharp eyes as I advanced like a gold-fevered greenhorn on the Old Wild West.

Still, I was less concerned about a war-party whooping out from the ripples of heat than I was the territorial strike of a coiled rattlesnake, scorpion, tarantula, Gila monster, or any other poisonous creepy-crawler hardy enough to survive in such a harsh and solitary place. At one point I happened upon a pile of blanched bone. The skeletal remains of a bovine-looking creature glistening in the low sunlight. It reminded me of a Georgia O'Keefe painting—the grim white steer's skull posed waywardly on the red desert floor. With all due respect for Georgia, it only inspired me to pick up the pace. And if the spiders, reptiles and bones weren't foreboding enough, about an hour into my trek, a flock of vultures appeared overhead. Huge, circling, sinister birds. The effortless grace of their slow glide too focused on potential fresh carrion to be fully appreciated.

A few more cars, and a motor home, went by. Again I was left unaided in the wake. I kept walking. Silently shadowed by the hungry birds, I must've put five very bleak miles between the truck and me, before at last I spotted a glimmer of hope on the horizon.

Another pickup. Much older than mine, it was parked on the side of the road. Flanked by a makeshift canopy, a large signboard leaned with entrepreneurial spirit against the truck's tailgate.

Getting closer, I read AUTHENTIC NAVAJO JEWELRY.

Beneath the canvas sunshield stood a short, ruddy-colored man behind a card table displaying sparkles of silver and turquoise. He looked to be in his mid-thirties, his straight black hair fashioned into two long braids that framed a high cheekboned face and hung well past his shoulders. He was obviously an Indian. Though hardly of the half-naked variety. He had on blue jeans, a clean white business shirt, and a handsome diamond-patterned snakeskin vest.

"Hello," I waved, approaching. "I'm sure glad to see you."

"How's it going?" he nodded.

"It could be better," I said. "My truck broke down a few miles back. I'm looking for a service station, or even a phone I could use."

"There's souvenir shop just up road." The man pointed the way. "They got a pay phone."

I needed to rest for a spell.

"Mind if I get out of the sun a minute?"

He motioned me under his canopy.

"Feel free to browse."

Grateful, I joined him in the shade.

"I make it all by hand," his sales pitch began. "Same way my ancestors did."

I considered the shiny assortment. Rings, bracelets, earrings, necklaces, belt buckles. "They're beautiful," I said. "Your ancestors would be proud."

"See anything you like I'll give you a fair price."

I shrugged. "Like I said, I have to get my truck fixed. Figure it's gonna cost me at least two hundred dollars to repair the radiator."

He nodded again. "Happens a lot out here. Gets pretty hot."

"Pretty lonely, too. You do much business?"

"Enough to scrape by." He told me, "I could make more selling to the stores, but then they turn around and overcharge people. Besides, I like the open space, room for the imagination to run a little wild."

"Yeah," I had to agree, "there's plenty of that. So, can you recommend a good mechanic?"

He paused, eyeing the work-in-progress in his hand. Then smiled decidedly. "Tell you what," he proposed, "I'm just about done with this watchband. For two hundred it's yours. Plus, I'll fix your truck for you."

I squinted at the offer.

"You know engines?"

"Engines, jewelry, pottery. You're talking to Joseph Hightower, my friend." He smiled. "A red-skinned Renaissance Man."

So it began: my unlikely introduction to the ways of the New Mexican Navajos . . . .

It took Joseph less than an hour to finish the watchband. Smooth polished turquoise set in cool pure silver. He shaped it to fit perfectly around my left wrist, and then carefully incorporated the Timex my dad had given me on the day of my high school graduation. It sparkled like a really sweet deal. Made even sweeter by the promise of a working radiator thrown into the bargain. Gladly, I paid the two hundred dollars. Then I helped Joseph break camp and load everything into the back of his pickup. On the drive to my truck I explained to him the nature of my journey. He knew the name Ford Sinclair but confessed that he was mostly unfamiliar with the art, and also the mystery of Sinclair's disappearance.

"We pretty much keep to ourselves out here," he told me.

As for my radiator, Joseph quickly diagnosed a problem with the cooling coils. The bad news was it wouldn't be an on the spot fix. The good news, he had the necessary tools and spare parts at his home to handle the job.

"We'll just tow it," he said.

Using a chain he kept in the cab, he pulled while I steered in neutral. We went another five miles beyond where I'd met him, and a few more to the south toward a blast of mountains that stretched along the border with old Mexico. This was reservation land. The dwellings were small and ramshackle. A modesty enforced by the agents of isolation and poverty—on a proud, forgotten people scratching an ancient existence from the scorched red earth.

We turned onto a parcel of property that resembled a salvage yard. There were old parts-stripped vehicles, washing machines, refrigerators, bathtubs, stacks of used lumber and pipe. The cannibalized remains of seemingly every appliance and basic convenience ever invented. And in the midst of the clutter, small and weather-beaten, stood a white adobe house. Our approach roused a muttly trio of dogs. Barking, they charged the trucks. "It's okay," Joseph assured me as he stepped to the ground. "They only bite cowboys."

I took his word for it, and eased out of the cab. The dogs growled, then sniffed at my crotch. Evidently they found the dried-sweat of my predicament somewhat endearing, as their tails started to wag in mongrel synchronization.

"C'mon." Joseph motioned to the adobe. A woman and two little kids were standing in the doorway, eyeing me like they'd never seen a paleface before. "Let's go get something cold to drink."

The woman backed the kids up as I followed Joseph inside.

"Woody Washborn, my lovely wife, Juanita," Joseph introduced us in the kitchen.

Lovely was right. "Nice to meet you, ma'am."

"And these are my children, Josey and Juan."

The kids peeked shyly around their mother's legs.

"Hello." I smiled at them.

"And this—" Joseph continued, turning to a very old man with long silvery-white hair seated on a rocking chair in the next room "—is my grandfather. Joe Spotted Owl Hightower."

"Sir." I bowed awkwardly to the old man, his face rusty and cracked like sun-baked New Mexican mud.

"Now." Joseph slapped his hands together. "What do we have to put out a man-sized thirst?"

They had cherry Kool-Aid. An icy glass for all of us, and we joined Grandpa Spotted Owl around a block a fragrant cedar that served as a coffee table.

"So, what brings you through the reservation, Woody?" Juanita asked politely.

"He's on a hunt," Joseph answered. "For a famous artist."

"Yes. His name is Ford Sinclair."

That drew Mr. Spotted Owl out of his silence. He spoke in a sliding, eliding language I'd heard in countless westerns. Navajo, I assumed.

"Grandfather asks what you want with this man?" Joseph translated.

"Ah . . . well . . . uh . . . this Sinclair, he's very wise, you see, and I need his advice. Kind of like a mentor, I guess."

"An earth guide," as Joseph put it.

"It was Grandfather who taught Joseph how to work with silver and stone," Juanita put in. "Just like his grandfather taught him."

"The problem is," Joseph explained to them, "this Ford Sinclair—he's found a good hiding place. Isn't that right, Woody?"

"The truth is I'd probably have a better chance of finding a hair in a haystack," I acknowledged. "But seeing I've come this far, I figure I might as well go the extra mile to California."

Spotted Owl spoke again.

"He says you must pray to the spirits for direction."

"Believe me, sir," I told him, "I'm open to anything that might help."

"In that case, maybe Woody should sit in on the *sing* tonight," Juanita suggested.

"Sing?" I asked.

"It's worth a shot," Joseph said. "What do you think, Grandfather?"

As the two men discussed the idea in Navajo, I detected a note of patriarchal reluctance on Spotted Owl's part.

"Sing?" I asked again.

"We have them once a month," Joseph informed me. "Normally outsiders are not allowed."

"Well, then, please, don't break any rules on my account. I'll just—"

Spotted Owl cut me off. His tone was heavy, judicial.

"But, seeing that your search is a humble one," Joseph translated, "Grandfather is willing to make an exception."

I hesitated.

"I'm honored, sir. Really. Thank you very much. It just that I . . . uh . . . what about my truck?"

"Not to worry," Joseph assured me. "I'll have you on the road in the morning."

I paused. Looked down at my newly, and beautifully, banded wristwatch. 7:15 p.m. Anxious as I was to get to L.A., how could I refuse such a gracious offer? I turned to meet Spotted Owl's venerable gaze. "This sing thing," I asked, "what would I have to do?"

The old man's voice inflected, lilting with intrigue.

"Just open your mind to the wisdom of the ages," was Joseph's interpretation.

The "sing" would begin at sundown. I was told it was best not to eat until after the ceremony; that the fasting was a practical as well as ritual consideration. They didn't go into the reasons why, and not wanting to be a bother I didn't question them further about it.

While Joseph and Spotted Owl went off to tend the final preparations, I remained in the house with Juanita and the children. I looked on as Juanita put the finishing touches to a wool blanket she'd woven on a loom, which, she told me, had been in her family for over a hundred years. Colored red, black and white, the blanket featured a sharp geometric design. She said it took several days to make one, and that they sold so well it was difficult to keep up with the demand.

"But this one isn't for sale." She smiled at me. "This one is for you."

"Oh no," I protested. "After all your hard work, I can't. It's much too generous of you."

When she insisted I offered to pay for it. Her lips frowned, insulted. Clearly I had no choice but to accept the blanket on her kind terms. It was a gift and she didn't want to hear another word about it.

At dusk Joseph and Spotted Owl returned. Everything was ready. The "sing" could begin. Outside, a group of five more men were gathered. Apparently my presence had already been explained to them; they greeted me with no surprise, no need for introduction. Just nods of silent acknowledgement before we all walked together into the last of the sunset at the back of the property. Where, maybe a quarter-mile from the house, a lone teepee stood.

"It's required that the door face east," Joseph told me as we approached the rawhide reminder of the past. "So we will see the sunrise of a new day."

New day? The implications wavered me. My body ached for a decent meal, a good sleep. I wasn't sure I had the staying power for another all night affair. But before I could think of a gracious way to bow out Spotted Owl entered the teepee through the door-flap, and the others followed, leaving only Joseph and I to join them.

"After you," Joseph motioned.

What else could I do? I took a deep breath, and ducked inside.

With Joseph comfortingly close behind me, my attention went first to a fire. A controlled, cedar-fueled burn on the ground at the center of the circle. The men stood around it. Smoke rising in a pale-gray ribbon, and out through the cone's open, ten foot high peek.

Steered by Joseph, I took my place directly to Spotted Owl's right. Between us, a moon-shaped mound of sand. An altar, I gathered: set with a bowl of water, a fan made from birds' feathers, a small drum of stretched animal-skin, and a wooden plate containing a pile of what looked like small black buttons. At Spotted Owl's lead we all sat down on a sort of prayer rug (each of us his own) and crossed our legs in front us, backs straight, faces eerily aglow in the firelight.

Spotted Owl began to speak, in Navajo, calling, I assumed, the meeting to order. His voice grow softer, more reverent as he removed from a leathery pouch attached to a strand of rosary beads around his neck a large button-like thing, about the size of a hockey puck.

"That's the father," Joseph whispered in my ear. "On the plate are the children."

I nodded. Interesting.

Spotted Owl held the "father" up toward the sky, and

delivered what sounded to be a short incantation of thanks. All quiet again but for the crackling of the fire, he returned the strange fetish to its amulet bag. Next, he raised the bowl from the altar, slowly to his lips, and took four very deliberate sips before passing it to the man on his left.

"Everything is done in fours," Joseph coached me softly. "Water, Air, Fire and Earth."

In clockwise succession the men sipped, four times. When Joseph handed the bowl to me, I drank as the others had. Passed back to Spotted Owl, the water was carefully replaced on the sand.

Taking the fan of feathers in hand, Spotted Owl rose to his knees. Again he worked left to right: fanning four wafts of smoke from the fire over each of us. Four deep cedar-scented breaths all around then the feathers were set aside. And he picked up the plate of small buttons. After placing four on the rug in front of him, he passed the dish, and each man chose his four, mine the last, and the plate was laid empty on the altar.

Water, Air, Fire, and now these buttons: Earth, I figured.

When Spotted Owl brought a button up to his face, we all did the same. A few solemn words—as if to announce our arrival at some moment of truth—then the old Indian placed the curious sacrament on his tongue, and proceeded to swallow it.

Joseph and the others followed suit.

Oh, well. When in Rome . . .

I likewise eased the button into my mouth. It had a kind of bitter taste. I closed my eyes, gulped it down. Not too bad, actually. I'd swallowed harder pills in my life. With the smell of burning cedar now pleasantly pungent, the process was repeated with the second, third, and fourth buttons. Once they had all been ceremoniously ingested, Spotted Owl moved on to the drum. He slipped it between his crossed legs. I gathered it was time to sing.

Reaching into a buckskin sack, Joseph brought out several painted gourds adorned with colorful beads. He gave one to each of us. Shaken, they rattled like maracas to the rhythmic "tom-

tom" beat Spotted Owl drummed on the taut skin. Then, accompanied by the rattles, he broke into a soulful chant, his voice deep, resonant, inspired . . .

"We will all sing four songs," Joseph whispered in my ear. "It will be your turn when the drum gets to you."

Had I been the old me, the very idea of having to carry a tune, a solo, anywhere, in front of anybody, would've caused me some alarm, to say the least. Let alone in a high plains teepee, surrounded by a strange congregation of serious Navajos. At that moment, however, I had more immediate issues to deal with—

A sudden dizziness came over me. I felt queasy. Nauseous. I could've easily gotten sick, vomitously ill. Only I had nothing in my stomach to throw-up. On the advice of my hosts, I hadn't eaten. A practical as well as ritual consideration, I recalled.

"Joseph, I don't feel good."

"It'll pass," Joseph said, his hand calmingly on my shoulder. "It's just the peyote—opening the doors."

"Peyote?" I dry heaved over Spotted Owl's steady song.

"You'll feel the light soon," Joseph continued. "Let it come. Go with it. It has much to show you."

It came in powerful vibrations. Like an earthquake, the tremors shook loose an avalanche of vibrant colors—red, blue, green, yellow, orange, purple—in my head. Intense, kaleidoscopic waves that rolled on through my body, to smother the sickness, quiet my panic.

As the initial rush subsided, I saw the faces in focus again. Sharper. More dimensional under the spell. I turned to the chanting, Spotted Owl's evensong now resonating from his mouth in vivid pictures: a hawk, a buffalo, lightning, a rainbow that arced over the fire and slowly melted into the flames. And the rising smoke sprouted rosebuds, which blossomed with all the colors of the bow, before, and behind, my eyes.

My heart pounded to the drumbeat. My breath one with the rattles. The song was inside me, and I inside it, each giving birth

---

to the other. I watched from somewhere beyond myself as the drum floated to the next man. A new voice in my ears, and the smoke began to stream in reverse—down from the sky and into the fire. I turned to Joseph. He was off the ground, levitated on his magic rug. He smiled at me as the rattle danced in his hand.

I closed my eyes. And there was my father. He was standing on top of the barn. He spread his arms, but they weren't arms, I saw, they were wings, white angel's wings, and with a flap he started to fly. He circled overhead, higher and higher, he climbed.

Go, Dad, go!

Then, suddenly, in mid-air, he stopped. He hovered there for a moment. Or was it an hour? I had no perception of time. Just space in which my mind could run wild. A realm without rules. Where a man was free to soar like a bird. *Fly, damn you, fly!*

But even here, in this magical place, when it came to Wood Washborn the laws of gravity were bound to apply. He began to fall, plummet—like the flightless spirit he'd always been—toward a stubbornly meaningless death . . .

"Woody?" Joseph's voice tugged me from the vision. When I opened my eyes, he had the drum, holding it out to me. While I was tuned-in to the high-flown frequencies of my own mind they'd all sung their fours songs. It was now my turn. I froze. What lyric could I possibly offer this peculiar assembly, sitting, as I was, so profoundly unversed in their native tongue, the elusive orthodoxy of their ancient religion?

"I don't know what to sing." An effort to speak coherently.

"Just let your breath move you. Like a wind chime," Joseph coaxed.

I accepted the drum. The skin stretched tight and warm to the touch. I stared into the fire. As I pondered its sway, my fingers began to tap lightly with the crackle, a slow hypnotic rhythm. It got louder, grew more familiar with every beat. Then I heard the whisper of a song in my head. I exhaled, and out it came:

"Amazing Grace . . . how sweet the sound . . . that saved a wretch like me . . . I once was lost . . . but now I'm found . . . was blind . . . but now I see." That was all I could remember. I waited for another draft from the depths. Instead, I heard a voice, in a language neither English nor Navajo.

"Bunn nwee, mohn ahmee."

I thought it was Joseph. But when I turned to him, it wasn't him; there was a man I did not recognize in his place. A white man. His long, handsome face shagged by a black mustache, the ends waxed into loose curls. As he got to his feet, I saw that his clothes were very old-fashioned, his shirt ruffled, blousy, seemingly Victorian. Looking down at me, the stranger nodded. "Bohn vwa-yazh," he said. Then he disappeared, casting no shadow, through teepee's flap door.

Bohn vwa-yazh. A Frenchman, I suspected. But why? Who was he? From what dim recess of my mind had he come? "Try the poisson cru, Woody." I turned to my left, to Spotted Owl, only the old Indian was gone. In his place there stood a young boy—his nose a red rubber ball, face grease-painted white, eyes sparkling blue under a wild yellow wig. His clothes a baggy clash of comical patches. Still, I knew at once the boy behind the guise. It was none other than Fordie Sinclair of the Big Little Circus, in the character of Omo the Clown. "It's my favorite dish, you know." His laughter, silly yet deeply haunting, fading into the night as he followed the mystery man outside.

"Are you okay, Woody?" Joseph. There on his rug again.

Spotted Owl? Yes. He too had returned.

Thick and slow, my reply stretched like pulled taffy.

"I-I-I N-E-E-E-D A-A-A-I-R-R-R . . ."

On shaky legs, I dropped the drum in Joseph's lap, and staggered from the cloistered weirdness of the teepee. Looking up at the stars, distant spangles of reality against the calm black sky, I tried to clear my head. It was like a dream within a dream within a heightened sense of wakefulness. I couldn't tell where the material world ended and the phantastic began.

A part of me understood: the boy-clown was only a hallucinatory figment of my peyote-fed imagination. Even so, another part of me called for him as if he existed beyond mere illusion.

"Omo!" I yelled in the dark.

From somewhere on the plain, a coyote answered with a howl.

"Maaarrraaa!"

And when I turned I saw it, the tree. The sculptured sycamore of Casa de Sol—so wonderfully carved in the figure of a nymph. Her arm extended toward the heavens. A gallows limb from which Carlos hung at the end of a rope noosed around his neck.

"Maaarrraaa!" he cried.

Then, the statue, it spoke.

"Don't you just love my moon, Woody?" The pale yellow crescent resting loftily in her open hand.

It was all a blur after that, images flashing too fast to comprehend.

The last thing I remember, a soft voice in my ear.

"*The journey is the destination,*" it whispered.

The next I knew something warm was caressing my face. Wet, resuscitative strokes. My eyes fluttered open, caught the long pinkish tongue of a dog as it reached for another lick. At first I thought I was still hallucinating. But the sudden smack of sunlight had a real sting to it. For better or worse, I was in command of my senses again.

I shooed the dog away and sat up. I was in the bed of my truck, covered by a blanket that looked vaguely familiar. Recognizing the red, black and white pattern as distinctly Navajo, it all started to come back to me: New Mexico, Joseph, Spotted Owl, the "sing." I glanced at my watch—polished turquoise and silver—10:15 in the morning. I must've fallen asleep, passed out. Someone must've placed me here, tucked me in for the night.

Turning, I saw through the cab windows that the hood was raised.

"Hello?"

The hood slammed down to reveal Joseph and Spotted Owl.

"Ah, you're awake," Joseph said. "Perfect timing." Wiping

grease from his hands with a rag, he came around to me. "I went ahead and replaced your radiator. It's not new but it should get you to California and back east again."

"California? Oh. Right. Los Angeles. Thanks for reminding me."

"Kind of a strange night, huh?"

"I'll say. That stuff really had me going."

"Yeah, it lets the spirits in, alright."

Spotted Owl joined us. He questioned me in Navajo.

"He wants to know if your visions showed the path you were looking for?" Joseph translated.

"They definitely showed me something," I answered fuzzily. "I'm just not sure what it all means."

The old man nodded, a hard-earned wisdom. "Carry them today," he said in surprising English, "and tomorrow they will carry you." Then, with a rare smile, he left us, walking tall in the direction of the house.

"If you have the time—" Joseph motioned to Juanita and the kids as they poured charcoal into a barbecue pit near a large picnic table "—we're gonna do a big cookout this afternoon. All the men from the sing and their families will be here. You're more than welcome to join us."

It was a tempting offer. The company of these good and unique people would be hard to beat. Only I had a long drive ahead of me; and the night had given me a lot to think about, try to interpret while it was fresh on my mind.

Joseph understood. "Yes, you have a very sly fox to catch. And his trail leads another way."

I hopped to the ground.

"Well. I guess this is it then."

"I'll tell everyone goodbye for you."

"Thank you, Joseph." I extended my hand. "It was an experience I won't forget."

"Been a pleasure doing business with you, Woody."

We shook on it.

"Now, enough said. You have a hunt to resume, a sun to follow," Joseph urged me. "As far as it takes you."

He opened the driver's side door, and closed it once I was behind the wheel. The engine started without complaint. Revving it up, I looked out at the teepee standing by itself in the distance.

"One last thing, Joseph."

"What's that, my friend?"

"I take it it was you who put me to bed."

He smiled. "Yes. I picked you up off the ground."

"And while you were at it, uh, did you say something?

"Something about what?"

"About a journey—the journey being the destination?"

He shook his head. "No. Never heard that before. Why?"

"Oh, I don't know." I shrugged. "Just thought I'd ask, that's all."

When I drove away the dogs ran after me. A dusty half a mile down the road they finally gave up the chase and turned back. Come feast time there would be bones thrown from the Hightower table for them to chew on.

As for me—I already had mine.

CHAPTER THIRTEEN

I got back on the I-10 headed west. Following the sun, I put New Mexico behind me and entered Arizona, a mostly empty continuation of hot desert but Joseph's radiator job did the trick, the pickup cruising along at a steady clip while I gnawed on store bought fruit, cheese, breadsticks, and the possible implications of my peyote dream.

The vision of Sinclair seemed only natural. He was stamped all over my consciousness; no great surprise that he'd seeped into my subconscious as well. But why the young Ford, Omo the Clown? And with the many things he could've said to me, why some obscure reference to poisson cru? Was it simply because I hadn't eaten, had food on my mind?

It made sense, I supposed.

Still, I couldn't help but wonder if there was more to it.

The Frenchman proved an even slipperier matter to grasp. To the best of my recollection I'd never met, nor given much thought to anyone from France. So who was that guy? How did he get in my head? "Bon voyage." Have a good trip. A good trip to where? I wondered. Los Angeles? Or maybe he was just speaking figuratively: Have a good peyote "trip."

Or could it mean something else? An allusion to a trip not yet included on my itinerary? Instead of answers, all I had were more questions. With no promise of enlightenment in sight, I wheeled past Tucson, then Phoenix. After that the landscape began a dramatic push toward the sky, craggy swells of mountains, one jagged surge followed by another. It was around six p.m. when I reached the Colorado River. On the other side California.

Across the border, the peaks continued to spike in majestic succession. With the sun nearing the horizon I passed through the upscale outpost of Palm Springs. From there things got increasingly more congested, the traffic growing heavier, buildings taller. Strip malls and billboards and cryptic graffiti; the ambient buzz that comes with higher concentrations of people conditioned to pick up the pace before somebody gets ahead of them.

Welcome to Los Angeles

It was well past dark when I entered the city limits. Having no business downtown, I drove on—looking for Hollywood. And less than an hour later, I was smack dab in the middle of it.

I'd expected a wondrous place, gilded in tinsel, glamour, a parade of shiny movie stars under strobe-lights of paparazzi flashbulbs. What I found was a tarnished, seedy, vice-ridden stretch of grim urban night. Along Hollywood Boulevard I saw ragged men and whorishly-dressed women prowling black sidewalks inlaid with gold stars: the renowned Walk of Fame. A trash-littered homage to the legends of the silver screen.

History . . .

Like 1973. The year Ford Sinclair brought his own brand of magic to the world of motion pictures. His first movie—which he not only wrote and directed but did all the music and camera work for as well—he called *Nomads*. A polished, semi-autographical gem, the story depicts the highs and lows and ultimate demise of a small, traveling circus. A hit with both audiences and critics alike, it went on to win Academy Awards for Best Screenplay, Best Director, Best Score and Best Cinematography. A grand slam.

Then, less than a year later, came *Con Man:* the title character a charming drifter who, after swindling the residents of a small town, has a sudden surge of conscience that compels him to confess his crimes. Only the people he duped don't want to hear it. Rather than be exposed as fools, they deny his guilt. They go so far as to pay him to shut up about it. Better to be taken, they figure, than let it be publicly known that they'd fallen for his grifter's tricks.

Perhaps the most curious thing about the tale was Sinclair's perspective on the subject matter. In a rare moment of accessibility, he told a reporter from *Daily Variety* that he very much identified with the conman. "His situation is not unlike my own," went the quote. Exactly what the similarities were, he refused to say.

Anyhow, the verdict was in: the musician turned playwright turned novelist turned painter turned out to be one heck of a filmmaker. For *Con Man* Sinclair received four more Oscars. Again Best Screenplay, Director, Music, plus the grand prize— Best Picture. Of course, true to form, he did not attend the ceremony to accept the awards. It just wasn't his style.

He did, however, bring home something from the experience. Between "takes" a beautiful young starlet caught his eye. Deanna Dees was her name; soon changed to Deanna Sinclair. And together they created a son, Fletcher Angus Sinclair.

The second wife and child being the reasons for my visit.

It was eleven p.m. by my turquoise and silver banded watch (too late to track them down now) when I spotted a cheap-looking hotel on the boulevard. I pulled into the parking lot. After spending two nights in the truck a real bed would be a nice change, I thought.

In the lobby sat a clerk behind the front desk. Unshaven, with a stubby cigar clamped between his lips, he eyed my suitcase like he'd never seen one before. When I asked if there was a room available he nodded blearily.

"Twenty bucks an hour," he grunted.

"How much for the night?" I asked.

That gave him pause. Through the smoke, he squinted over my shoulder. "You alone?"

"Yes, sir, it'll just be me."

An ash dropped onto the counter as he shrugged off his surprise.

"Whatever floats your boat, kid."

I paid a cut-rate, long-term price of sixty dollars.

"The elevator don't work." The clerk slid me a key. "You'll have to walk up."

No problem. I took the stairs. A dim burned-out-bulb climb to the third floor. My room was at the end of the hall, and when I pushed open the door it dawned on me why someone would opt to stay for no more than an hour. The wallpaper was faded, peeling; drapes limp, frayed; the carpet a worn, matted, dirt-brown shag. Oh well, I sighed wearily, at least there's a bed. A double-bed, in fact, with what appeared to be a small parking meter built into the headboard. MagicFingersMassage it read above a coin slot designed to take Quarters Only.

A two bit back rub was more than I needed. Saving my loose change, I passed on the magic fingers and flopped face-up on the saggy chintz covered mattress. My reflection staring down at me from a large square of mirrored tiles stuck to the ceiling, I watched myself yawn.

"Goodnight, Woody."

Dozing off, I tried to keep one eye open—to see what I looked like asleep.

It didn't work.

I was, however, startling enough, the first thing I saw when I awoke. Hardly a pretty picture. I looked thin, drawn, haggard almost beyond recognition. And smelled even worse. I noted the time: seven a.m. That gave me a few hours to shower, change clothes, grab some breakfast before finding my way to Universal Studios.

I knew from an article in *People* magazine—a sort of fluffy profile piece on the hot young actors in Hollywood—'that Fletcher Sinclair now had his own production company, with an office on the Universal lot. Just three years older than me, Fletcher had starred in the teen horror flick *Vampires Suck*. As well as the two sequels: *Vampires Suck Again* and *Vampires Still Suck*. All three were box-office hits. Of course, artistically speaking, they pale (and then some) when compared to his father's films. Even so, who was I to detract from the son's success? On a mere mortal level, Fletcher Sinclair was doing pretty darn well for himself. Furthermore, although his fledgling company had yet to produce anything, I'd gathered from the article that the young man possessed ambitions higher than *Vampires Suck 4Ever*.

In any event, it wasn't his career that concerned me.

Like everything else about the hotel, its water pressure left much to be desired. Under a barely warm trickle, I eked out a shower before slipping into a clean white dress shirt and khakis pants. With the key returned to the dayshift desk clerk, I then fueled-up on two Egg McMuffins at a nearby McDonald's, and from there hopped on the Hollywood Freeway headed north. According to my map Universal was just over the hill in Studio City.

It wasn't hard to find. At a little past ten o'clock I arrived at the front gate guard station. "Yes, my name is Woodrow Washborn. I'm here to see Fletcher Sinclair," I said to the uniformed lady guard inside the booth.

Scanning a clipboard, she shook her head.

"I don't see your name. What time was your appointment?"

"My appointment . . . uh . . . well . . . the thing is I got into town kinda late last night. So I didn't really have a chance to make a . . . a formal appoint—"

"In other words, you don't have one."

"That would be one way of putting it, but—"

"I'm sorry. If you're not on the list I can't let you pass."

"Then why don't we call him now. Let him know I'm here."

"I'm afraid it doesn't work that way. You'll have to back up, turn around and go make your call elsewhere."

"And what is his phone number again?"

"Have a nice day, sir."

There was a firm finality in her tone. She was only doing her job, and wasn't about to risk it on my account. If I wanted in I would have to come up with a Plan B. Which, as fate would have it, didn't take very long at all. I was driving away to look for a payphone when a sign—advertising a public tour of the studio—caught my eye. It gave me an idea.

"I'll take one ticket for the next tour, please."

It was easy as that. I paid the fee, killed a few hours wandering through the Universal theme park, City Walk, and then, at two in the afternoon, I boarded a sort of open trolley car along with a dozen or so other sightseers, and off we went, onto the sunny studio lot.

In a smooth, practiced voice, our guide called our attention to the various attractions. Each had to do with the one of the studio's more famous movies: the spooky Bates house from *Psycho*, *King Kong*, a *Jaws* inspired shark that jumped frightfully from a pool of water. Stuff I would've thought really interesting had there not been an ulterior motive behind my visit. Namely, Fletcher Sinclair.

When the trolley stopped in front of a huge, airplane hanger-like building, the guide informed us it was actually a soundstage. "Our newest and largest stage," he said. "Inside we have the lunar landscape from the soon-to-be-released *Apollo 11*. Now, if you will all follow me, we'll step inside and walk on the moon for a moment."

We piled out onto the pavement.

"Again," the guide reminded us, "this is a jobsite. So, for your own safety, please, stay with the group."

He led the way through a big bay door, the others herded close behind him. Only I hung back. This was my chance. I waited until they'd all gone inside, to leave their footprints on the faux-lunar surface, then, seizing the opportunity, I sneaked off down the road, trying to exude some semblance of authorization.

So far, so good. In the bustling sprawl of soundstages, office buildings, cottages and trailers no one gave me a second glance. I was just another body on the move, dodging golf carts, forklifts, bicycles. It had the feel of an industrious, campus community.

"Excuse me." I approached a freshman-type standing over a basket attached to the handlebars of his bicycle, sorting mail like he had to deliver it. "Maybe you can help me. I'm trying to find Fletcher Sinclair's office."

"Fletch'n'Bone," he replied without looking up.

"What?"

He huffed like he had enough to do without playing Information Guy.

"Fletch'n'Bone—that's the name of his company."

"Oh, right, of course, Fletch'n'Bone. So you know it."

"Trailer 22."

"Yes. 22. And that's uh . . ."

"Go to the next intersection, take a left, it's about a hundred yards down, name's on the front, you can't miss it."

The kid knew his beat. A relatively short walk later there it was: Fletch'n'Bone Productions.

"Can I help you?" asked a pretty young woman from behind the reception desk just inside the door.

"I hope so." I smiled innocently. "I'm here to see Fletcher Sinclair."

"Is he expecting you?"

Here we go again.

"Not exactly, but—"

"Do you work on the lot?"

"No. I don't but—"

"Can I see your gate pass, please," she snipped.

"If you'd just tell him I'm here, I'm sure—"

"I'm calling security." She reached for the desk phone.

"No. Really. That won't be necessary." I withdrew in retreat. "I'll just go. No problem. Sorry to have bothered you."

I was halfway out the door when the phone started to buzz. With her eyes still fixed on me, she pressed a blinking button. "Yes?" she answered.

"Judy, I'm at a loss in here." A male voice over the intercom. "Whaddaya know about the Amish?"

"The Amish?" she frowned.

"Yeah. You know, hats, beards, buggies. Amish people."

"Yes, I understand. But all I know is what I saw in that Harrison Ford thing: *Witness*."

"Well, I need some background. History, religion—"

"The Amish are Protestant," I cut in. "They broke from the Mennonites in the 17th Century."

"What? Who's that? Judy?"

"I have no idea." She shrugged. "Some kid. He just walked in un-announced."

"My name is Woody Washborn. I was born and raised in Amish country."

Silence. Broken by a clatter of footsteps coming down the hall. Followed closely by a very handsome young man dressed in faded denim and cowboy boots. His tanned, square-jawed face framed by a sandy brown lion's mane to his shoulders, I recognized him immediately. He was none other than the hunky vampire slayer, *aka* Fletcher Sinclair.

"So, you're Amish, huh?" His father's blue eyes took me in.

"Not exactly," I told him. "My mother was until she married my dad."

"Close enough." He turned to the desk. "Judy, hold down the fort. I'll be over at the commissary with . . ."

"Woody," Judy huffed.

"Woody—my man!" He slapped me flush on the back.

On the walk across the lot, Fletcher pumped me for information regarding the Amish. I was no expert on the subject but gladly shared with him the things my mother had told me about her life growing up in the fold, and what I'd picked up from those rare encounters with my grandparents Lapp and the others.

Preoccupied with my estranged kinfolk, Fletcher never thought to ask how I'd gotten to him, or why I was there. He led me into the studio's cafeteria, directed me to a corner table then went to the counter to get us some coffee. Seated, I scanned the big room. Well past lunchtime there was only a smattering of afternoon snackers in the place. I panned back to Fletcher. He took two large Styrofoam cups to the cash register. There he had a brief, breezy conversation with another very familiar face standing in line to pay. Could it be? They parted on a private laugh, Fletcher bringing the drinks to the table. "Here ya go." He set one down in front of me. "Ice mocha."

"That guy you were talking to. Was that Tom Hanks?"

"Yeah." He sat opposite me. "We have the same agent."

"He's a terrific actor," I gushed as Forrest Gump ambled out the door.

"It's all about landing the right role," Fletcher said. "Like this thing I'm after, the story of a young Amish man who gets drafted into the army during Vietnam. Now does he stick to his beliefs, pacifism; or does he join the battle, patriotism? It's a fat part, Woody. And I want it. Or course, so does every other hot shit actor in my age range."

"Your last movie was a hit," I said supportively. "That should give you some advantage."

"Typecasting," he complained, "it's a bear trap. I've always played the streetwise smart ass. I gotta show them naïve. You know, fresh off the farm."

"Then you should go hangout in Bird in Hand for a while."

"No time for that. The sharks are already circling the meat."

"Well. I'll keep my fingers crossed for you."

We paused to collect our thoughts and sip the trendy mocha java on the rocks. Prompted by the lull, I broached my own agenda. "Anyhow, about the reason I'm here . . . uh . . . you see, I'm very interested in your father."

I felt a sudden chill from Fletcher's side of the table. His eyes hardened, nostrils flared reflexively. "Fuck my father!" he scoffed. "Far as I'm concerned Ford Sinclair is dead."

The harsh sincerity in his voice took me by surprise. Clearly, I'd poked my nose into an unhealed wound, certainly not my intention. Still, I was desperate for something in the way of a lead. Insensitive as it was, I had to know. "So you haven't heard from him?"

"From him? Nada. About him? So goddamn much I wanna scream every time his name is mentioned."

"I'm sorry, I don't mean to upset you. Only it's very important to me that I find him."

Fletcher sagged in his chair.

"I was three years old when he ran out on us. And I've spent every day since then trying to forget him. Do you have any idea how it feels to never just be you? To always be thought of as your father's son?"

"Yes," I answered. "In fact, I have a pretty good idea how it feels."

"And my mother . . . she gave up her career, her friends, her sense of identity for that son-of-a-bitch. Then he dropped her. Like she was some puppet he got tired of manipulating."

"From what I've read, though, he never stopped supporting her."

"Never stopped *haunting* her is more like it. She's wasted twenty years and counting waiting for him to come back to her. No. All the money in the world won't make up for what he took from us." He paused for a moment, stewing in the loss. Then, "What about your dad—was he there for you?"

"Yeah. But he was just, you know, an ordinary guy."

"Well that's more than I got. Ford the fuckin' flake. I hate him. Always will."

We drank the rest of our coffee in silence.

Outdoors, Fletcher returned to the less emotional matter of the Amish.

"So, basically they're a patriarchal society. Who see modern conveniences as an improper display of vanity."

"Basically."

He looked off for a moment—above the tops of the buildings toward a rugged hillside in the distance. His profile, itself cast from a patriarchal mold, suddenly brightened under the tan. When he turned back to me his eyes were dancing to a mischievous rhythm.

"Woody, I just got an idea." He flashed a movie star smile. "How'd you like to go to a *party* tonight?"

"Party? What kind of party?"

"Ever heard of Howard Klein?"

In fact, I had. "Howard Klein. He produced your father's films."

"He's also producing this project we've been talking about."

There was a golf cart parked at the curb. On a whim Fletcher hopped in behind the wheel. "C'mon," he hurried me, "let's take a ride."

Feeling again like an accomplice to a crime, I slid reluctantly onto the seat beside him. "Hang on," he said, then stomped on the foot peddle, and off we lurched. A nutty dash of golf cart larceny added to the troublesome trail mix of my soul.

As he weaved recklessly through the traffic, away from his trailer, Fletcher let me in on the brainstorm. "I'm thinking if I show-up at Howard's party with you—it'll look like I already have connections to the Amish."

"But I'm not Amish," I reminded him.

"Hey, Woody, baby, this is Hollywood," he reminded me. "The land of make-believe."

INTERIOR. UNIVERSAL STUDIOS' WARDROBE DEPT. LATE DAY.

Open on a pair of plain black shoes. Tilt up to a pair of plain black trousers, a plain white shirt under a plain black jacket . . .

Hold on a medium shot of my face. A plain black wide-brimmed hat placed ridiculously on my head.

                                ME
                    This is not going to work.

     Reverse angle

FLETCHER

Whaddaya mean? You look great. If I didn't know better I'd assume you rode into town on a buckboard.

ME

Fletcher, there's no way I can pull this off.

FLETCHER

I'll pay you. Five hundred dollars. Consider it a professional acting job.

ME

But I can't act! I couldn't even make the cut at the community playhouse back home.

FLETCHER

All you have to do is be true to your roots.

ME

True? Look at me—I'm dressed in a lie here!

FLETCHER

Hey, you've got more truth on your side than the Godfather did.

ME

What?

FLETCHER

Brando. Don Corleone. At least you have Amish in your blood. Marlon doesn't have a drop of Italian in him.

Close up on me. A portrait of dread.

*   *   *

The Pacific Coast Highway.

At a little past eight that evening I was seated next to Fletcher in his sporty silver Porsche convertible. He was doing close to ninety miles-per-hour. All I could do to keep that dopey black hat from flying off my too small head.

After "wardrobe" we'd returned to the trailer to get our story straight for the party. While Fletcher was back in his office changing into a sharp white Armani suit Judy the receptionist had looked at me like I was a mental case trick-or-treater and she was fresh out of candy.

Now, insanely, I was on my way to ring Howard Klein's doorbell.

"One more time," Fletcher said for tenth time. "From the top."

Breathing a heavy sigh, I indulged him.

"We're cousins," I repeated. "Your mother and my mother are sisters. When you were a kid you spent summers on our farm."

"Bird in Hand. Lancaster County. Southern Pennsylvania."

"What if somebody asks me an Amish question I can't answer?"

"Improvise," Fletcher directed. "Change the subject. Excuse yourself to go to the bathroom. Whatever. Just *stay* in character."

CHAPTER FOURTEEN

The Porsche zoomed north along the shoreline. With the sun resting on the horizon—the water a rippling red—we were bound for Malibu. For Howard Bigtime Hollywood Producer Klein's summer getaway.

Fletcher pointed it out to me as we approached. It was lit-up like a swanky beacon at the sandy edge of the ocean. We turned into a driveway already lined with cars, serious cars, Ferraris, Mercedes, a Rolls Royce, under the watchful eye of a dark little man in a red service vest. He signaled for us to stop.

"How do you feel?" Fletcher asked me.

"I feel like a fraud," I answered uneasily.

"No, cousin Woody. Not a fraud," he insisted. "A thespian!"

When the valet stepped to the driver's side door Fletcher climbed out with motor running. I took a deep breath to calm my jitters then did the same. Leaving the car in the valet's care, we walked the walk to the front door of the elegant beach house.

"Here we go, Woody. Showtime."

I winced as he rang the bell. On cue the door swung open to reveal a stiff-looking gentleman dressed for duty in a black bow tie and tails. "Good evening, Mr. Sinclair," he said. His eyes startled wide when he got a load of me.

Now, I've been to a few parties in my life. But I've never made an entrance that turned so many heads as I did on this night. Ushered into the foyer, we were immediately the focus of attention. A curious hush fell over the two dozen or more oh-so-chic guests gathered in the sunken white living room.

"May I take your hat, sir?" asked the doorman, professionally polite.

"No!" Fletcher answered. "He wants to keep the hat on."

"Yes, sir," the man nodded somewhat awkwardly before returning to his post by the door.

"Thanks a lot," I grumbled to Fletcher under my breath.

"Lawrence Olivier," he whispered back. "The character comes with the costume."

"Fletcher!"

The crowd parted as a short, stocky, mostly bald older man in a black velvet jumpsuit rushed to greet us. "So glad you could make it."

"Wouldn't've missed for the world, Howard," Fletcher grinned, and the two converged in a big, backslappy bear hug.

Easing out of the embrace, Fletcher introduced me.

"Howard, I'd like you to meet my cousin Woody. Cousin Woody, Howard Klein."

The legendary producer considered me shrewdly.

"Interesting look, Woody. Hasidim, or has Versace gone very retro?"

"Neither, Howard," Fletcher scammed. "Cousin Woody is of the Amish persuasion."

"Of course." Our host apologized, "Forgive my ignorance. I should've realized."

"That's okay," I assured him. "It was news to me, too."

"Actually, this is quite a coincidence. Because I just happen to have a picture on my plate that features an Amish fellow."

"Really?" Fletcher played dumb. "Sounds interesting."

"But hey—no shoptalk tonight," Klein decreed. "Tonight we leave business for pleasure. Now come, join the party. We will drink, eat and make merry!" He escorted us down into the living room crowd, and over to where a bar was set up. Telling the tender to take good care of us, he then excused himself to go mingle amongst his other guests.

Fletcher ordered a vodka martini. In keeping with my Amish temperance, we decided I should stick with mineral water. Besides, I had to stay on my toes.

"So, whaddaya think, Woody?" Fletcher asked as we scanned the swell faces. "The operators of the dream factory."

"Fletcher, I still don't feel right about this."

"Of course you don't. Such vanity. Must seem an arrogant display to humble lad such as yourself."

"You know damn well that's not what I mean."

"I'm counting on you now, Woody. Don't let me down, man."

I sighed. "How long do we have to stay?"

"Just take it easy, relax, you're doing fine. If you really want to hear some good-old-days stories about The Flake talk to Howard. He loves to tell them, ad nauseam. He's even got an original Sinclair hanging in the den."

"A *painting* . . . can we go see it?"

"I'd rather pluck my eyes out. But don't let me stop you."

"Fletcher!"

We turned to a very well preserved older woman in a smart gold lamé cocktail dress gliding toward us. "How nice to see you again, dear," she beamed, a bit tipsy already, I suspected.

"You're looking lovely as ever, Gloria."

They kissed the air at both cheeks. Then, not so subtly, she segued to me. "And who, I am dying to know, do we have here?"

"Gloria Klein, my cousin Woody."

"Let me guess," she smiled warmly. "Amish."

With a twinge of guilt, I nodded. "Yes, ma'am."

"You know," the lady Klein proposed, "odd as it may sound, our cultures have a great deal in common. I mean the film business—it's a very exclusive, close-knit community. And we live by our own rules. And we tend to distrust strangers."

"And we've been known to shun people on occasion," another woman joined in, only half joking.

"Seriously," Gloria Klein went on. "We pull together to make movies much like you Amish pull together to raise a barn."

"Yes," a man interjected, "but I doubt they have prima donnas who refuse to come out of their trailers."

I was soon surrounded by a distinguished flock of executives, producers, lawyers, agents and bejeweled Hollywood wives taken in by the hoax. Squeezed out, Fletcher winked at me from the perimeter. (I must confess) Encouraged by all the attention, I actually started to get into it. It was fun being interesting. They laughed at my quaint Amish wit; stood rapt as I wove my imposter's web of horse and buggy lies. Heck, I was beginning to believe them myself. Until—

"So, tell me, Woody," a woman probed deeper, "as a former teacher, I'm curious about your educational system . . ."

Uh-oh.

" . . . What is the curriculum in Amish Schools?"

I flinched. "C-c-curriculum?"

"Other than the 3Rs, what sort of courses do they teach?"

Good question.

With all eyes on me, ears hanging on my every word, I drew a blank. Cornered, cracking under the pressure, I couldn't even think to make up an answer. I looked to Fletcher for help, but he wasn't there. Confident I had everything under control he'd drifted off somewhere. I was now alone on the stage.

"You were saying?" the woman persisted.

In lieu of a ready improvisation, I ransacked my brain for a way to smoothly change the subject. "Uh . . ." Still, nothing came. I felt a drumroll in my chest. "Well . . ."

Mayday! Mayday!

Suddenly I remembered—the last refuge of knaves and bullshitters.

"Excuse me, but I uh . . . I have to go. To the bathroom."

Fleeing the scene, I heard Gloria Klein remark to the others, "I don't believe they have indoor plumbing where he's from."

Thank God the john was unoccupied. I ducked inside, locked the door behind me. I could've kicked myself for letting Fletcher talk me into such a crazy scheme. The thought of being exposed as a total sham in from of all these classy people made me want to climb out the window and run for the hills. I cringed at myself in the seashell-framed mirror above the sink. I was sweating bullets under that heavy black hat and thick wool suit. I turned on the faucet, splashed my face with cold water. Enough was enough. I had to be gone from this party.

There came a knock at the door.

"I'll be out in a minute," it pained me to say.

Okay. Suck it up, Woody. It's almost over. Just go find Fletcher and make him take me back to my truck. If he resists, threaten to spill the beans to Klein. By any means, get the hell *out* of there. I opened the door and scurried off, weaving quickly through the crowd in search of my counterfeit cousin. I checked the parlor, dining room, back deck, kitchen. Fletcher was nowhere to be found. At a loss, I peeked into the den. He wasn't there, either. On the far wall, however, I spotted something from which I could not turn away. It was the painting Fletcher had told me about: an original Sinclair.

Alone in the room, I crossed to the finely framed work of art, eyeing it with a charged wonder. One of the *Everglade* paintings. A lush green swamp at golden sunrise. Softened by a ghostly pale mist. At the bottom of the canvas, just above Sinclair's signature, a large alligator lurked hungrily in the primordial muck. I could almost smell the cypress. Hear the morning songs of birds in the trees, the baritone harmony of bullfrogs. A strange and dangerous place. And Sinclair had gone out there alone. Six unsheltered days in a lightweight canoe, armed with only a machete and paint brushes. His emergence brilliantly marked by three of his most famous paintings.

Rumor has it that he actually did four. That one was lost to the glade when he had to fight off a poisonous viper on his paddle back to dry land. A story Arthur Brimm suspects is merely a tall tale—invented by the slick art dealer who first sold the works.

Anyhow, three survived. One of them now so close I could've reached out and touched it.

"Mesmerizing, isn't it?"

Startled, I spun around, and there was Howard Klein smiling

proudly up at the canvas. "Your Uncle Ford gave it to me the night I gave him the green light to make *Nomads*. Hard to say which I prize more—the movie or the painting."

"They're both very special, sir."

"He was by far the best I ever worked with," the producer proclaimed. "And I've worked with some of the biggest."

"Oh, I know, sir."

"Ford had a way of channeling the art he wanted to make into the mainstream," Klein went on. "What's more he made it seem effortless. He'd juggle composition, dialogue, lighting, wardrobe, everything down to the smallest detail. And at the same time he'd look over at me and say, 'Don't you worry, Howard. I'll have it on your table in time for dinner.'

"And somehow he always managed it. He brought both pictures in ahead of schedule and under budget. Like it was the easiest thing in the world."

"So, what happened to number three?" I asked.

"Ah, the Captain Cook story." A heavy sigh. "It was his dream project. Said he had it in his head since he was a boy. Wrote the script and drew-up a complete storyboard in less than a month, an epic, mind you. At the time it promised to be one of the grandest productions ever put on screen. Of course with two box-office winners and a half-dozen Oscars under his belt, Ford expected the studio would gladly put up the financing we needed."

"Only it didn't work out that way."

"It's all part of the game, Woody. Let's make a deal. We said twenty-five million, they said twenty. Hell, once they realized Ford wasn't going to play they offered thirty."

"Which he refused."

The producer shook his head, over what might have been.

"He took the haggling personally. He saw it as an insult, an affront to the vision. The last thing he said to me was, 'Howard, I can no longer indulge the bookkeepers' view of the universe.'"

"Even if it meant the end of his Cook dream."

"He had a deep stubborn streak, your uncle. Once he got something in his head that was it. He packed his bags, went up

into the mountains with Deanna, and never came back." Howard
Klein swallowed, winced, after more than twenty years still a
hard pill to choke down. "A goddamned waste is what it is."

I found Fletcher in the dining room. He was at the buffet table,
munching on a sushi roll.

"Not cool," I scolded him, "leaving me like that."

"Try the beluga, cuz. It's from Mr. Hito's."

"I've had enough. Let's blow before something goes wrong."

"Check this out, Woody. Looks like you have an admirer."

I followed his sightline—across the room—to a stunningly
gorgeous redhead in a snug green mini-dress. She was staring at
me. The instant our eyes met it hit me who she was. My breath
taken, I turned back to the table.

"That's Samantha Gillette," I gasped.

"Mmmmm-mmmm!" Fletcher confirmed. "She looks even
fresher than the caviar."

For a red-blooded heterosexual male in the 1930s, it was
Jean Harlow. In the 40s, Rita Hayworth. The 50s, Marilyn
Monroe. And for me, at the lusty dawn of the new century, it
was Samantha Gillette. The flawless image I'd mooned over in
darkened theaters magically sealed off from the real world. Now
here she was, in the flesh, near enough that I could feel her sultry
gaze heating the scruff of my neck.

"See that guy she's with," Fletcher dished. "That's Nicky Quinn."

I sneaked a peek. He looked to be in his mid-thirties, a few
years older than Samantha. His Adonis blond hair slicked back
in a short playboy's ponytail, he was rapping possessively in her
ear. Still, her eyes remained fixed on me.

"His old man was the Q in TVQ Broadcasting," Fletcher
went on. "Word is he left slick Nick a tidy two hundred mil."

"Good for him. Now let's get out of here."

"He fancies himself a stud. But at the moment she seems
more interested in you."

"Fletcher, please, I want to go."

"C'mon." He grabbed my arm. "I'll introduce you."

"No!" I planted my heels. "It's too much."

"Don't worry," he tugged. "I'll catch you if you faint."

He had to practically drag me over there. Samantha Gillette's face, perfect and creamy, dimpled with a ripe-lipped smile as we approached.

"Hey, Sam," Fletcher instigated.

"Fletcher Sinclair, I was beginning to think you were ignoring me," she chided playfully.

"Not a chance, baby," Fletcher volleyed. "Nobody in their right mind could ignore you."

Her jade green eyes ("bewitching" to quote Roger Ebert the movie critic) flicked flirtatiously to mine. "And this must be the cousin everyone's talking about."

"Samantha Gillette, Woody Washborn."

"Hello, Woody," she purred, offering me her hand.

Star struck, it was all I could do to keep from swooning. My palm damp, clammy, pressed against hers: America's Sweetheart. "Miss Gillette, it is a pleasure to make you. I mean meet you. Make your acquaintance."

"I'm afraid he's a little nervous," Fletcher jumped in. "Not quite the scene he's used to."

"Of course not." Samantha sparkled. "All this posing and pretense. It must seem rather shallow to someone like you."

Ironic; given that I was the biggest poser and pretender on the premises. But I was far too swept-up in the thrill to brood over it now. "I'm a big fan of your work," I gushed. "I've seen every film you've been in."

"Since when do the Amish go to the movies?" Nicky Quinn wanted to know. A chilling, if not unreasonable, question.

"Oh . . . uh . . . well . . . ummm . . ."

"Strictly speaking, it's not really allowed," Fletcher came to my rescue. "When it comes to Samantha, however, Woody bends the rules a bit. He stands outside the local drive-in and watches her through the fence."

I cringed. Too cornball. She'll never believe it.

Samantha's eyes narrowed. "Now that—"

Oh, God, here it comes.

"—is the most flattering review I've ever received."

I exhaled, shocked, the corn had worked

"Nicky, I could use another drink." Samantha handed Quinn her champagne flute, it was still half full.

"Me, too," Fletcher chimed in. "C'mon, Nick, this round's on me."

Quinn paused. Clearly he was not a man accustomed to playing the gofer. Then again he wasn't a glamorous movie star, either. And at this party one Samantha Gillette trumped even two hundred million inherited dollars. A fact he had to concede. So off he went, with Fletcher along for the laugh, through the crowd in the direction of the bar.

"You must be roasting in that heavy suit," Samantha said once her date was out of sight.

"Yeah," I replied. "It's part of the sweaty and itchy collection."

"What you need is a cool ocean breeze." She took my arm. "And I know just where to find one.

"Now? What about your drink?"

She smiled. "Let's take a walk, Woody."

She led me through the parlor, then out onto the back deck, and down the steps toward the water. On the moonlit beach, we strolled, a very odd couple indeed, the shoreline all to ourselves.

Slipping off her high heels, she walked barefoot on the sand. Samantha Gillette! Princess Hedra in *Galaxy Storm*, Nurse Lucy for *The Asylum*, Miss Nelson from *Gang'sta High*, one of *People* magazine's "50 Most Beautiful People." Confiding in me the insecurities of her fame.

"You would not believe the phonies I have to deal with. Either they're looking to get into my limelight or into my pants. Mostly both."

"Must be hard finding someone you can trust."

"Humility. It's the hardest thing to find in this business.

Everybody's always trying to be bigger than life." She hugged my arm. "That's what makes you so refreshing, Woody. You're not about image or celebrity. You're . . . *real*."

"Yeah, well, the clothes don't always make the man," I said guiltily.

"I bet where you're from everyone's nice. Good, loyal, down to Earth, uncomplicated people."

"In Bird in Hand you learn to appreciate the simple things. Otherwise you go mad from the boredom."

"Do you have a girlfriend?"

I couldn't help but laugh at that, in light of the hardly uncomplicated mess I'd made of my relationship with Kelly Ann.

"Last I heard, I don't."

"Now that surprises me," Samantha replied.

"It does? Why?"

"Because what's more simple than the birds and the bees? It's the most natural thing there is, right?"

I shrugged. "I guess."

"And I can't imagine anyone more in touch with nature than strong young Amish man," she said, and what a delivery! To the sound of the breaking waves, and their ebbing retreat back into the darkness, she was everything Samantha Gillette was supposed to be: heroine, soul mate, ruby-lipped muse.

While I, in my flimflam black hat, played the part of a rat.

"Miss Gillette—"

"Please." She took my hands. "Call me, Sam."

Those moonstruck green eyes, so bright and trusting, beamed straight to my conscience. Fletcher forgive me, I could not perpetrate the lie any further. "Sam, there's something I have to tell you."

She pulled my hands flat over her hips.

"Woody, I know what you're going to say."

"You do?" The drive-in nonsense, she hadn't bought it after all.

"You're thinking this is crazy, that we're from totally different worlds. That I'm in the fast lane and you belong behind a plow.

But don't you see," she emoted, "that's what makes it so electric, so magnetic. The irresistible attraction of opposites."

"Sam, I'm not quite as opposite as you've been led to believe."

"You don't have to pretend with me, Woody." She pressed herself against me. "I'm a girl who likes her romance old-fashioned."

I'd seen her movies enough to know what was coming next. Her lips swelled to meet mine. A deep, glossy, R-rated kiss. Her tongue flicking, probing, thrilling as her manicured nails raked a most incredible thrill down my spine.

"Woody, I have a confession to make," she purred.

"Confession?" I panted.

"Yes. There's something I've been wondering about all night."

"What?"

Her hand slid around my waist, then lower, between my legs.

"I've been wondering if Amish men are circumcised."

She gave me a squeeze. I grunted. She kissed me again to shut me up.

"Don't tell me," she whispered. "I want to find out for myself."

She pulled me by my belt toward a talus of fallen rock at the foot of a sheer bluff. "Where we going?" I asked, stumbling in tow behind her.

"I'm leading you astray," Samantha replied matter-of-factly.

A nook between the boulders insured us an uncertain degree of privacy. She spun me around. Her eyes aglow, like two polished emeralds on fire, she asked, "When you were watching me through that fence, Woody, what was it you really wanted to see?" She slipped the thin straps from her shoulders. "Was it *this*?" Like a dream the dress slid down, and off the slope of her breasts. High, creamy-white, perfect mounds topped by ripe strawberry areolas. "Or was it *this*?" she toyed, the slight jut of her rib cage giving way to a flat, softly muscled belly. Pushed snug over the crescent flair of her hips, she let the dress spill to the sand, a rippled green puddle about her feet. Now wearing only the glint of diamond earrings and a shimmer of moonlight, she stood straight, perfectly erect. My breath caught in my throat. The fleecy trim between her legs the same lustrous red as the locks that framed her flushed angel face.

She came towards me. Running her hands hypnotically over her body—the firm, graceful curves that had inspired my most lascivious, celluloid fantasies—she said, "I've been offered millions of dollars to do a nude scene. And still, I told them no." She was so close now I could smell the desire wafting up from her sex. "But I'm saying yes to you, Woody. It's all yours. Free and easy for my fine Amish stud."

I stood spellbound as she reached out, tugged loose my belt. Her fingers worked nimbly the buttons on my fly. "Now," she cooed, "let's see what you have for me," and dropped to her knees. Her gaze fixed squarely on the bulge in my crotch, she licked her lips, anticipating the hard evidence of my seduction. Then, slowly, allowing the suspense to build, she eased down my pants, drawers and all, until finally my erection leapt free.

"Ahhh . . ." Her breath hot on my throbbing flesh "so you are circumcised." She took it in her hand. Samantha Gillette! "Tell me, Woody," she stroked: "those proper young ladies at home, do they touch you like this?"

"Nrrrr" was my answer.

"Salt of the earth. I want it, Woody. I want every inch of your innocence."

Her mouth opened. Round and ready to take me in.

"Samantha!"

She drew back, startled away from the true commencement of my corruption. "Shit!" she whispered. "It's Nicky."

"Nicky?" Instantly the blood began to drain from my loins.

"Samantha!" he called again.

She jumped to her feet. I yanked up my pants. Scrambling into her dress, she told me to "Stay put. Don't come out till we're gone."

"Sam!"

"Here I am."

Brushing sand from her behind, she hurried clear of the rocks.

Nicky's voice, "I've been looking all over for you. What the hell you doing out here?"

"Nothing," she said and scurried from my view. "Just taking a walk."

"Alone?"

"Of course alone."

"So where's the kid?"

"Kid—what kid?"

"You know damn well what kid."

"Nicky, please—"

"Get out of my way!"

"Nicky, stop!"

There was no place to hide. I was trapped. Nicky Quinn filled the only exit. His face twisted with rage at the sight of me; my shirt untucked, fly half unbuttoned. "I knew it," he growled. "A wolf in sheep's wool."

Samantha came up behind him. "Nicky, now don't get crazy." Slipping through a gap, she stepped in between us.

"So, you're gonna protect him," Nicky sneered. He lashed out, grabbed her violently by the hair. "And who's gonna protect you?"

"Nicky, let her go!" I heard myself blurt.

He bared his teeth at me. "Oh, don't you worry, Amish boy." He threw Samantha aside, to the ground. "This is about you and me now."

He came at me. Arm cocked. In range, he swung—a wild, looping roundhouse. Instinctively I ducked under it, and countered with a right hand. A sharp, tight-fisted hook I never knew I had in me. And even more to my surprise the shot landed. Clean, flush to his nose. A lucky punch that dropped Nicky straight to his knees, his hands cradling his face.

"Oh my God!" Samantha cried.

Nicky groaned, blood streaming through his fingers.

Samantha rushed to his side. "Nicky, are you all right?"

"He broke my nose," Nicky gurgled.

Samantha screamed at me "You hit him!" in disbelief.

"He was hurting you," I reminded her.

"You're not supposed to go around beating people up!"

"But he swung first."

"You're *Amish*!" she railed. "You're supposed to turn the other cheek!"

"I'm sorry," I said. "Here, let me—"

"Stay away from us!" America's Sweetheart snarled. "You people are animals!"

I wasn't sure what to feel worse about: Nicky's nose, or that I'd given the entire Amish world a black eye.

"C'mon, baby." She helped him to his feet. "Let's get you to a doctor."

As she crutched Nicky back toward the beach house, Samantha Gillette snapped a last look over her shoulder.

"You took advantage of me!" she declared.

CHAPTER FIFTEEN

"Whup Ass Woody Washborn," Fletcher cackled over the wind as we sped south on the PCH. "I love it!"

We'd left the party abuzz. While word of my run-in with Nicky Quinn spread through the crowd like a wildfire in the Malibu hills I lingered on the beach until Fletcher came looking for me, and then waited in the Porsche while he went back into house to say goodnight to the Kleins. He'd come out laughing, and had yet to stop.

It puzzled me. "I thought you'd be mad I broke character."

"Mad? Woody, you were great, man. Cracking Quinn was a stroke of genius."

"How so?"

"Think story, Woody. If the Amish kid knows how to fight then it adds a whole new dimension to his reluctance to go to war. It gives him more depth, makes him more dynamic. Howard ate it up. Not only is he gonna have it doctored into the script, he promised me first shot at the part. You were perfect, Woody. I owe you. And a lot more than five hundred bucks."

"Forget about the money. It's not what I'm after."

"Then how does this sound? My mother, she was the last person to see The Flake before he split. She's still living up at the ranch. It's a two-hour drive from the studio. If you're interested I'll give her a call first thing in the morning. See if she's willing to meet with you."

"Yes. Please," I said eagerly, "I'm very interested."

"In the meantime, you can crash at my place."

"Actually, if it's not a problem, I'm thinking it would be kinda neat to spend the night at Universal."

Fletcher was happy to oblige me.

"I've got a sofa-bed in my office you can sleep on."

We arrived at the studio's employee entrance gate around midnight.

"Working late, Mr. Sinclair?" asked the guard on duty.

"No rest for the wicked, Stan," was Fletcher's reply.

Signed in, we drove onto the now quiet lot. Inside the Fletch'n'Bone trailer, Fletcher led me to his office. It was furnished with a glass-top desk, TV, VCR, CD player, *Vampires Suck* pinball machine, and a leather sofa, which he pulled out for me to sleep on.

"Make yourself at home," he said. "Only I wouldn't go wandering around the grounds if I was you. Security can get pretty gnarly."

"Don't worry. I'll stay put," I assured him. "I've had enough excitement for one day."

"All right then. So chill out, get some shut-eye, and I'll see you in the morning."

"Please, tell your mom I'd be extremely grateful for even five minutes of her time."

"Let's just hope she's up for some company," Fletcher said with a shrug, as if that was seldom the case, and then he was gone. Bound for his own beach house in Santa Monica.

Left alone, I stripped off the Amish garb. Feeling somewhat like myself again, I took the liberty of browsing the office in detail. A library of video tapes on a rack under the TV snagged my attention. Curious, I scanned the titles for *Nomads* or *Con Man* but neither was included in the collection. Nor did I find among the stacks of CDs on the player any discs acknowledging the music of Buster Sinclair. Evidently Fletcher was sincere in his aversion to all reminders of the celebrated father he barely knew.

Drained, I stretched out on the bed. My hand still hurt from the first real punch I'd ever thrown. Massaging my bruised knuckles, I allowed myself a smile. The reviews were in.

My performance had drawn raves.

I was up before the sun. Dressed in my own clothes, I was waiting by the door with my fingers crossed when Fletcher entered the trailer at a few minutes past seven. From the grin on his face I detected good news.

"I called mom early," he reported. "Figured yea or nay you'd want to know soon as possible."

"And?"

"She went for it, man. You are persona grata at the ranch."

I sighed my relief. If she'd said "no" I don't know what I would've done. I had nowhere else to go, but home, and the prospect of returning to Bird in Hand with the Deanna rock left unturned seemed yet another testament to my shameful proclivity for underachievement. At least now I had one more stop to make between Hollywood and hometown humiliation.

Fletcher drew me a map. I was to take Vineland Avenue north to Sunland Boulevard; Sunland to Mount Gleason Avenue; Mount Gleason to the Angeles Forest Highway, which would take me high into the San Gabriel Mountains. From there it got a little trickier—winding roads through the wilderness. The ranch to be found on a secluded hilltop miles removed from its nearest neighbor.

"This is my cell-phone number." He wrote it down at the bottom of the paper. "If you get lost call me."

I was hot to roll. Fletcher walked me to the truck. In spite of the fact that I'd picked at the deep, unhealed wounds left on his heart by a father seemingly intent to neglect, he'd embraced to me. Treated me (albeit in a devilish sort of way) like a—well; like a long lost cousin.

I thanked him. Wished him much luck landing the Amish whopper of a role he'd gone to such extraordinary lengths to bait.

"Just do me one more favor, Woody," he said as I was about
to drive off. "If somehow you do manage to catch up with Ford
the Flake . . ." He smiled " . . . *bust* his fucking nose for me."

Sadly, I understood, the smile was only an actor's mask.
Underneath the façade he could not have been more serious.
However obscured by the rising star brightness of his future,
Fletcher Sinclair remained the abandoned, unforgiving son.

Fade out.

To the credit of Fletcher's directions, I didn't get lost. Leaving
the valley behind, I climbed toward the rugged spine of the San
Gabriels, and then followed the mapped out twists and turns
along unpaved roads until I arrived just before ten a.m. at the
bottom of a lonely rise. There was a large boulder beside two
tire-worn ruts running straight up the face of the hill. Fletcher
had drawn the rock to landmark the path as the only way to the
ranch.

The "retreat" according to Arthur Brimm. Designed and built
by Sinclair as a kind of refuge where artists could come, stay,
work, socialize, and otherwise feed off each other's talents, visions.
A place to inspire and be inspired. Sinclair had put millions of
dollars into its creation. His last known address.

I wheeled up the bumpy drive. A good half-mile later, the
slope suddenly leveled off at the top to reveal the front of a large,
log-fashioned house crowded by unchecked woods. I braked to a
stop behind a late-modeled SUV parked before the flagstone-
pillared porch. Stepping out of the truck, I looked back to admire
the view—white-capped peaks, green valleys, a distant dark blue
lake under an endless clear blue sky. Breathtaking . . .

"Woody?"

I turned to the voice. It belonged to a woman.

"Yes, ma'am," I answered through the front door screen.

"I told Fletcher, no pictures." Her tone guarded, yet soft.

"No, ma'am. I don't even have a camera with me."

She pushed open the door, took a cautious step out onto the

porch. In her mid-forties, she was still very beautiful. Her eyes dark like her hair. The sunken, high boned cheeks of a fashion model. Full lips pushed into a girlish pout. Dressed casually in a black t-shirt, jeans, and boots, she looked every inch Fletcher Sinclair's mother.

"I don't mean to be suspicious," she explained. "It's just that the shutterbugs who come snooping around—reporters and tourists—they have no respect for privacy."

"Believe me, Mrs. Sinclair, the last thing I want to do is bother you."

"Yes. Fletcher said you're a nice young man."

"He's quite a guy himself." Approaching slowly, "You must be very proud of him."

"That I am," she said, adding, "He inherited his father's charm."

I stopped at the stairs. "I take he also told you why I'm here."

She nodded. "You were drawn by your admiration for Ford."

"Yes, ma'am. Very much so."

She paused. Lifted her gaze to take in the view. Inhaling a deep breath of the clean mountain air, a slow smile stretched across her face. Then her eyes returned me. "Do you ride, Woody?"

It seemed less a question than an invitation.

"Ride, ma'am?"

"It's such a lovely day for it."

She led me directly to a redwood building maybe a hundred weedy yards from the main house. A stable. Loose boards and broken hinges spoke to its disrepair. We went inside. There were enough stalls for a dozen horses, all empty but two. They held a fine gray mare and handsome black stallion.

"We used to keep it fully stocked," Deanna remembered. "We had many guests who rode. But not the Appaloosa," she was quick to add. "Trojan was strictly a one-man horse. Anybody other than Ford, forget it. He'd throw them like a big bad bronc." She ran a hand atop the gate to an empty stall. "He died just a few years ago. Old age." With a sigh, she brushed the dust from her fingers.

I studied the once promising starlet as she saddled the animals. She was very gentle with them, wistfully so. It reminded me of Alice Faye with her birds, an attempt to fill a void in their lives: the inexplicable loss of a brother. Husband. Unlike Olivia Sutton Sinclair Woolbright, who'd come to accept the fact that Ford had dumped her, Deanna Dees Sinclair gave off an aura of steadfast denial. It enveloped her in a dim, desperate light. Like a last layer of defense against twenty years of unanswered prayers.

"There," she said, both saddles securely in place. "We're ready to go."

She handed me the reins to the male, and then mounted the female in one graceful move. I'd ridden a couple of times back home, but they were old field nags—a far cry from the groomed, well-bred steed now awaiting my reluctant rump.

"Easy, boy," I appealed, sliding an unsure foot into the stirrup. Visions of air-bucked rodeo riders flipped through my head as I pulled myself up, swung my leg over, and straddled the beast. It snorted. Skittish under my clumsiness.

"Buster, behave!" Deanna chided.

At her command the stallion huffed and puffed, then, obediently, he settled right down. Ironic, I thought: *a Buster she could tame.*

"We'll take it slow," she said, then tapped the mare with her boot heels and off we went at an easy trot. My horse content to follow hers along a flat dirt path through the overgrowth.

Moments later we slowed to a walk as she guided me passed a collection of broken down cabins. "These were the guests quarters," she told me. "At times we had as many as twenty artists in residence. Some stayed for weeks."

"Like who?" I asked.

"Oh, everybody who was anybody. Marlon Brando, Bob Dylan, Salvador Dali, Mia Farrow, Stanley Kubrick, Henry Miller, Miles Davis. I could go on and on."

I wished she would. Instead, she picked up the pace and continued the tour. She showed me the decrepit remains of several art studios, a sauna house, the "saloon," a drained swimming pool with weeds growing out of cracks in the concrete. It was like an exclusive ghost town. Gone overnight from boom to bust. A sense of desertion personified by Deanna herself. The lady left behind to keep a lonely torch burning.

"And here we have the pavilion," she said as we arrived at a large, rounded, dome-topped stone structure. The windows boarded over with rotted sheets of plywood. An impressive ruin in the making, it appeared.

"On any given day you could've dropped in to find Lenny Bernstein working on a new score, or Twyla Tharp putting together one of her wonderful dance routines. Ford designed it so the acoustics are absolutely incredible."

Seeing the crumbling mortar, I recalled Howard Klein's lamentation:

A goddamned waste is what it is.

Deanna laughed, nostalgic. "I remember one hot summer night. Truman Capote got drunk as a skunk and locked himself inside, because Ford wouldn't throw Gore Vidal off the property. He stayed put, without food, for nearly forty-eight hours. Finally we had to shut down the air-conditioning and sweat him out."

Her laugher faded into the past.

"Seems like only yesterday," she sighed.

Suddenly I understood Fletcher's anger. His hatred for the man who'd betrayed his mother with a kiss she still could not bear to wipe away.

"You must really miss it," was all I could say.

"Ah, but it's not over, Woody." She had to believe. "When Ford comes home we'll pick up right where we left off."

We rode back to the main house. After hitching the horses to a post, Deanna led me inside. It had the feel of grand ski lodge on a mountain where it no longer snowed. Welcoming, yet hollow. She took me through a spacious den area furnished with overstuffed chairs, sofas, a stone fireplace cold in a corner; passed a grand dining room where the famous and fashionable once gathered at the long oaken table to break bread and savor the bounty of their many gifts.

At the end of the hallway, Deanna pushed open a door, and we entered a study. It exuded a kind of simple elegance. The floor was polished hardwood, warmed by deep Oriental throw rugs. An old desk sat under a sunlit bay window. Lining one wall, an extensive library. On the opposite wall a rough wood mantel holding an antique humidor above a small granite fireplace. A spent log smoldered on the irons.

"This was Ford's sanctuary," Deanna informed me. "He spent hours and hours in here." She must've noticed me eyeing the log. "Oh. Yes. I light a fire every morning. Ford loved the smell."

"Did he work in here?"

She smiled. "I used to listen through the door." A light, naughty laugh. "A few times he almost caught me."

"And what did you hear?"

"Thinking," she said. "That was the only sound I ever heard. Ford's thoughts, they could be very loud, deafening at times." She paused. Tuned-in to the echoes. "Still—resonant as there were . . ." She shook her head, suggesting some failure on her part " . . . I could never quite comprehend what was going through his mind."

She crossed to the desk, into the sunlight, running her hand along the back of his chair. "He was sitting right here the last time I saw him. I'd just put Fletcher to bed. I came in to ask if he would be much longer. But he didn't answer me. He kept staring out this window.

"What is it, my love? What do you see?

"He took my hand.

"'I see the world turning, Deedee. The world turning.'

"He said, no, he wouldn't be long. So I went upstairs to wait for him. Only after a while I fell asleep. And the next morning, when I awoke . . . he was gone."

My heart went out to her. Still, I had to ask, "Would it be okay if I looked around for a few minutes?"

She turned. The smile came back to her face.

"I'll go put on a pot of tea."

Left alone in the room, I focused my investigation on the small things Sinclair had dispossessed. There had to be some indication, hint, a clue to what was going through his mind that night. I scanned the rows of books. Handsome, leather-bound volumes arranged alphabetically by author. I noted Alger, Asimov, Auden; Balzac, Blake, Byron; Chaucer, Chekhov; Dante, Dostoevski; Ibsen, Joyce, Lewis, London; Melville—

Melville. I stopped. *Moby Dick, Typee,* and there, pressed between them, a title that widened my eyes. *Omoo.*

I pulled it from the shelf. Put my finger over the last O.

Omo. As in Omo the clown.

I cracked the book open. From the prologue I read: Omoo . . . a person who wanders from island to island. *Buster's Island Dream* came to mind.

Herman Melville. Followed in order by Michener, James. *Return to Paradise.* Hmmm.

I went back to the works by Jack London. *Call of the Wild* and *South Seas Tales.* Interesting.

I returned *Omoo* to the shelf then moved on to the desk. As I considered the bareness of its top, it occurred to me—there were no mementos, no photographs, none of the awards or golden Oscars that distinguished Sinclair's life anywhere on display. Nothing at all to suggest a sentimental value.

Where were they? What did he do with them?

I slid out the top desk drawer. Fountain pens, charcoal pencils, a fancy ivory letter opener. I checked a lower drawer, empty. The middle drawer, nothing. Then the bottom drawer. Bingo! A manuscript. The yellowed bulk of a screenplay. Its title printed in big black block letters. "COOK"

I brought it up into the light, and flipped the cover page—to finely detailed charcoal drawing of the captain's 18th Century sailing ship. It's name printed clearly across the bow. *Endeavour.*

I turned to the next page, the text, and began to read

EXT. TOP DECK. SOUTH PACIFIC.

As I poured over the indelible black type, I could feel the sea spray on my face, the trade wind at my back, billowing the sails, transporting me back in time. To a voyage of discovery more than two hundred years ago . . .

"Tea's ready."

She startled me. I turned to her, the paper suddenly heavy in my hands.

"I'm sorry," I said. "I should've asked if I could read this."

"It's a great script," Deanna smiled. She didn't seem to mind.

"He ever say why he abandoned the movie? I know he felt insulted by the studio, but still—to walk away from his dream project."

"He was the most sensitive man I've ever known," Deanna answered. "Yet he also had the thickest skin. No, Woody, it had nothing to do with the studio, or anyone else. Whatever made him walk away from it, it didn't come from outside. It was something in him. Something that, to answer your question, he was not inclined to share."

I looked out the window. Weeds had reclaimed a private stone courtyard. I tried to imagine how it must've looked on that night more than twenty years ago, the open, tended garden Sinclair had known. But in spite of my efforts to take in the view from his perspective, I could not see it . . . *the world turning*.

We sat down to our tea in the parlor. Between us, a round, glass-topped coffee table. Over the steam of hot chamomile, I was all ears as Deanna recounted for me her first meeting with Sinclair.

"I had just turned nineteen. I'd been in Hollywood less than a year, having come by Greyhound bus from Indianapolis. So my résumé was pretty thin. Modeling work mostly. Several local television commercials. My film experience amounted to a few small roles, pretty much window dressing to start, but they were gradually getting more substantial. My star was rising, as they say.

"Anyhow, when my agent told me I'd been cast as the waitress in *Con Man* I figured it would be a couple of days, a nice credit, a union scale paycheck and that would be that. At the time I only knew Ford by reputation. Since *Nomads* had hit big he was the talk of the town. But even then he wasn't one to go parties or attend premieres. So I'd never seen him in person. Not until I showed up on the set to do my first scene."

She gazed deep into her tea. A portal back to the day that had, for better or worse, changed her life.

"I was sitting in make-up," she continued. "My hair in curlers, reading over my lines, just trying to get myself together. And when it came time to put on my blush I looked in the mirror again, and there he was, standing in the doorway. For what reason only he knows, because as soon as our eyes met he sent everyone else out of the room. He was so focused on me I thought there was a problem, that he was going to fire me for some reason. But he didn't say a word. He just stared at my reflection. I'd never seen such intensity. Like the sun shining through a magnifying glass. This white, silent, heat. Until, finally, after what seemed like an hour, he spoke to me. And do you know what he said?"

"No, ma'am."

"He said, 'Young lady, you have angels dancing in your eyes.'"

She sort of swooned in her chair. As she had in the make-up chair, I imagined.

"And that was how it began." She smiled. "From that moment on I was his."

"Then Fletcher came along."

"It took almost two years of trying before I got pregnant. Ford already had the name picked out," she told me. "From Fletcher Christian"

"Mutiny on the Bounty."

"It was the bedtime book Carmen read to him when he was a little boy. I suppose that's what led to his interest in the Cook story."

I sat back to digest the information. I was watching the steam swirl up from my teacup when suddenly I noticed something: a large book resting on a shelf under the tabletop. It had a man's face on the cover. A hauntingly familiar face.

I leaned forward and slid it out for a closer look. It was a painting, a portrait. The title of the book written in jolting red above the man's head. *The Life and Works of Paul Gauguin.*

It was a self-portrait. The artist ruggedly handsome behind a thick black moustache. A Frenchman! It zapped me like a cattle prod—it was *him*. The man who'd appeared to me in my peyote vision. "Gauguin."

"Yes. Ford's favorite painter," Deanna confirmed. "He considered him something of a kindred spirit."

More to do with the subject matter than the technique, I remembered from Jack Buzbee. A fascination for the primitive. Oceania.

"Mrs. Sinclair, would you happen to have an atlas I could look at?"

"An atlas?"

"A world atlas, with maps and stuff."

"Yes. Ford has several of them in his library. Why?"

"I'm not sure. It's just a . . . can I see them now?"

Again Deanna humored me. We returned to the study, where she pointed out a bottom shelf lined with a number of references books: encyclopedias, dictionaries, almanacs and, as promised, a collection of atlases. There was one for the world, one for just the U.S.A, for South America, Europe, Asia, and—well, what do you know—one exclusive to the South Pacific. I took the latter to the desk, and opened it to a full-page map of the islands known in Gauguin's time as Oceania. The most prominent of them being Tahiti.

I flipped to a map that was just Tahiti and considered the island in detail. The capital, Papeete, was clearly denoted. As were (in slightly smaller print) Cook's Anchorage . . . Gauguin Museum . . . and (smaller still) a place called the Maraa Grotto. Maraa. I put my thumbnail over the last letter.

"Mara," it read.

"That's Ford's daughter's name," Deanna didn't have to tell me.

"Mrs. Sinclair, do you know about poisson cru?"

"Of course," she said. "A tuna dish, with coconut. Ford taught Rosa, our cook, how to fix it."

I nodded. "It's Polynesian, isn't it?"

"Yes. Why do you ask?"

To whom it may concern. Gone fishing.

"Thank you, ma'am, very much. You've been more than kind." I slammed the book shut. "But I have to go now."

Puzzled, Deanna walked me to my truck.

"Are you sure you can't stay for lunch?"

"I'm sorry. I wish I could. It's just that I have some last minute arrangements I need to make."

"Another day then." She smiled. "Perhaps the next time you visit Ford will be here. I'm sure he'll appreciate your enthusiasm."

I took a long, last look at her. A warm, lovely, fragile woman. I could only hope that her unwavering faith would someday prove well placed. That from out of the blue into which he'd disappeared, her love would finally return to her.

"As usual Ford had it right, ma'am:"

I returned her smile.

"You really do have angels dancing in your eyes."

CHAPTER SIXTEEN

I drove directly to Los Angeles International Airport. Drawn there by bits of deductive reasoning the sum total of which amounted to something only slightly more rational than a crazy hunch.

Still, the clues were compelling:

Omo(o).

Island Dream.

Endeavo(u)r.

Noble Savage.

Mara(a).

Poisson cru.

Gauguin.

Captain Cook.

Fletcher.

The Mutiny on the Bounty.

And the through-line that tied them all together . . . Tahiti!

I parked in the long term lot and made the rounds of airlines that served the island. Air Tahiti didn't have anything leaving until the day after next. Hawaiian Air was booked solid for a week. My persistence paid off, however. Air France had a seat available that very night. But, on such short notice, it would cost me—nearly three thousand dollars for a round-trip ticket.

Also, I would need a passport.

I ran to a payphone and dialed an operator who connected

me with the L.A. branch of the U.S. Passport Department. I was told that for a rush-job fee of one hundred and thirty-five dollars I could have the document in my hand by the end of the business day. Provided I could submit, in person, my application to their downtown office within the hour.

I would have to move fast. Which, I figured, was for the better insomuch as it left me no time to entertain whatever second-thoughts I may have had. Because I knew—even out there on the fraying fringe of reason—that it was an obsessive, quixotic thing to do. A whim so farfetched it required a full and immediate commitment before I had a chance to sensibly change my mind.

I ran back to the Air France reservation counter and slapped my credit card down on the high smooth top. It was one of those things, like selling the farm, that was easier done than imagined: the seemingly harebrained purchase of a non-refundable cabin-class ticket for an eight-hour non-stop flight to . . . what? A vague notion. The distant remains of ancient undersea volcano somewhere in the middle of a not so pacific ocean. It had all the makings of a fool's errand. A very expensive one at that. Only I could see no way around it. Giving in to the practical, to the unjust laws of probability, would mean giving up on Sinclair. And giving up on Sinclair was tantamount to giving up on myself. It was either onward into the great unknown, or backward—to what I knew too well, and dreaded more than anything: a regrettable return to Bird in Hand with yet another failure to my name. After all, who there (aside from my mother, and only because she was my mother) would believe that I had actually blown a cool trumpet with Oats Sleet? Had written a love sonnet that melted the fair Mara's heart? Had, with my very life on the line, painted a portrait that captured in a very real way the biting essence of Jack Buzbee? That I had in fact played a starring role opposite Fletcher Sinclair with enough of what it took to hoodwink a who's who in Hollywood?

Mr. Crino wouldn't believe it. Nor Mrs. Kincade or Mr. Coho or Doc Carney or Miss Delripple. And certainly not Kelly Ann. I had no proof. Nothing to show for it all. If I went back now, without Ford Sinclair's feather in my cap, I would be what I'd always been: Woody the dreamer, the wanna-be, the wacky Washborn who thought he could fly.

I *had* to keep going.

I pulled out of the long term after a pricey short term stay and raced for downtown Los Angeles. On the way I made a quick pit stop, as directed, at a travel agency where I got my picture taken for the passport. It reminded me of the mug shot I'd posed for in Key West. That same shell-shocked expression on my face.

Then I sped on—pushing the tired pickup until it squealed to a halt in front of an imposing-looking federal building distinguished by an American flag flapping in the smoggy breeze. Just in the nick of time to fill-out the necessary paperwork, pay the extra charge for expedited processing, and then wait for two anxious hours before finally I was officially issued a little blue passport book with my face and my name on it.

Thus, I was ready for some serious travel.

It was slow going back to the airport. A rush-hour crawl along the 405 Freeway, but that was okay. I had a few hours now to catch my breath, get at least a tenuous handle on my thoughts.

I had a week on Tahiti ahead of me. I would need some sort of basic plan. For starters a place to stay while I conducted my manhunt. A cheap rented room near a main road seemed a logical first step. From there I could work my way around the island, see if by chance one of the locals might recognize Sinclair from the pictures in *Half a Life*.

It was the best I could come up with.

Parked again in the long term lot, I found a terminal bookshop where I bought a *Lonely Planet* guidebook for Tahiti and French Polynesia. It was already past eight o'clock when I arrived at my departure gate, giving me almost fours before my plane left. In the meantime, I took a seat facing a glass wall overlooking the runway. Watching the big jets come and go, I consulted my maps—devising what I hoped would prove an appropriately flexible, effectively methodical, and not entirely delusional strategy . . . .

"Ladies and gentleman, bohn-swahr, this is your captain speaking. I would like to welcome you aboard, and to let you know that we should be in the air in just a few minutes. So, buckle up, relax, and enjoy what I expect will be a smooth and pleasant ride."

It took eleven minutes to be exact. At precisely 12:05 a.m. Air France Flight 070 left the ground at LAX—climbing with a thunderous roar to cross more than four thousand miles of Pacific Ocean. Bound for a place called Papeete on the island of Tahiti.

Cramped into a vibrating window seat in the very last row, I gripped the armrests so tight on takeoff my knuckles turned a bloodless shade of white. My stomach flipped, flopped, dropped queasily into my lap as I watched the red runway lights recede into the distance. The thrust, the ascent, the sudden realization that this was not a dream, that I was actually hurtling headlong toward the monomaniacal manifestation of my obsession, I'm not sure which was more unsettling. All combined, they induced a cold sweat dizziness. A sense of being at the mercy of alien forces.

My ears popped.

My head clearing just enough as we leveled-off at thirty-odd thousand feet to half-focus on something other than the pink paper barf bag tucked into the seat pocket in front me, I opened the guidebook. Taking a deep breath of re-circulated air, I thumbed through the pages to an abridged history of my now inescapable destination. Tahiti:

— largest of what are now known as the Society Islands.
— located between the Equator and the Tropic of Capricorn, midway between South America and Australia.
— created some two million years ago by volcanic eruption.
— populated approximately two thousand years ago by people from Southeast Asia.

Credit for its discovery, however, was given to the English

explorer Samuel Wallis, in 1767. He was soon followed by a Frenchman named Louis-Antione de Bouganville, who coined the expression "noble savages" to describe the proud and primitive inhabitants of this "new earthly paradise."

Then, in 1769, came Captain James Cook, sailing aboard the British flagship *Endeavour*. His was a three month stay, accompanied by a number of artists who provided the Old European World with its first visual images of a land where near-naked young women danced "a very indecent dance" and sang "most indecent songs" while "keeping time to a great nicety."

Hmmm. I couldn't help but wonder: Were these the visions sailing through Sinclair's mind when he, too, christened his own seaworthy vessel—centuries later and with only a slight variation in spelling—the *Endeavor*?

I doubted it was simply a coincidence. But did it meet the criteria of a legitimate clue? An even remotely possible indication of his present whereabouts? The evidence, circumstantial at best, continued to twist my brain as I read on . . .

In Cook's wake arrived the *HMS Bounty*. The storied mutiny led by Mister Fletcher Christian against the cruel Captain Bligh. About which Carmen Sinclair had read aloud and repeatedly to her budding genius of a little boy as he lay in his circus bus bunk at bedtime.

It was a hundred years after the crew of the *Bounty* that Paul Gauguin first stepped foot on the Tahitian shore. His paintings to come—portraits of the "primitive"—destined to leave an indelible late-19th Century Polynesian imprint on the collective human soul. He took us there; transported the world to the Ile du Vent in the plain wooden box where he kept his magic oils.

Pondering the seeds of Sinclair's imagination, I closed the book and looked out the window at the high black night beyond the powerful drone of the engines. Riding on two riveted wings and one shaky prayer, the odds of my finding Sinclair on the island were, even optimistically thinking, rather long indeed. Not much better, I figured, than my chances of stumbling across Cook, or Christian, or Gauguin still combing the beach for firewood.

Still, I was curious. Eager to see for myself what had inspired the men who'd inspired the man.

I reclined in my seat and shut my eyes. I tried to sleep but was wound too tight to doze off. Maybe some music would loosen me up. I plugged in my complimentary earphones and flicked through the dial until I heard the sweet voice of jazz— Billy Holiday. *God Bless the Child*. It took me back to Keisha. The way she smiled at me. Her scent. How she'd opened her arms and crossed her fingers to wish me luck. My very own Euterpe swaying to the smooth saxophone sounds of Lester Young. "Ol Lester" Oats had called him, recalling that night at the Gum Drop when young Buster had wowed the room. Harlem. Far away and further still with every beat of my heart. Time passing, in reverse, counter-clockwise as we sped westward. I checked my watch. Turquoise and silver. It was now eleven a.m. in Bird in Hand. Eight a.m. in Los Angeles. Five a.m. on Tahiti.

I was getting older as the day got younger.

Suddenly a piano filled my head. The distinct, airy virtuosity of the boy wonder himself. *Buster's Island Dream*. It quickened my pulse. Gave me a chill. Another coincidence?

Or could it be . . . an omen?

With Chet Baker's breezy trumpet filling the refrain, I relived the exhilaration of my own solo. My levitation. The miracle on 127th Street. Those few phenomenal moments when I wasn't Woodrow Wilson Washborn IV, the floundering farm boy; I was Woodman! Freewheeling and feeling it for sure. *BETHUMP!* Again I was silenced prematurely. This time not by a New York City police raid but by a shudder of turbulence that jostled me from my reverie. The Fasten Seatbelt light flashed on. "Ladies and gentleman, we are beginning our descent," said the pilot in his calm French intercom accent. "Please, prepare for landing."

I made sure that my safety belt was securely fastened. My seat returned to its upright position. That familiar first flight flip-flopping in my gut, I watched through the double-paned window as the plane banked downward, the cold white haze giving way to a clear morning blue sky. And far below us, rising out of the ocean vastness, there dawned the sudden reality of a great, green mountain; its cratered peak, crowned by a cottonlike cloud, looming majestically over a jagged jumble of smaller ridges, lush valleys, and finally a narrow white band of sandy beach. *Tahiti.* Ringed by a glow of still turquoise water streaked by dark corral reefs. I'd never seen anything quite so beautiful. Or so obviously cut off from the world.

We skirted the snaky coastline until a long black ruler-straight landing strip came into view. The flat gray roof of a large building— Faaa Airport—growing closer in the early morning light. My heart began to pound. This was no movie, no book, no painting; I'd flown well-beyond the safety-net of vicarious existence.

For better or worse, this was what *my* life had come to.

"Ohr-vwahr," bid the attendant repeatedly as we filed off the plane, and down the portable metal staircase to the tarmac.

The first thing that struck me was the heat. It pressed from all directions, like a clammy hand squeezing the sweat from my jet-lagged body while the sun beat with the intensity of a high-powered grow lamp only inches above my already light head.

We were escorted to an open terminal. At the entrance we were greeted by two young Polynesian women (*vahines*, they are called) handing out little yellow flowers. "Ia ora na." They smiled prettily; suppressing the urge, I supposed, to dance that "very indecent dance" I'd read about.

On cue the music began. A native quintet in blue floral-patterned shirts strummed guitars and ukuleles, harmonizing in a language loosely rounded by a lyrical succession of vowels as we stepped inside the terminal. I had no idea what they were singing but it sounded very sincere in its welcome. Which was much more than I can say for the next voice I heard. Amplified, it directed us—first in French, then English—to form neat, straight lines at several glass-enclosed booths, and have our passports ready for inspection.

I fell in as instructed. My line moved right along. At least it did until I stepped up to the window. The man behind the glass examined my picture. Then, through a little metal vent, he hit me with a question I wasn't entirely prepared to answer. "What is the nature of your visit?" he asked.

"Uh . . . well . . ." Did he want a full accounting? That I'd come on a mission to find a man who didn't wish to be found? Who, in all probability, wasn't within thousands of miles of this island?

Given my lack of response, the man's eyes narrowed suspiciously.

"Business or pleasure?" he pressed.

"Business," I said and left it at that.

"And what is your business, sir?"

On second thought—"Pleasure," I waffled.

He was clearly in no mood for my nonsense.

"Let me see your ticket, please." The "please" purely perfunctory.

I slid my flight information through the slot to be scrutinized.

"You are here for one week?"

"Yes, sir."

"And where will you be staying?"

"Staying?"

"Do you have a reservation somewhere?"

"Uh, well, not exactly. You see, I'm—"

"You must have a place to stay!"

By now the people in line behind me had started to grumble. At a loss, I fumbled through my guidebook until I came to the section on budget accommodations. I'd earmarked a couple of possibilities. The first being a nearby guesthouse called the Chez Fifi. I went with that.

"Here." I pointed it out to him "The Fifi."

He paused. Considered it. Frowned. But, rather than waste anymore of his valuable time on the likes of me, he finally relented. With a huff that said, *I'm giving you the idiot's benefit of the doubt*, he grudgingly stamped my passport. Good riddance!

From there it was on to the baggage carousel. A respite of a sort as I was able to claim my suitcase without further incident.

Only I wasn't done yet, and sure enough my sigh of relief was cut rather short when I got to the next checkpoint: Customs.

Again, "What is the nature of your visit?"

This time I was ready for it. "Pleasure," without missing a beat.

Again, a mistake. Because evidently answering too fast arouses the same sentinel suspicions as responding too slow.

"You will have to open your bag, sir."

Maybe I just looked guilty; like a smuggler, or terrorist, or international fugitive on the lam. In any case, I unzipped the Samsonite and flipped back the lid. A blush of embarrassment on my cheeks as the agent searched my balled socks and folded underwear for narcotics, or explosives, or whatever else he thought I might be hiding in there.

Satisfied that I'd packed nothing more sinister than a hard-bristled toothbrush, he sniffed, like I'd ruined his day. My clothes now a ransacked mess, he abruptly dismissed me with a wave. "Next!"

Welcome to paradise.

I zipped up and beat it . . . .

My next order of business was to secure a week's worth of the local currency. In that regard a Banque de Polynesie located near the exit proved convenient. Using my credit card, I obtained one hundred and twenty-five thousand Pacific francs in exchange for one thousand dollars American. The cash securely pocketed, I then ventured outside. Into the equatorial swelter.

My eyes squinted against the blazing sun. Where was I? I didn't know east from west, north from south, a kilometer from a long walk off a short pier. Nudged by the uncertainty, I approached a man who looked darkly native as he retrieved luggage carts from the parking lot. "Excuse me, sir."

His brow furrowed.

"Do you speak English?" I asked.

He shook his head, no.

Undeterred, I opened the guidebook and pointed. "Chez Fifi?"

"Ah, wee," he nodded, "Pahns-yohn," then aimed a benevolent

finger across a busy street at the bottom of a hill—directing me to a narrow side-road running straight up the steep slope toward a cluster of modest single-story dwellings.

"Le Fifi!" he said like he knew it well.

In a daze I started up the hill. I was shagged, sweating, and after a hundred yards or so I must've looked as lost as I felt; because a thin, brown Tahitian boy—shirtless and shoeless and dangling a live gecko lizard by its tail—turned from what he was doing to level a curious gaze on me.

"Ess suh kuh zhuh puh voo ay-day?" he asked.

I stopped. "I'm sorry but I don't speak French."

"American?"

"Yes. The United States."

A wide grin stretched across the boy's face. I guessed he was fifteen, sixteen years old at the most.

"It is okay, man. I talk good English." He beamed. "New York Yankees, Disneyland, Snoop Doggy Dog—I know it all."

"Do you know where I can find the Chez Fifi?"

"Sure thing, dude. Right there behind you." He pointed to a rough cement driveway running alongside a long one-story building bannered by a load of laundry hung to dry on a make-shift clothesline. "Why? You looking for a place to crash?"

"Yes, I am. A pahns-yohn."

The boy wrinkled his small brown nose.

"The Fifi, it is not bad. But you can do better."

"Oh, yeah. Like where?"

His dark eyes brightened, shrewd beyond their years. "You just follow me," he said. And setting the little lizard free, he padded up the hill.

I hesitated. My guidebook made no mention of any other guesthouses in the vicinity. Sensing my reluctance, the kid looked back and waved me on. "Sa va! I got your back, homey!"

The way he said it—so exotically oblivious to the incongruity of "hood-speak" under the tropical mise en scene of an ancient volcano, like a Polynesian parody of MTV—I couldn't help but laugh.

"So what's your name?" I asked him as we rounded a high bend where the road turned from brick to dirt.

"Omai," he told me and spit on the ground.

"Omai." It rang a bell. I knew it from somewhere. Then it came to me. Sinclair's screenplay. Yes, of course, O-m-a-i. "That was the name of the boy Captain Cook took back to England with him."

Omai sighed at the thought of it. "I wish somebody would take me somewhere," he said.

"Why—don't you like it here?"

"It is the only place I ever been," he shrugged. "I would like to see more."

"Like what?"

"New York, New York. Gay Paree. I want to see a big city, with buildings to the sky. And snow. I go ski, skate on the ice." He paused to kick a fallen coconut out of his path. "I watch the airplanes,' he continued. "All day, all night, they come and go. Remind me there is more world beyond the sea."

I knew the feeling. Even without the water Bird in Hand had seemed to me as remote as his island. "So, how did you learn to speak English?"

"I buy a book," he said. "Then I go to American movies, listen to rock and roll and rap music. To practice I go to ferry dock on Papeete. I talk with the tourist. They say I got good ears."

"I'd say they're right."

"And you? What is your name?"

"Woody. Woody Washborn."

"And where you come from, Woodywashborn?"

"Pennsylvania. It's a state."

"Philadelphia. Fourth of the July. Elton John."

"Elton John?"

"Philadelphia freedom," he sang, a sunny soprano, "I love love love you, yes I do . . ."

He was a charmer, alright. But getting back to the matter at hand: "So where's this guesthouse you're taking me to?"

"Do not worry, Woodywashborn. It will be dope, man."

"How much do they charge—per day?"

"One thousand five hundred francs. A good deal."

It sounded pretty good (given that *Lonely Planet* priced the Fifi at two thousand a day.) I was calculating the overall savings in my head when a pair of red and brown roosters crossed the road in front of us. They crowed as if to announce our arrival.

"This way." Omai veered onto a foot-worn path, toward a small clapboard structure topped by a low sheet-metal roof in the shade of green banana trees and drooping palms. Vibrant yellow and orange hibiscus flowers swayed like a sweet-scented lei around the otherwise humble abode.

"Mere!" Omai called out as we approached an open entrance draped by mosquito netting. "Noo zavohns un veezeeterr!"

At that a dark-skinned woman appeared in the doorway. Plump in a full-length blue and white floral wrap, she could've been a model for Rubens as well as Gauguin. As Omai spoke to her—his mother, I gathered—she looked me over through the thin mesh. In reply, her voice was cool, guarded.

"She ask how long you want to stay?" Omai translated.

"A few days." I sensed she wasn't in the habit of taking in boarders. "A week at the most."

Hearing it from her son, she tilted her head in a way that suggested a weighing of pride against the prospect of a few extra francs. When she finally answered her tone was distinctly non-negotiable.

"She said you pay three days now," Omai relayed. "Four thousand five-hundred francs. Five thousand if you want breakfast in the mornings."

That seemed reasonable. Less than fifty dollars including three meals. A real bargain, in fact. But there was something else about the offer I found hard to walk away from. They needed the money, I suspected. More than either was inclined to admit.

"Fine," I agreed. "Five thousand it is."

"You will not be sorry," Omai bubbled. "Ma-ma is a yum-yum delicious good cook."

The terms settled, we stepped inside to close the deal. A small, very low-tech kitchen, where Omai's mother warmed incrementally to the idea as I counted five one-thousand franc bills onto the table.

"Mairsee, Muss-yuh," she said. Then, turning to an old rust-stained refrigerator, she took out a gray clay pitcher, and filled a glass with a yellowish red juice. "B'yen-vuh-nu." She pushed the cold glass into my hand.

"Fresh squeeze mango." Omai grinned. "No charge." He gave me a wink. Only the first of many *uncommon* courtesies to come, it implied.

CHAPTER SEVENTEEN

"I got the feeling your mother wasn't expecting a guest."

"That is because you are the first," Omai said as he led me down a narrow dirt path behind the house. Having insisted on carrying my suitcase, he used his free hand to hold back the low palm branches for me; his version of the red carpet treatment. A short walk, less than twenty yards or so, before we came to a squat cinderblock structure, no bigger than a tool shed, nestled under a canopy of lush flora. "This is were my brother chill when he come home. But most of the time he work on Bora Bora. Barman at the Club Med there." He pulled open a raw plywood door. "So it is all for you, Woodywashborn."

He ushered me inside. It was one square room, with one screened window and a single twin bed opposite a metal toilet and tiny sink. Not exactly a Motel 6 but it was neat, clean, and relatively cool in the shade.

Omai laid my bag on the bed. "This mattress—not too soft, not too hard, good springs—you sleep very comfy."

I looked out the window. Through a break in the trees I could see the irregular green hump of another island in the near distance. Moorea. The home, according to *Lonely Planet,* of what has come to be known as Cook's Bay. A stop I would have to make if all else failed.

But first things first: "So I take you know Tahiti pretty well."

"Like the back of my hand, dude," Omai said, as though he'd waited all his life to use that line. "I ride my bicycle all the way around, many times."

"Then maybe you can help me with something." I opened my suitcase and took out the Sinclair biography. "You see I'm here on a kind of mission." I showed him the front cover. "I'm trying to find this man. Ford Sinclair."

Omai eyed the photo intently.

"He's older now," I told him, "sixty. So add twenty years. Maybe some gray hair. He might even be bald. About my height."

"American?"

"Yes. And he plays the piano. Paints, too. You know, an artist."

"Like Gauguin."

"Exactly. So what do you think? Does he look familiar at all?"

"I think . . ." he shook his head " . . . no. I do not remember this face."

"Here." I flipped to a shot of Sinclair snapped on the set of *Con Man*. "Take this." I ripped the page from the book. "And this." I handed him a two thousand franc note along with the photo. "Show it around. Maybe one of your friends will recognize him."

Omai's face lit-up as if it was Christmas morning and he'd been a very good boy. "Are you a gumshoe, Woodywashborn?" he asked. "Like *Magnum P.I.*?"

"P.I., well, that would be a stretch. But I am serious about finding Sinclair."

"Then I am your man," Omai declared. "We make a posse."

"Just be careful," I told him. "I'm not looking for any trouble."

"Ah, don't you worry, boss. I will be a good detective. Omai is on the case," he said, and with that he rushed out the door. A gung-ho recruit if ever there was one.

As for me, exhausted, I sat on the bed and thought about a nap. But the day was still young, and I could hear my father's voice in my head "make your hay while the sun is shining." So I dragged myself up and over to the sink. Splashed cold water on my face. I'd come too far to lay down now.

I consulted my guidebook again. Under "Getting Around" it read: "Le Truck, the standard public transportation on Tahiti . . . a fifteen minute ride from the airport to the center of Papeete . . . will stop for anyone who hails them."

I traipsed back down to the bottom of the hill, and waved to the first le truck that came along. Sure enough it stopped to let me on. It had no doors, no front-facing seats like a bus, just a long wooden bench the length of either side. At the wheel, a shirtless Tahitian man. He grinded the gears and the truck rattled out of tune along the four-lane Boulevard Pomare.

Being the only non-Polynesian onboard, the natives eyed me curiously. Since I had their attention, I plucked a few words of French from the guidebook's glossary, and strung them together as best I could. "Excusez-moi, madame," I said to a lady with a purple flower in her hair seated beside me. I showed her Sinclair's cover picture. "Avez . . . vous . . . vu . . . cet . . . homme? Ford Sinclair."

She smiled at the touristy mangling of her colonial language. She seemed to appreciate the effort, though, and must've got the gist because she studied Sinclair's face for a thoughtful moment before shaking her head. "No," she answered.

Still, I was encouraged by the exchange. She'd understood me. Which meant, on a rudimentary level, I could communicate my search. By the time we reached downtown Papeete I'd posed the question to each of my fellow passengers. Unfortunately, they all responded in kind, with a "No." They had never seen the man.

I got off the le truck at the end of the line—near the ferry dock—at a cross-street appropriately named Rue Paul Gauguin. It ran through a bustling commercial district, congested and colorful with a loosely territorial succession of bazaar-like shops displaying racks of exotic handicrafts, flowery fabrics and a wide variety of seashell accessories. Getting right down to business, I proceeded to stop at every shop, troubling the salespeople to look the photos and repeating, over and over again, in the clumsiest of French—"Avez vous vu cet homme?"

The replies unanimous. "No."

I walked for hours in the heat. Street by gritty street, mile after mile, getting nowhere. By mid-afternoon I was sweat-logged, woozy from hunger. I lumbered into a little café with a menu posted in the front window that offered poisson cru for one thousand francs, and dropped onto a seat at a table under a ceiling fan which turned too slowly to provide much of a breeze.

My waitress—pretty as Gauguin's *Vairoamati*—had a working grasp of English. She was just fluent enough to take my order and, after laying her lovely almond-shaped eyes on Sinclair's face, to serve me up a warmed-over "No, I do not know him" for an appetizer.

But the fish was fresh, the coconut sauce cool, and the service came with a smile. A meal deserving of a nice tip, I thought. Only the waitress politely refused to accept it.

"It is not our way," she informed me.

Back to the streets . . .

The Rue Jeanne d'Arc, Rue Colette, Rue de General de Gaulle. Frankly, I was beginning to rue the day I'd first heard the name Ford Buster Sinclair. My head felt light, my eyelids heavy, a blister nagged at the heel of my foot. Still, I hobbled along. And on the Rue du 22 Septembre I happened upon a huge, canopied marketplace. The Marche du Papeete.

Two open floors high, the market covers an entire city block. A flocking spot for locals and tourists alike, it dates back some two hundred and fifty years. I saw it as a chance to concentrate my efforts under a few merciful acres of shady roof.

On the lower level, I worked my way through a timeless maze of make-shift stands and stalls selling everything from strange-looking fruits and vegetables to homemade bath and body oils extracted from island-grown vanilla plants and tiare blossoms; from hanging carcasses of butchered meats to tables lined with whole sharks, wahoo, mahi mahi, tuna and swordfishes. All tended by shiny native women in florid sarongs (*pareus*, they call them) brandishing fan-shaped branches to shoo away the flies.

Bounteous entrepreneurial simplicity. Yet not so much as a flicker of recognition when it came to Sinclair.

I went up the stairs to the second floor, where the goods were of the clothing, craft and cultured black pearl variety. My luck, however, fared no better than it had below. Wherever my man was, he wasn't to be found patronizing the old Papeete Market.

I stepped out from under the roof, into the sunshine again, and headed toward the Boulevard Pomare where I'd gotten off the le truck. There was still a few hours of daylight left so I crossed the boulevard to canvass the waterfront—a long stretch of wharf at which numerous boats of various sizes and amenities were docked. Most conspicuously, a titanic *Renaissance* cruise ship that rose like a glossy white iceberg over the bay, promising a flotation of luxuries Captain Cook and his crew could not have imagined even in their most fanciful, scurvy-fevered dreams. But then again there were no bare-breasted young vahines in pirogue canoes paddling out to welcome this vessel as they had way back when to greet the arrival of the sea-worn *Endeavour*.

On a much smaller scale, I pondered several handsome yachts in mooring, and also a ferryboat, the *Ono Ono*, which, according to *Lonely Planet*, made daily runs to and from Moorea. That island clearly visible in the distance as I sat on a bench to take an inventory of my situation.

Come tomorrow I would have six days left to cover the rest of Tahiti. I had more than enough money to do it, but still nothing the least bit tangible to go on. I'd walked for nearly eight hours, questioned hundreds of people. And all I had to show for my efforts were a mild case of sunstroke, a slight limp, and a gnawing sense of futility.

I tried to shake it off. Look on the bright side, Woody: You have six days left, eight hours less to walk, hundreds of people you no longer have to wonder about, only a mild case of sunstroke, just a slight limp, and, although you came up empty, you can now, by process of elimination, pretty much rule out Papeete as Sinclair's possible hiding place.

Enough, I consoled myself, to justify at least an illusion of accomplishment.

I le trucked back to the airport then climbed the hill again to my little room behind Omai's house. It was nearly dark now. I figured I'd turn-in early, get a good night sleep, then resume the hunt fresh in the morning.

I was armpit deep in a sponge bath when a knock came at the door.

"It is me, boss." Omai entered, bearing gifts. "You hungry maybe."

He set a plate heavily slabbed with grilled pork, fried potatoes, French bread and fresh pineapple on the small wooden table flanked by two folding chairs.

"I thought the deal only included breakfast."

"Ma-ma, she always cook too much for dinner. So bonapatee."

"Thank you, Omai. You've gone beyond the call of duty."

"We must keep strong." He sat across from me. "To be a detective is hard work."

"Speaking of which, did you show Sinclair's picture to anybody?"

"Oh yes." Nodding emphatically. "I go to every house in the hood." He shrugged. "But nobody know the dude."

"Yeah. I heard the same thing all over Papeete."

"Tomorrow I make the net more wide. Drag the airport, the markets on Pomare."

"The airport. Right. I didn't think of that. Way to go, Omai. Between us we should cover a good bit of ground."

"And you—what ground you will cover?"

"I'm gonna hit the Gauguin Museum. Also the Maraa Grotto."

"You must ride on le truck that say Papeari. It stop at the bottom of the hill at eight in the morning. Take maybe just more than one hour to the museum."

"Eight o'clock." I yawned. "Okay. So we have our assignments. We'll meet back here tomorrow night. Hopefully one of us will have something positive to report."

"Do not let today bummer you out, boss." His optimism unfettered. "If this Ford Sinclair on the island we will find him."

I smiled wearily. "If you say so."

"Now I split." He hopped to his feet. "Fa'aitoito ananahi," he trilled in what I took for Tahitian on his way out the door.

"Hey, Omai."

He looked back. "Yo, boss?"

I flashed him a thumb up.

"Thanks again for the eats, man."

He returned a thumb in kind.

"Roger, Houston."

And off he went.

I was digging with my bare hands at my father's grave.

Uncovering the coffin, I forced back the lid and found the body lying facedown. I turned it over, but it wasn't my father. It was Sinclair. His flesh half-rotted away, mouth oozing worms. Then, from behind me, there sounded a haunting laugh. I spun around, and there standing over me was my dad. The weathervane still lodged in his bloody chest. "You broke my heart, son," he said to me as he slowly pulled out the arrow. His heart impaled, eviscerated, yet still beating . . .

I awoke from the nightmare to the crowing of roosters. Harsh morning light pouring in through the window. "Damn!" I sat up. Leaving the bedding soaked with sweat, I plodded across the room, feeling unrested and hollow, to my reflection in the little round mirror on the wall above the sink. My face was sunburned, a punky patch of stubble on my chin, dark quarter-moons under my red-rimmed eyes. I looked like hell.

"Who are you?" I asked myself.

When no answer came I leaned on the edge of the basin and took a deep breath. "Get a grip, Woody."

Omai's mother was busy brooming off the loose brick entryway as I approached the house.

"Bohn-zhoor, Muss-yuh." She waved me inside.

There was a single place setting on the kitchen table. She motioned for me to sit then went to the stove, where, after lighting two gas burners with a matchstick, she proceeded to whip-up a ham and cheesy three-egg omelet in one ancient-looking iron skillet while rolling a jumbo-sized crepe in another. Together, they barely fit on the big plate she put in front of me. With a half a pineapple and a tall glass of coconut milk on the side, the breakfast more than surpassed my expectations. It was more, I suspected, than they could possibly turn a profit on. I felt a little guilty about that.

"Mahnzay, mahnzay," she urged me. Then hovered rather maternally over my shoulder to make sure I ate it all.

"Omai—" I asked between bites, tilting my head on the back of my hand to mime "—sleeping?"

"No, no." She walked her fingers toward the door to indicate that he'd already left the house, and then pointed to the biography I'd laid on the table, making it understood that her son had gone out to look for "Seenclair."

Anxious to get back to the hunt myself, I wolfed down my breakfast, cleaning the plates to her satisfaction before miming my compliments to the chef. Our endearing game charades thus concluded for the time being, I then bid the kind lady a fond adieu, and went quickly on my way out mosquito net door. Fully fueled for *Operation Island Dream: Day Two* . . .

At the bottom of the hill I waited for a le truck that read Papeari. And sure enough, at a few minutes past eight, one arrived. "Gauguin Museum?" I asked the driver. He nodded, "Wee," so I got onboard. My kidneys sorely aware of every bump in the road as the truck rattled south along the sunny coast.

Again I was the only non-Polynesian passenger. Again I showed Sinclair's picture to each of my fellow riders on the chance that it might ring a bell. Again my luck ran cold. Another succession of "nos" and shrugged shoulders.

Five miles. Ten miles. Twenty. The further we went the more rural things got, the shoreline increasingly less developed; just a smattering of sleepy village markets, small white churches and simple tin-roofed dwellings set amid the lush flora that fronted the snaky ribbon of beach. And of course the ever-present palm trees—tall, frond-topped, bowing toward the sea: an awesome study in deepening blues broken only by the far tumble of white-capped waves.

As I took it all in the le truck stopped intermittently to let people off. By the time we reached the village of Papeari (about an hour and a half from where I'd gotten on) there were but five of us left. We rode in silence for another few miles, then stopped again, and when nobody made a move to get out the driver tooted the horn. "Gauguin," he called back.

I looked around. There was nothing but woods as far as I could see. "Gauguin!" the driver repeated. Confused, I stepped down to the ground and questioned him through the open cab window— "Museum?"

"Wee." He motioned impatiently to a rather inconspicuous sign posted at the start of a tarred side-road running into the woods. *Gauguin Museum/ Botanical Gardens*, it read. "Duhsahn." His hand out for the fare.

I fished all the coins from pocket and let him take what was owed. The next thing I knew, I was standing there alone, two hundred francs lighter, in a noxious cloud of backfired exhaust. Evidently I had to walk the rest of the way.

Following the blacktopped road, I felt a bit like Dorothy in the forest of Oz. In search of a mysterious wizard concealed behind a curtain of shadows. The only sounds the rustling of leaves in the trade wind and the strange chatter of birds in the dark trees. No cars or tour buses to suggest there was anything of interest up ahead.

I'd hiked about a half-mile when the road dead-ended into a clearing of dirt parking lot. Off to one side I spotted the subtle façade of a building nestled in the foliage. Arriving at the open entrance, I noted a placard fixed above it:

MUSEE DE GAUGUIN

I went inside. Under a high thatched roof, I came to a rough wood counter. Behind it, a young vahine. Looking up from her boredom, she smiled at me. "Bohn-zhoor, Muss-yuh."

"Bohn-zhoor," I echoed.

From just that much she gleaned I wasn't French. "Welcome to the Gauguin Museum," she accommodated me. "The price of admission is six hundred francs.

I paid it. There was no one else in sight.

"Kinda quiet today, huh?"

"Yes." She nodded. "It will be nice for you."

"Have you worked here long?"

The question surprised her. What business of mine how long? She answered hesitantly. "Two years."

"The reason I ask is—" I set the bio face up on the countertop "—I'm looking for this man. Ford Sinclair. He's an artist, and big fan of Gauguin. So I'm thinking he might have come here."

As she considered the picture I went through the "old photo, he's sixty now" routine. She heard me out then shook her head. "No. I do not remember seeing him."

I flipped the book open to the inside shots: Sinclair at a piano, on stage in *The Messenger*, aboard the *Endeavor*, with Olivia on their wedding day, posing in front of an *Everglade* painting, with Deanna and baby Fletcher at the ranch.

"I'm sorry," she said conclusively. "But again, no."

With a sigh, I closed the book.

"Then I guess I'll just have a look around."

*   *   *

The complex consisted of four separate old-styled buildings. Passing through the first, a gift and souvenir shop, I strolled along a stone walkway flanked by tracts of manicured green lawn and fragrant gardens . . . to the next building, the *Memorial de Gauguin*.

In front of it stood a crude, rust-colored, spookily humanlike sculpture, about five feet tall. A tiki, I read, carved from red volcanic rock to represent a pagan Polynesian god, who, it was warned, would seek a mighty revenge should the idol ever be defaced or moved in any way. A rather unnerving thought, seeing how it had been taken from its original place on the island of Raivavae and brought to Tahiti in 1933. And then relocated again to the museum in '65.

The last thing I needed was another curse put upon me.

Not wanting to disturb the gods further, I moved on. At the entrance to the memorial loomed a full-wall portrait of the artist it stood to commemorate. The dark, penetrating gaze, long mustached nose and thick, powerful looking neck of Paul Gauguin. The man I'd seen half a world ago through peyote-opened eyes.

Stepping inside, where ceiling fans turned lazily to heighten the ambience, I perused the glass-encased intimacies of Gauguin's life. There were photographs in sepia tones, newspaper and album accounts of his early years, his family, his evolution from ordinary stockbroker to extraordinary *artiste*; from a devoted husband and father to the solitary drifter who, like Sinclair, had deserted his wife and children.

Given the apparent lack of security there were none of his original paintings on display, only pallid reproductions of his work. More interesting was an assortment of personal and domestic items, which provided a glimpse into the practical aspects of his stay in Oceania: his sun hats, clothing, furnishings, walking sticks, a sewing case—odds and ends that brought the humanity of a daily existence to the myth.

Of all the relics on view, however, perhaps the most curious was a great stone obelisk standing at least seven feet high and four wide in the middle of the gallery room. Gauguin, I read, had it shipped from the French town of Brittany—the one place he'd felt truly appreciated as an artist—to a lagoon in Papeari. A very heavy good luck charm, indeed, and it struck me as kind of sad; to think that Gauguin, unlike Sinclair, had been so poorly received in his own time that he felt compelled to lug a ton of rock thousands of miles, and across an ocean, to remind himself that somewhere somebody had recognized his genius. It seemed a maddening weight to bear.

The next space I entered contained a collection of his writings. They revealed an intense and articulate man, convinced that one day his vision would be universally understood, that, at last, he would be considered a painter of major significance.

How right he was, I thought.

They also reasserted his fascination with "the wild and the primitive," and expressed his dismay at the encroachment of the outside world on his beloved island. "Tahiti is becoming completely French," he wrote. "Little by little, all the ancient ways of doing things will disappear."

Moving on, the walkway took me to a third building, its otherwise flat roof suddenly rising like a tall, upside-down ice cream cone in the center. A sign above the door read, *Maison du Jour*.

Inside, I was at once drawn to what looked like a dollhouse, under glass, set on a table in the middle of the room. On closer examination a place-card explained that it was in fact a scale-model of Gauguin's Tahitian home. Impressively reconstructed in fine detail from raw cuts of wood and thatching, it offered two elongated floors. The lower featured a kitchen and dining area, a sort of den complete with hanging hammock, and an open garage where a wagon was parked, as if waiting to be hitched to a Lilliputian pull horse.

On the upper floor, aside from a small bedroom, it was all one big studio. A tiny easel conjured up the image of the artist at work, his canvas exposed to a gentle trade breeze. I watched him paint a masterpiece in my mind.

Had Sinclair done the same? Might he have stood on that very same spot, on a day not unlike today, to pay his pilgrim's homage to the ghost of Gauguin?

Maybe.

Or *maybe not*. Turning to a door, I opened it on an adjacent room. It was cool in there, air-conditioned. The climate controlled to preserve a collection of artifacts—each boxed in glass and on a pedestal—sculpted by Gauguin's own hands. Bronzes. Vaguely human figures with round cold eyes and threatening mouths. Dating back to 1892, considered to be one of Gauguin's most productive years, their resemblance to the tiki suggested that he had, by then, strayed far from delicate influences of "civilized men," and was now fully basked in the aesthetic sunlight of the "savage." By the sheer force of his will he had blazed a trail through a cultural divide. A path into a dreamscape that others were bound to follow.

Was Sinclair among them?

The questioned remained.

Lastly, I toured a gallery exhibiting the paintings of artists inspired by the master to capture the island in the oils and watercolors of the 20th Century. These were skillful works as well (I would have been proud to call any of them my own) but still they lacked the wonder and natural rhythms of a Gauguin. He was a singular occurrence, I understood. A divine fingerprint left on the global canvas of our collective consciousness.

From the gallery I crossed the lawn to the black sand beach, and sat on a rock looking out over the water. There I pondered the final chapter of Gauguin's life. How—decrying the loss of the "ancient ways"—he'd fled this place to take refuge on the yet un-colonized Marquesan isle of Hiva Oa, almost a thousand miles from here. Where he ultimately died, and was buried a pauper in 1903.

It wasn't an encouraging thought. If Tahiti had gotten too crowded for a recluse a hundred years ago, it seemed all the more unlikely that Sinclair would risk it today. Not exactly the sort of revelation I'd hoped for.

It was a few minutes past two o'clock when I finally walked away from the museum. Before heading back up the road, I stopped at the ticket hut for the Botanical Gardens. I didn't see any point in taking the tour so I just showed the admissions man on duty Sinclair's picture. And got another "no" for the effort.

I had to concede, I'd come to a dead-end, literally and figuratively. The only thing to do was return to the far southern extension of the Boulevard Pomare. Where under the broiling sun, I waited . . . and *waited* . . . over an hour for a northbound le truck that did not come. Anxious, I flagged down an old man riding by on a bicycle not much younger than he was.

"Le truck to Papeete?" I asked him.

A sudden flash of sympathy in his eyes told me it wasn't good news. His tongue wagged incomprehensible French but his hand language—a tap on his wrist where a watch would be, followed by a finger slash across his throat—was universal. I'd missed the last truck back to town.

As a gesture of advice, the old man stuck out his thumb. I watched him peddle slowly down the road a ways, then turned my attention to hitching a ride. With the futility of begging a lift in New Mexico still fresh on my mind, I wasn't surprised by the half-dozen cars that passed me by. It was the seventh, a shiny white Jeep with two surfboards strapped to the roof, that kind of threw me . . . when it actually stopped to let me in. There was a man behind the wheel, a boy about my age riding shotgun. They were Germans but spoke enough English to make it clear they were only going as far as the Papara Village resort. I located it in my guidebook. It appeared to be just down the coast from the Maraa Grotto. Figuring I could walk from Papara to Maraa to check out the grotto, and then hitchhike again from there, I hopped aboard.

We chatted breezily en route. I learned that the two were in fact father and son. And as I listened to their story—how they had come to Tahiti, just the two of them, to surf the big waves together—I couldn't help but feel a twinge of envy. They shared an interest, a bond beyond the obligations of blood. Something my dad and I never knew. Aside from my mother, what was important to me meant nothing to him, and vice versa. We'd never found our common wave. It seemed we were always on opposite shores of a philosophical ocean, a frustrating static between us.

What made it sadder yet was that neither of us was really to blame. We were simply, in spite of our genetics and the name we shared, two very different people . . .

"Hey!"

Earth to Woody.

"We are here," said the father.

Jarred from my own familial thoughts, I realized that the Jeep had come to a stop at the end of a long loose stone driveway. The man pointed to a sign. "Papara Village."

"Oh, right."

I hopped out.

"Thanks a lot, guys. And good luck surfing."

"Auf Wiedershehen." The son waving as they continued down the graveled drive toward a woodsy hamlet of bungalows framed by the sea.

Alone again, I set off on foot. My eyes peeled for the Maraa Grotto.

Some two hours and ten miles later I was still walking, withering in the late afternoon heat. Either the map had deceived me, distance-wise, or the grotto wasn't clearly marked and I'd passed it. Whichever the case, my spirit damp with sweat, I considered giving up on it, begging a ride back to my guest-shed.

"Not yet." I pushed myself. "Go the extra mile." At least then I could say the heck with it and not feel like a total hypocrite.

Whether or not I would have ultimately walked as big as I talked, I don't know. Because it was only a few hundred yards further down the road that I spotted a signpost in the shape of an arrow. *Grotto Maraa*, it read.

The path ran inland through an acclivity of green trees and ferns at the base of a volcanic bluff. Following it, I soon came to the gaped mouth of a cave. Toward the sound of dripping water, I entered.

It was dim and cool inside. A vault-like cavern. A good fifty feet wide, forty deep, maybe fifty high—there was water raining down from the domed dark gray ceiling. Into a fresh crystal clear pool. Indeed, a very strange and wonderful sight to behold.

"Bohn-zhoor." The voice startled me.

I turned to a low corner and saw a young Polynesian couple bathing waist-deep in the pool. Both of them smiling, beautiful, their shiny brown chests bare, au natural, without inhibition.

"Bohn-zhoor," I replied and quickly averted my eyes.

"Ahntray la oh," said the girl. She swept a little splash invitingly in my direction.

I hesitated. Blushed at the idea of taking off my clothes in front of them. They giggled at that—in a way that made me feel silly, prudish; but at the same time the sheer innocence of their laughter served to put me at ease.

Ah, what the heck. When in Eden . . .

All New World modesty aside, I set my books down on a rock where they wouldn't get wet, and proceeded to strip to my Fruit of the Loom.

"Tarzan," the boy applauded as I waded, the water raining on my head, into that cold grotto pool.

OHHHHHHHH YEEAAAHHH! my brain screamed. After so many "nos." Yes! Yes! Yes! at the redeeming chill that ran up my spine. Skin tingling, goose bumped. Greedy for more, I flopped face first below surface. A rapturous, seemingly sacramental immersion. Yes! There was something holy about it. A lustration. A rite of passage. A . . .

(I could think of only one word to fully describe the sensation)

. . . a baptism.

CHAPTER EIGHTEEN

I floated up the hill toward Omai's house. It was dark by then but I was still flying high from the grotto. I'd stayed there longer than I'd planned, yet not long enough. It was a hard place to leave. A spiritual, intoxicating experience.

After an exchange of "Oh-ruh-vwahrs" the young sweethearts had left me alone to revel in my enchantment. Fearing it might somehow break the spell, I hadn't imposed Sinclair upon them. Although, when they were gone, my thoughts soon drifted to Mara.

Was she, as I suspected, named after the Maraa Grotto?

If so, how did Sinclair know about it? Did he simply pluck it from the page of a book? I found that difficult to believe. There was no way to comprehend the inspiration, exhilaration, of the cave without actually bathing in its water. He was here, I told myself.

But when?

I rehashed what I knew about the years before his daughter's birth. He'd gone directly from the circus to the Gum Drop, and from the Gum Drop to Europe on tour with his jazz band. And then it was back to New York, a smooth transition from musician to playwright. Unless—

I recalled a short passage in the bio. Just a paragraph, it mentioned that Buster, after he quit the quintet, had dropped out of sight for three weeks. How, upon his return, he claimed he had rented a cabin in the Adirondacks to unwind, by himself, from the pressures of the road. Only Brimm could not verify the story. It was just assumed Sinclair had told the truth.

Had he? I wondered. Could he have slipped away to Tahiti, instead? Snuck off to the island of Cook, Christian, and Gauguin, for an impressive dip in the grotto pool and his first taste of poisson cru?

When I got to my room Omai was waiting outside the door.

"Yo, yo, boss." He sprang to his feet. "Did you have a good day?"

"It definitely had its moments," I said.

He shrugged. "I start to be worried. Think maybe you get lost."

"I missed the le truck. Had to hitchhike back."

"Be cool if Ford Sinclair pick you up, hey?"

He followed me inside.

"You find the museum okay?"

"Yeah, I found it. No leads, though. What about you? Get anything?"

He shook his head. "It is a very tough case, boss. Nobody give me a clue. But—" he was quick to add "—we not beat yet. Could be we make a crack tomorrow."

"I've decided to rent a car for the day. Figure that way I can circle the whole island."

"And I will go to the hospitals. And to the pharmacies. Maybe Sinclair he get sick some time."

"Yeah. Maybe. Right on, Omai, that's some sharp detective thinking."

He swelled. "Good thing you hire me, hey?

"A very good thing," I nodded. "You're a regular Doctor Watson."

His eyes narrowed. "Doctor Wat?"

"Watson. You know—Sherlock Holmes."

"Holmes. Ah!" His eyes widened. "Wee! He wear a funny hat, yes?"

"It's called a deerstalker."

"No shit, Sherlock!" Omai remembered from somewhere.

It pulled a much needed laugh out of me. I reached into my pocket, "Anyhow, I'd say you've earned yourself a raise," and gave him another two thousand francs for his time and expenses.

In return he offered to go raid the refrigerator again. Still too buzzed from the grotto to eat, I told him, thanks, but no thanks. "At ease. Take the rest of the night off."

He saluted, "Whatever you say, boss," then he threw up his hand as far as he could. "High five!"

I slapped him one. "Bunn nwee, my dear Watson."

I could hear his voice—rapping over the low rumble of a jet taking off from the airport—as he followed the dirt path toward the house " . . . my name is O Dog and I gotsta say, I got my props from da man today, now I so fine, stand in line, dig my shine when I bust my rhyme . . ."

With boy and plane both fading into the distance, I stretched out on the bed and stared at the ceiling. I watched a gecko crawl, inverted, along the roughhewn wooden beam that supported the roof. It stopped directly above my head and looked down at me. Beady-eyed. Translucent. Its tongue flicking, in and out, a tease, like it knew something, the answer I was searching for, but had been sworn to secrecy.

"What is it? Tell me. Please!" I begged. A desperate plea that hung in the air until the roosters awakened me the next morning from a deep and dreamless sleep, and I saw that the little lizard was gone.

After a second round of breakfast charades with Omai's mother I walked to the airport where I rented a car from Avis. Nothing fancy, a compact economy vehicle; all I would need to circumference the island via the coast roads.

By eight a.m. I was on my way. I set a clockwise course, which took me first to the south along the western shore. When I came to the Maraa Grotto again, I felt an urge to pull over and treat myself to another dip in the cool cave pool, but I fought the temptation. Instead, I sped up. *Onward* . . . .

A while later I wheeled past the familiar black side-road that led to the Gauguin Museum. From there the trail was new to me, a growing sense remoteness as the humble palm-shaded homes and dusty markets stood fewer and farther between. I stopped routinely—at the markets, gas stations, uncovered wagons stinky with the morning's catch of fish for sale—anywhere there was even a small group of locals gathered.

Still, nothing panned out. Not I person I spoke to had ever seen, or heard the name, Ford Sinclair. At midday I rounded the bottom of the island and arrived at the narrow isthmus that connects Tahiti Nui (Big Tahiti) to Tahiti Ito (Little Tahiti). The smaller a sort of ovoid peninsula centerpieced by a lush volcanic mountain all its own.

Following the arc of a calm blue bay, I was wowed by the rugged, unspoiled beauty of Ito. Its pristine black sand beaches obscured only by the occasional drape of fishing nets hanging to dry in the sun. The flora unchecked but for rare patches of clearing where sleepy, old-styled villages stood. But while the pace was much slower than on Nui, the responses to my inquiries in regard to Sinclair elicited the same negative responses as they had in busy downtown Papeete: a Polynesian French medley of definite "Nos," "Nons" and "Aitas."

I approached elderly women hawking handicrafts on spinney front yards, a clique of teenagers smoking cigarettes beside a waterfall, road gangs of dark-muscled men laboring with picks and shovels in ditches along the roadside. Some shook their heads. Others shrugged their shoulders. All looked at me like I was from another planet.

Finally, I relented, and left them to their world. They deserved it. A way of life well preserved despite the intrusions of Wallis, Bougaiville, Cook, the Bounty, and now Avis.

Back on Big Tahiti, I continued north on the eastern shore. It offered a steady rise in population and, consequently, more gathering places to sweep for information. Only by then the theme of the day had, at my expense, been established. These people knew nothing of Ford Sinclair.

When I reached the congestion of Papeete the sun was a great red ball on the watery horizon. And with dusk the circle was complete—I'd gone all the way around the island. Back at the airport again, I returned the car to the rental agency, then walked back up the hill, reflecting on what had proved to be an incredibly scenic and discreditably unproductive trip. Picturesque, but a bust just the same.

"You must keep the faith, Woodywashborn," Omai consoled me as his mother slid a generous slab of breadfruit onto my plate. "You still have four more days to look."

They'd put off their dinner on my account, waiting so I could join them at the kitchen table. "Look where?" I brooded. "We've pretty much covered the island. I'm chasing my tail, man. He's not here."

Interpreting the mood, Omai's mother chimed in French. "What did she say?"

"She say," Omai translated, "that the ocean is very deep. Because you do not catch the fish does not mean there is no fish to catch. I could maybe mean only that your line it not long enough."

I turned to the woman. Along with the free meal she was serving up food for thought. I mirrored her smile. Her logic, like the smell of her cooking, too good at that moment to resist.

Famished, I swallowed them both.

The next morning I cast my line toward Moorea.

I angled into Cook's Bay aboard the ferryboat *Ono Ono*. It was just a half-hour hop from the pier at Papeete, where Omai had seen me off. I'd wanted him to come with me, to keep me company if nothing else, but he said he had other plans—without going into details—and I trusted his instincts enough by then to let him chart his own course.

Mine was set on an island nearly one-tenth the size of Tahiti. Moorea the favored destination of vacationers, honeymooners, backpackers and even Tahitians looking to get away from the crowd for a few days. For me, however, the eponymous acknowledgment of Cook was the draw. The brave captain who's adventures in the South Seas had touched Sinclair so profoundly.

The bay was serene this morning. It sparkled like a smooth blue sapphire in the early sunlight. Alone on the water, the ferry backed up to its mooring posts at the dock, and once the ropes were secured the gangway went down, and I ventured ashore. Overshadowed by a sleeping giant of a volcano, the wharf didn't amount to much: a couple of little snack bars and souvenir stands were all. I went directly to the ferry office, where I showed Sinclair's picture to the lady working the window.

"Avez vous vu cet homme?" I asked for what had to be the thousandth time. And like the nine hundred and ninety-nine that preceded it, the answer was a courteous but discouraging "No."

"So what about transportation?"

Again, the news wasn't good. She told me not to count on the le trucks to get around, that they were in short supply and unreliable. A taxicab was an option, although a very expensive one. She suggested I rent a car or a motor scooter at one of the hotels to be found on the far side of the bay.

I decided to play it by ear. Go with the flow in the hope that something positive might develop if I left myself more open to happenstance. So, bound for no place in particular, I just started walking. Humbled between the towering volcano and the vast blue sea.

I stopped at the hotels, at campsites, outdoor cafes, a pineapple juice factory that was open to the public. It was all very laid-back in a slow, lazy, touristy kind of way. People pedaling by on bicycles, baking on the fine white sand beaches, snorkeling in shallow lagoons, canoeing beyond the reefs where the water was deeper and bluer.

Eventually, I lost track of time, it was easy to do, the seductive lull of exotic isolation. Palm trees swaying postcard perfect to the carefree song of a balmy breeze. Still, despite every pacifying distraction, the sense of mission weighed heavy on my mind.

The mere presence of so many visitors from places where Sinclair would be recognized only made it more unlikely that he could hide here with any lasting success. At some point, somehow, someone would have blown the whistle on him.

Hot and thirsty from thinking on the move, I wandered into a quiet little café called Cook's Cabin to deliberate over a cold drink. Under the whirl of ceiling fans I sat at the bar. Two stools down an elderly white man in a tank top that revealed a faded red tattoo of an anchor on his upper-arm was flipping through a copy of *Field & Stream*. Published in English, I noted.

"Are you an American?" I interrupted him.

Turning to me, the old man thought about it for a moment, as though he couldn't remember. Finally, he nodded. "I was." Smiling at the recollection, "But that was a long, long time ago."

"So what are you now?"

"An ancient transplant," he said. "Re-rooted more than fifty years deep in Moorean soil."

When I told him I was from Pennsylvania, he countered with "Michigan. Born and raised in Detroit." He went on to tell me in colorful detail how his fate had brought him to the islands, as a twenty-five-year-old communications officer—Ensign Andrew P. Wilson—with the U.S. Navy during World War II. "I fell in love with the place at first sight," he said. "The people, the weather, the water, everything about it.

"Anyhow, after we won the war I went back to Detroit. Spent a winter working at a Chevy plant, assembly line, freezing my miserable ass off, until finally I said to hell with that. I quit, packed by bags, took a train to Frisco, and then hired on as a swabby on a merchant ship headed west. Didn't get off till we docked at Vaiare. That was 1946. And Moorea's been my home ever since. I married a vahine, started a family. That's one of my boys there." He pointed to the bartender. "Andre."

I could see the resemblance, the son handsomely darkened by a tint of Polynesian blood. "Yesiree," his father continued, "it was all untapped back then. Hell, when I opened this joint there was nothing else for near a mile."

"So you own it."

"Built it with my own two hands, I did."

Interesting. "So you must know a lot of the people who live here."

"Just about everybody," Mr. Wilson asserted. "And most of their grandfathers too."

"What about this guy?" I slid the biography along the bar top. "You ever see him around?"

"Ford Sinclair," he read off the cover. "They still haven't found that son-a-gun, huh?"

"No, sir."

I explained to them that was why I was there. I touched on the Gauguin/Cook/Christian connections, and they seemed to get a kick out of it. The elder Wilson knew about Sinclair from the magazines and newspapers sent to him by his sister in Battle Creek, Michigan, over the years. But both father and son were quite sure they had never seen the man in person. Nor had they heard a word of gossip to suggest he'd ever stepped foot on Moorea.

"And believe me," Mr. Wilson said, "when a stranger takes up residence people talk." He slid the book back my way. "So I'm afraid you've come to the wrong place, Woody."

I slumped on my stool. "Yeah, well, I can't say I'm surprised."

Wilson did what he could to lift my spirits. He had Andre refill my glass with ice tea "on the house" then regaled me a while longer with stories of his navy days, and how, when he was a kid, he used to play hooky from school and sneak into Tiger Stadium to watch baseball from the bleachers on sunny afternoons.

Convinced that any further search of the island would prove fruitless, I cooled my heels, appreciating the company, until it was time for me to shove off if I wanted to catch the day's last ferryboat back to Papeete.

Graciously, Mr. Wilson nixed the idea of me walking.

"I can handle the bar. Andre, you give our young friend from PA. here a ride to the quai." In parting the old ex-patriot shook my hand firmly. "Be sure to give my regards to the States, Woody.

And if you're ever in the neighborhood again don't forget Cook's Cabin."

I told him I would, and wouldn't. Then, leaving the old navy man to the little parcel of paradise he'd long claimed for himself, I followed Andre outside. There was a dusty Puguet parked under a carport off the café.

"So what will you do now?" Andre asked as we drove the bay road toward the wharf.

I sighed. "I don't know." But who was I kidding? "Yes I do. I'll go back to Tahiti, waste my time there for a couple more days, and then admit defeat and go groveling home to Bird in Hand. Where I'll have to eat humble pie for the rest of my life."

"At least you tried." Andre shrugged. "That's something."

At least you tried: *kind words reserved for losers*.

"Yeah, but to try and try again, and never succeed, that's something else. That's making a damn fool out of yourself."

There was nothing Andre Wilson could say to console me. There was nothing anyone could say.

Or was there?

The *Ono Ono* ferry returned me to Papeete at 6:15 p.m. By 7:30 I was flopped on my rented bed staring up at the ceiling again. Waiting, in a funk of depression, for the gecko to reappear. What did it know? I wondered.

The Tahitian art I'd seen on my forays around the island gave traditional reverence to the gecko; bestowing upon it an aloof, mystical wisdom. Drained of all other hope, I desperately needed some of that old reptilian magic right about now.

I was still waiting for the lizard to crawl to my rescue when, at 8:45, there came a sharp rap at the door.

"Woodywashborn!" Omai's voice cracked.

"It's open."

He rushed into the room, out of breath.

"Buhn noovell, boss! I get a bite!"

"What?"

"Sinclair! Sinclair!"

I shot up. "You found him?"

"No. But my cousin Alf. You know, like on TV."

"Your cousin's on TV?"

"No. The little hairy thing. From out in space. *Alf.*"

"Yes, I know, Alf from Melmac, I've seen the show. Now what about your cousin?"

"He captain on a cargo boat. Go from island to island. Bring food, water, oil, tires for cars—"

"Omai, please, just cut to the chase. Sinclair."

"Okay. Today I go the dock on Motu Uta. I show the picture to Alf."

"And?"

"And he think maybe he see the face before."

"He thinks maybe? What does that mean?"

"It mean maybe he think harder if he see some—" He rubbed his thumb and fingers together. Some money, I understood.

"Did he say where he thinks maybe he saw the face?"

"He say we meet him tomorrow morning. Six o'clock. You pay he tell more then."

I got to my feet. The blister nagging at my heel, I limped to the window, and looked out over the airport. A jet (possibly the same one that would take me back to the States in seventy-two hours) had just lifted off. As I watched the blinking red lights shrink into the blackness, I fought to keep my hopes down. I wasn't sure I could take another disappointment.

Then, very clearly, I saw myself on the plane. Strapped to my seat, to my failures, looking down on the island, and wondering: *What if . . .*

"Six o'clock." Recalling how I'd had to cut short my dreams and drag myself from my bed every morning to milk the cows at that ungodly hour, I yawned. No rest for the witless. So be it, I decided. On with the fool's parade. "Then we'll have to leave here by five."

*   *   *

The roosters looked at us cockeyed as we descended the hill in the pre-dawn darkness. Their feathers ruffled at the audacity of us being up and about before they could crow the alarm. It went against the natural order of things.

We caught a groggy le truck to Papeete. From the wharf it was a thirty minute or so walk before, at sunrise, we crossed the bridge to Motu Uta: a coral reef islet where the cargo boats dock to load and unload their freight.

At ten till six we arrived at the bollards where the *Mana Mao* was berthed. A modest vessel, to put it politely: battered, dirty, and, at barely fifty feet in length, smaller than I'd expected.

"The name, *Mana Mao*, it mean Spirit Shark," Omai informed me.

The bow area was open, crowded with large wooden crates, centered by a heavy-duty crane that lifted the cargo on board while several hard-looking natives worked in the harsh floodlights to accommodate the load.

"Which one's Alf?"

"I do not see him," Omai said. He scanned toward the stern, to a forklift moving pallets stacked high with boxes up a rusty metal ramp and into the hull. "There he is." He pointed. "Alf!"

A big man, heavyset, shirtless to display a shark tattooed across his chest, glanced over at us from near the bottom of the ramp. He appeared to be in his mid-thirties, a wild tangle of raven black hair framing a wide, serious face. His dark eyes sized me with some reservation as he approached.

After a brief exchange in French Omai made the introduction. "Alf Teariki, Woodywashborn."

I put my hand out. "Nice to meet you, Alf."

Forgoing the shake, he nodded curtly, and Omai continued in French. The only words I understood were "American . . . artiste . . ." and finally, "Ford Sinclair."

On cue, I held up the bio. "This is him. Twenty years ago."

"Eel ee ya ven ahn," Omai translated.

"Puh-tetre." Alf shrugged.

"He said maybe he see him."

"Where?"

"First he a businessman, boss. Show him the money."

"Tell him I'll pay five thousand francs."

"Ten thousand," Alf responded shrewdly. Then something in French.

"For ten thousand francs he tell you and take you on the boat."

I locked eyes with the big skipper. He was clearly not a man to haggle with. Furthermore Omai had assured me he could be trusted. "All right," I agreed. "Ten thousand, including the ride."

I pulled a roll from my pocket, peeled off five two thousand franc notes and handed them over. His palm sufficiently greased, Alf allowed himself the trace of a smile. "Huahine," he said.

"Huahine? What's that?"

"It is a small island," Omai put in. "Take near eight hours to go there."

Alf expounded: Huahine was a regular stop on his route. He'd seen the man in question on a number of occasions picking up supplies at the wharf there. He didn't know the man's name, had never spoken to him, but it seemed he lived on the island, and was about sixty years old.

It wasn't much to go on, and a long way to go, at that. As a favor to Omai, Alf sweetened the deal—when we got there he would take me to an old panhandler who worked the dock and knew Huahine better than anyone.

"Capitaine!" a deckhand called from the gunwale. "Noo som pray de parteer!"

"Un meenut," Alf yelled back. Then he turned to me. "What you do, gar-sohn? You come or no?"

"Bon vwayazh!" Omai waved from the pier as I set out to sea aboard the *Mana Mao*. "Good luck to you, boss!"

Consigned to a little poop deck (for my own safety, Alf had insisted, although I suspected it was more to keep me from getting in his crew's way) I watched the volcanic skyline of Tahiti, and then Moorea, recede into the white water in our wake.

Three choppy hours later there was nothing but ocean and sky in sight.

A lonely place on the planet, indeed.

I opened the guidebook to the section on Huahine. Like Tahiti it was divided into two sub-islands, Huahine Nui and Huahine Ito. The split, according to legend, having come when the god Hiro plowed through the igneous rock in his mighty canoe.

In all, it covered an area of seventy-five square kilometers. The entire population was a sparse five thousand, with farming— vanilla, melons, citrus—and fishing the primary livelihood. I contemplated the map. I noted the wharf at Fare. Mount Turi. The Ancient Stone Fish Traps. Then, off the western coast, something jumped out at me—

"Well I'll he darned."

—a small inlet. *Cook's Bay*.

"They got one, too." I took a deep breath, reluctant to make too much of it. Still, in spite of all the dead-ends I'd come to, it gave me a charge; a faint glimmer of hope that flashed, like a distant lighthouse, through the layers of fog that had frustrated my search from the outset.

At least it was something.

At midday the three-man crew joined me on the poop to eat their lunch. When they realized I didn't speak French they quickly lost interest and talked exclusively amongst themselves. Whatever my business with the captain, it didn't concern them. I was just another piece of cargo, one they wouldn't have to hoist, so it was simply "Bohn-zhoor" and "Ohr-vwahr" and then they were gone, all hands back to their respective decks.

But I wasn't alone for long. A few minutes later Alf appeared—with a hero-like sandwich and a can of Coca-Cola. "Dayzhuhnay," he grunted. "For you."

"Thank you. Mairsee," I said appreciatively, "bookoo."

He took a seat facing me and rolled a cigarette while I went to work on the ham and cheese on crusty French bread. Lighting up, he watched me eat, the shark indelibly inked across his chest. Between bites, I pointed to the tattoo. "Mao," I said by way of conversation.

"Wee," he nodded. "*Jaws.*" And to prove he wasn't just talking about the movie, he lifted his right pant leg to showoff a nasty configuration of thick purplish scars that ringed his calf muscle from knee to ankle. Serious teethmarks. Evidence of a vicious, barely survivable attack.

"Wow!" I gasped. "What the hell did that?"

"Tiger shark." He grinned, proudly, like it was a badge of honor. "A seven feeter."

It bloodied the imagination. Talk about a nightmare.

"You must've been terrified."

He laughed it off. "Say la vee." Taking a last drag from his cigarette, he flicked it into the ocean. Then got to his feet. Damn lucky to still have two legs to stand on. "Huahine—three hours more," he said; his wide brown shoulders filling the narrow companionway as he headed back toward the bridge.

Left to myself again, I scanned the surface of the water. My eyes peeled for anything that even remotely resembled a dorsal fin.

Say le vee?

Not where I was from.

CHAPTER NINETEEN

L *and ho!*

The island of Huahine a solitary stroke of dark green between the vast blues of sea and sky. We entered the Avamoa Pass, to Haamene Bay, and then the sleepy little port town of Fare. As the crew secured the mooring ropes, I surveyed the wharf. A smattering of people were milling about a pavilion stocked with bulks of produce, a flatbed truck laden with shiny fish, a lunch van; against a backdrop strip of small shops on either side of what appeared to be a popular grocery store.

I spotted Alf standing on the dock. He called out orders to his men, then turned and waved for me to join him. Promptly, I climbed down a ladder to the gangplank and went ashore. By the time I reached Alf he'd already locked in on the target. "Say luh ohm," he said, pointing to an old Polynesian man in shabby clothes seated on a bench under a shady tree while he fished the slow stream of passersby for a handout.

Alf snapped his fingers. "Dohnay-mwa. Luh book."

I gave him the bio. Followed him across the pier.

"Bohn-zhoor, Alf," the man chirped at our approach. "Komahn tallay voo?"

"Tray b'yen, Oopa. Ay voo?"

"Ahhh. Pa mahl," the man shrugged.

"Oopa, zhuh voo prayzahn—Woodee Washaborn."

The old guy smiled up at me. One rotted tooth left in his mouth. "Ahn-shantay, Muss-yuh Woodee."

Bohn-zhoor, sir. It is my, uh . . . playzeer."

The intro out of the way, Alf got right down to business. Showing the man Sinclair's picture, he questioned him in French.

Eyeing the photo, Oopa squinted intently.

"Well?" I asked.

He shrugged again. "Puh-tetr."

I looked to Alf for translation.

"He say, uh, poseebel. Maybe."

Now schooled in the "maybe" game, I dug into my pocket and pulled out a one thousand franc note. "For you," I said, and forked it over.

"Ah, Woodee," Oopa grinned. "Tray zhahntee—a gentleman."

"Dahkor," Alf pressed him. "Metuhnah pahsay."

His tongue loosened by the grease, Oopa dusted off some English.

"The photo . . . it look . . . uh . . . alike . . . man . . . live Tefarerii."

"Tefarerii." I opened the guidebook to the earmarked map.

"Huahine Ito." Alf pointed to a spot near the southeast corner of the smaller island. "Vwa-la. Terarerii."

"He live big house," Oopa added. "Sur l'ohsayahn."

"On the ocean?"

"Wee. Ocean."

"Do you know his name?"

"Name? Ah! Nohn. Wee. Muss-yuh Roget."

"Roget. But he's American?"

"No no. Eel ay Frahnsay." ·

A Frenchman. That didn't bode well.

Unless it was part of the trick—a false identity? After all, it seemed highly unlikely that Sinclair had avoided detection for so long living under his own name. He had to be operating under an alias. But a Frenchman? More than likely Mister Roget would prove to be none other than Mister Roget. Then again, there was only one way to find out for sure.

"Okay. So how can I get to Tefarerii? Le truck, taxi?

"No," they answered in unison. I would have to rent some wheels, a car or scooter. And however I chose to proceed I would be on my own, because Alf had had enough of it. He'd done what he'd agreed to do and, under no further obligation, was in a hurry to get back to the *Mana Mao*. He made it understood that they would unload some cargo, take on some more, and then continue their route to the next island, Raiatea, come morning.

"What about me?" I asked.

He said they would dock again at Fare in three days time before returning to Papeete. If I was willing to wait until then I could rejoin them for the last leg, free of charge. Only I didn't have that long. I was booked to depart for Los Angeles in just a little over forty-eight hours now. In that case, Alf advised me to fly back to Tahiti. He showed me the Huahine airfield on the map. From the pier I could walk there.

Finally, he offered me his hand.

"Oh-ruh-vwahr, Woodee Washaborn. Bunn shahns."

We shook on it.

"Steer clear of those sharks, Alf Teariki."

Oopa directed me to a rental agency on the strip. Rather than pay triple the price for a car, I opted for a scooter instead. The time noted on the lease receipt read 16h. 4:00 p.m. That gave me a good three hours of daylight left. More than enough, I figured, to drive the fifteen or so kilometers to Tefarerii, and back again, before dark.

So, with a provided crash helmet two sizes too big strapped on my head, I straddled the motorbike. And off I went.

The breeze soothing against my sunburned face, I followed the paved main road south along the shore where Haamene Bay segued into the calm blue waters of Cook's Bay. Unlike his arrival at Tahiti, where Wallis and Bougainville had preceded him, James Cook was the first European to visit Huahine. But by all accounts he did not receive the characteristically warm Polynesian welcome.

As far as the natives were concerned E-N-D-E-A-V-O-U-R spelled trouble. They received the captain and his crew as anomalous entities to be viewed with suspicion, contempt—the sense of dread reserved for things unknown, uninvited, unneeded.

For Cook, the thrill of a paradise found.

For the Huahineans, the threat of a paradise lost.

Still, despite the intrusion of strangers, and the colonizations that followed, the signs of change were surprisingly minimal. Somehow the island had managed to maintain its natural charm; it remained largely undeveloped. Once beyond the outskirts of Fare the land grew increasingly more wild, virginal, suggesting a steadfast resistance to the depredations of "progress."

The Maohi of old would be proud of their descendants, I thought as I crossed the bridge from Nui to Ito, where the golden green aura of preserved innocence shined even brighter. Lush and fragrant. Time seeming to tick backward as I continued along the coast, now to the northeast, flanked on my left by the turquoise splendor of Maroe Bay, and on my right by the volcanic rise of Mount Pohue Rahi.

There was little traffic to contend with. Aside from the occasional truck or tractor pulling open trailers loaded with freshly harvested fruits I had the road pretty much to myself. Although, at one point, I did pass a tour bus parked at a gazebo flagged with colorful pareus for sale; the tourists, in loud flowered shirts, Bermuda shorts and wide straw hats, fondling the vibrant fabrics like archaeologists who'd just discovered a secret vault draped in Golden Fleeces.

Pressing on, I rounded the top of Ito, and then preceded south. Soon the pavement came to an end and the road narrowed to a hilly ribbon of dirt. There were no homes, no trapping of inhabitation in sight. Pressed between high jungle on one side and the rocky beach giving way to perpetual ocean on the other, I stopped for a moment to consider the map. Using my thumb to measure the distance, I figured it was another three or four kilometers to Tefarerii: a small inland village, according to Oopa, which could not be seen from this road.

Nor would I be able to see Roget's "big house"—as it was

supposedly set back in a thick covert of woods that buffered a short stretch of the shoreline up ahead. I'd been told to go very slow when I got to the woods, to keep my eyes peeled for a tire-worn path that arced toward the water. The path, Oopa had assured me, would be Monsieur Roget's driveway.

All that in mind, I went to the throttle again . . . up and over a long, dusty incline, which descended to a flat but snaky section of track that nearly fish-tailed my rear wheel out from under me. *Easy, Woody, steady now.* Don't be too anxious. This isn't about speed; endurance is what got you here. So just stay focused and on the bike and get there in one piece. After that, be it yes or no, at least you'll have your answer.

Carefully, I negotiated the last few zigs and zags. Then, coming to a straightway, I was afforded a clear and rather encouraging view: a borderline where the open beach ended and the promised greenery of trees began.

When the water disappeared behind the dark tangle of leafy branches and liana vines, I slowed to a crawl, searching the wooded fringe for the path Oopa had warned me was angled to be missed.

Is that it?

No. Just a chink in the brush.

But there was something else. *Could it be?* Yes! Two strips of bare earth running diagonally under a natural bower of low boughs and high bracken. Tire ruts. A driveway, albeit in the most primitive sense of the word.

I turned, followed it. With little more than an arm's length of head clearance, the path arced through the covert for almost a hundred yards, where at last it fanned out to reveal a grove of tall palm trees, botanical columns, too many to count, all standing perfectly vertical, as tall as fifty feet above the grassy ground, and just far enough apart to allow in long streaks of late-afternoon sunshine, which painted the big house they surrounded with a golden, impressionistic light.

I hit the brakes. It was so peaceful, so transcendent a scene, I felt compelled to the silence the scooter's motor; its whine sounding suddenly corrupt, out of place in this remote patch of Eden.

I got off the bike and put down the kickstand. As I walked toward the house there was something very familiar about it, like I'd seen it before. Then suddenly it came to me—the model of Gauguin's home on display at the museum. Two elongated stories, rough wood, pitched roof. Except this one was topped with gray clay tiles instead of thatching, and there were screens over the windows.

Still, the resemblance was remarkable.

I cleared a lump from my throat. Then called out, "Hello?"

Getting no reply, I climbed the three steps to the porch, and knocked at the front door. "Hello?"

No answer. "Anybody home?"

Nothing was stirring, not even a gecko.

Taking a deep breath, I tried the knob. When it turned, unlocked, the temptation to push my luck further proved irresistible. Ah, what the heck. I was just about to poke my head inside when a faint waft of laughter froze me in mid-trespass. Only my ears twitched. Where did it come from? Then it sounded again, light and playful—carried by the ocean breeze blowing in from somewhere behind the house.

I went to investigate.

Walking along the side of the house, I passed an open carport built into the ground floor. Gauguin had kept a wagon in one very much like it. But in this space there was parked a muddy white Land Rover, and two matching red scooters. Hearing another peal of laughter—now accompanied by the sound of splashing water—I veered onto a footpath crowded by a gauntlet of wild hibiscus and jasmine bushes, which took me nearer to the shore.

The flowers stopped at the edge of a bank. It sloped into a sort of cove area trimmed by a crescent of white sand beach. And then, further out, through the glare of sunlight reflected off the water, I saw the sources of the laughter: two young vahines, wading hip-deep in a lagoon that sparkled around them like a pool of electric blue diamonds. Their high brown breasts covered only by shiny locks of dark, sea-soaked hair.

I couldn't take my eyes off them. Beautiful, exotic creatures, like beings from some enchanted mythology—*water nymphs*—frolicking in the shallows calmed by a natural break wall of black coral reef. My mouth awed open, I watched as they took turns diving beneath the surface, again and again, diving, rising, laughing . . .

What was the objective of their game?

Finally, one of the girls sprang up, a surge of excitement. "Ruhgarday!" she cried, her right arm thrust triumphantly toward the sky. "Zhay un!" Something yellow and sleek and wriggling clutched in her hand.

Well, I'll be darned. She'd snatched a fish.

Her celebration, however, was short lived. When she saw me there, she froze. Then sounded her alarm. "Eel ee ya un ohm!" she yelled, aiming a finger at me like it was a spear and I the reincarnation of Captain Cook.

As the two women stood tense in the water, I caught a rush of movement out of the corner of my eye. It was a man—appearing from behind a crag of black rock. Under a wide straw hat, he moved shirtless, a faded blue pareu wrapped around his waist. Tanned a deep bronze, his body was lean but for a bit of paunch that betrayed a significant accumulation of years.

When he spotted me, he slowed to stop at the shoreline.

"Kuh voo lay voo?" he barked, his eyes hidden by a pair of dark aviator sunglasses.

"Mister Roget?" I asked.

"Wee," he responded with authority. "Raypohns tout de suite—kee voolay voo?"

"I'm sorry, sir, but I . . . uh . . . no parlay voo Frahnsay. Only English."

"He ask what you want?" said the vahine with the fish.

Given the awkwardness of the situation, I decided to just put it out there, cast my line and see if anything bit. "If he can spare of a minute or two, I'd like to ask him a few questions."

She relayed the request. His reply was curt.

"Are you reporter?" the girl translated.

"No," I answered. "My name is Woody Washborn."

"Then what business do you have to ask questions?"

"They have to do with a man I'm trying to find." I concentrated on what I could see of Roget's face, looking for a reaction, a flinch, grimace, some sort of tip-off. "Ford Sinclair," I said.

Nothing. Not so much as a twinge to suggest I'd touched a nerve.

The girl relayed his reply. "He no know a man name Ford Sinclair."

I considered him physically. He was smaller than I envisioned Sinclair to be. But then again I'd formed in my mind the picture of giant; a presence bigger than life, who shook the ground when he walked. It was, I realized, an exaggerated, distorted image. One I had to shrink into focus or it would trick me, trip me up. Because in reality, at close to six feet tall, he was about the right height. And although the hat and glasses shaded his face, he appeared to be in the ballpark of sixty years old. So, in general terms, the description loosely matched.

"Tell him that Ford Sinclair is a very brilliant man. A *great* artist."

I watched for the hint of a flattered smile as the vahine echoed my sentiments in French. Roget's expression, however, remained inflexible. His response ready, without a pause—

"There is no such artist here," was the interpretation.

—perhaps a little too ready; recalling my brush with the customs agent at Faa airport.

"That's too bad, sir. Because you have a very interesting way of fishing." I motioned to the young women, so perfectly in their element, one still clutching her barehanded catch. "It would make for a wonderful portrait. A painting I'm sure Paul Gauguin would appreciate."

"Say preevay ici!"

"This is private property!"

"Eel fo parteer!"

"You must go!"

"Yes, sir. Wee. I will go. It's just that I came a very long way to get here. So, please, if you could take off your hat and glasses for a moment, well, it would really mean a lot to me."

Hearing it from the girl, he dismissed it with a laugh. His answer:

"He say faces are not like snowflakes. Many can look the same. You know the story of the Prince and the Pauper."

"Zhuh swee Jean Roget."

"He is Jean Roget."

"Donc voo poovay parteer."

"Now you can go."

"Ohr-vwahr," he said conclusively.

Yeah, right. Ohr-vwahr. And don't let a coconut drop on your head on the way out. But what else could I do? It was either go down there and forcibly remove the hat and sunglasses, or respectfully concede the moment and beat of mannered retreat.

Grudgingly, I opted for the latter.

"I'm very sorry to have bothered you, Mister Roget. It seems I was given some wrong information. So uh . . . I'll just . . . well . . . parteer."

And with that I turned, and walked away.

Was he or wasn't he? I couldn't be certain. An unexpected twist— for I'd been sure that if I saw Sinclair I would know him, through any disguise. That, however, was not the case. Either I'd over-estimated my ability to pan fact from fiction, or I was so blinded by delusion, denial, I just couldn't bring myself to accept that Roget was, truly, who he claimed to be.

Seated on the motorbike again, I spotted the two vahines

peeking around the back corner of the house at me. Lovely but not quite stealthy spies sent by the man, no doubt, to confirm my departure.

Recalling how I'd already spent one night in jail for trespassing, and with no desire to compare the Huahine lockup to the grim cage on Key West, I compliantly started the engine. Then slipped on my helmet; the girls' eyes pushing at my back as I swung a U-turn and I scooted up the path toward the road to Fare. To Tahiti. To Los Angeles. To Bird in Hand, where, upon my return, I would be hailed the *Unconquering Zero*. It was a prospect daunting enough to stop me at the end of the driveway.

There was something stuck in my throat. Some sound bite from my exchange with Roget that refused to be swallowed. I closed my eyes, rewound the scene in my head, and then I let it play again—this time without the visual distractions—just the audio:

" . . . a reporter? . . . no such artist here . . . snowflakes . . . now you can go . . ."

"Damn it!" What was I missing? A slip of the tongue, a false note; it wasn't just my imagination, I'd heard it. Something slippery, teasing. Think, Woody, think!

Still, I couldn't dislodge the clue.

On the road again, I glanced up at the sun setting behind the jagged crest of the volcano. In another few hours it would sink into the ocean, and night would fall, like a seamless black velvet curtain on the third, and final, act of the farce that was my madcap odyssey.

I had nowhere to go now but home. Home? Heck, I didn't even have that anymore. The place I once called home, the farm, was sold. Lot, stock and barrels of Washborn sweat and blood—swapped for a certified cashier's check and a chance to chase a dream too elusive to be sane.

As the covert thinned to open beach, my vision started to blur, the wind cooler against my face. I had to pull over, and when I checked my reflection in the side-view mirror, I saw tears streaming down my cheeks. I was crying—the real me, stripped of all pretense—awash in a torrent of shameful self-pity. Weepy, wacky, wayward, worthless Woody Washborn. Exposed, he stared back at me in the round, rented glass.

Only then did it hit me. Like a lightning bolt through the rain of tears, it shook loose the provocative sound bite from my throat. *The Prince and the Pauper.*

Yes, I knew the story. I'd seen the movie. Adapted from Mark Twain's tale of two young men, the mirror image of each other. And I remembered something else. In the film, the two title-roles . . . they weren't played by look-alikes, or identical twins, or whatever. No. It was only an illusion, a bit of cinematic magic. Both parts— the Prince and the Pauper—were in fact portrayed by the *same* actor. His name escaped me but it was irrelevant. The point was he pulled it off. The audience, myself included, fooled into believing that one could be two.

So what if the trick was reversed?

Then two could actually be *one*.

I hid the scooter in a clump of bushes, and sneaked back to the house through the woods.

Using a copse of low fronds for cover, I spied beyond the palm trees a light now yellowing a large ground-floor side window. A silhouette—distinctly male—passed behind the screen; followed by the slender, topless figure of a woman. There was no sign of the second vahine but I assumed they were all three inside now. Their suppertime, perhaps. Or maybe my visit had spooked them off the beach, sent them scurrying behind walls in case I had a mind to return.

I checked my watch. It was a ten minutes past six.

Dare I creep closer? Play the Peeping Tom? No. Too risky, I decided. Better to sit tight, keep my distance; maintain a shadowy surveillance and see what Roget's next move would be?

While I waited an ominous black cloud appeared overhead. Its threat of rain proved far from idle. After a thunderous overture, a flash, tropical downpour began. It raged for more than an hour.

When it finally passed, I was left soaked to the bone, cramped in my crouch, surrounded by steamy, bug-buzzing darkness. And still, I stayed put. Enduring the mosquitoes, the miserable wetness, the intrinsic indignities of a lone scavenger sniffing the night air for a scrap of meat, I was resolved to remain there till morning if I had to. Sooner or later Roget would come out again, hopefully without the hat and glasses, and I'd have another chance to look him over, reevaluate him in the light of a new day.

As it happened, however, I didn't have to wait that long.

At around eight p.m. a lone figure stepped from the back of the house. By the light of a kerosene lantern in his hand I saw it was Roget. The lamp leading the way, he walked quickly in my direction. Afraid he'd somehow gotten wise to me, my first instinct was to turn and run for the scooter. But, on second-thought, I held my ground. If he was man enough to brave a confrontation, apparently unarmed, then how could I cower away from it and justify whatever sense of self-respect I had left?

Besides, I was too tired, too wet, too hungry, too fully invested to turn tail on the truth. I was about to stand up and face him—get it over with, play out the endgame right there and then—when suddenly the lamp veered from its course, toward a part of the woods nearer the sea. He wasn't coming for me after all; he was entering the underbrush a good twenty yards from my position.

When the flora swallowed the light I emerged from my hiding place and crept to the spot where he'd gone in. A little opening there, barely a path, running parallel to the shoreline. The lantern's ghostly-white glow shrinking as it pushed deeper into the jungle.

I followed it. Unsure what I would do if he turned around, I kept a cushion of thick night between us. He continued down the narrow trail for another two, maybe three, minutes, until, arriving at a high dead-end wall of vegetation, he stopped. So I stopped; holding my breath as he raised his hand above his head, then lowered it. Then raised and lowered it again. And then, with a creak like a rusty hinge, the light was gone.

Once more in the dark, I shivered under my drenched clothes. Was it a trick? Had he lured me down this path to bushwhack me? I stood very still, listening for some rustle of a sneak attack. But, aside from the pounding of my own heart, all was quiet. My fear suppressed by cautious curiosity: Where the hell did he go?

Blindly, I inched forward. And when I arrived at the spot where the light had vanished, the mystery of its disappearance was easily solved—there was a door standing before me. An entrance to a *barn*, it seemed; the rest of it hidden behind a wild shroud of climbing ivy and tangled vines, under a canopy of leafy trees. As if the jungle had conspired with the architect to keep its construction a secret.

The door's two rusty hinges explained the creaking sound I'd heard.

Evidently Roget had gone inside.

In search of a window to spy through, I waded into the bramble. It was tough, thorny going. As I slogged my way around the structure, I came upon a generator in the back, but not so much as a peephole anywhere to be found. Whatever Roget was doing in there, it wasn't for the benefit of prying eyes.

At the front again, I hunkered down in a jumble of bougainvillea and frangipani bushes thick with sweet-scented white, pink, and yellow flowers, where I waited on pins and needles for the man to come out. I squatted there until my legs stiffened. Knelt until my feet fell asleep. Sat till a creepy night crawler sank its muddy mandibles into my ass. A miserable two hours passed before the door finally creaked open, and the lantern's flame burned a fresh hole into the darkness.

Blanched by the light, Roget pulled the door closed behind him. Then he reached up, over transom board, and brought down a key, which he used to lock the door before returning it to the ledge. There was nothing to suggest he suspected a stakeout. His stride relaxed as he followed the path back toward the house.

When the lamp faded into the distance, I slunk from the bushes. My next move had already been decided. Feeling my way through the lush black night, I went straight for the key.

CHAPTER TWENTY

There comes a moment in everyone's life, I suppose, when your existence appears to be validated. *Justified.* Like the first time a new mother brings the babe to her breast, or a mountain climber stands at the top of the world, or the scientist discovers through his microscope the cure for some epidemic social ill. When the stars align and the payoff proves far greater than the sum of the risks.

For me that moment came when I entered that jungle-draped barn on the island of Huahine, and flipped a switch I found next to the doorframe, and the overhead lights went on. "Hooo-leee cow!" A thrill ran through my body like I was a part of the electrical circuitry. My eyed shocked wide by a sight beyond even my wildest expectations.

There were sculptures. At least a dozen. Abstracts and statuary, ranging from bust-sized to more than ten feet high, exquisitely carved from a variety of stones and indigenous woods.

And paintings. Hundreds of them. Portraits, still lives, land– and seascapes, hanging chockablock on the walls. A veritable treasure trove of *masterworks*!

And at the center of this unlikely gallery—a shiny black grand piano.

My legs shaking in awe, I approached the keyboard. A Steinway, no less. An instrument fit for the stages of Carnegie Hall, La Scala, Staatsoper, locked secretly away in a humble barn at the base of a sleepy volcano in the middle of nowhere. Unable to resist, my finger touched down on one of the ivory white keys, and a deep note resounded, in perfect tune, the crude space surprisingly rich in its acoustics.

I noticed there were several stacks of composition paper neatly arranged along the smooth-topped length of the instrument. Sheet music. The staff lines scaled in pencil, a staggered progression of clefs, dots and doo-hickeys I couldn't even begin to interpret.

The titles, however, were handwritten in legible English:

Symphony #2
Symphony #3
Tone Poem (E Minor)
Sonata 7 (B Flat Major)
Nocturne
Jazz in G Minor

But none of them had a byline. Come to think of it—I scanned the walls again—the paintings were all unsigned as well. The artist seemingly content to remain anonymous. My pan settled on a kind of plasterboard cubicle jutting out from a far corner. Attached to one of its walls was a workbench cluttered with photography equipment. Up close, I counted six cameras, twelve different sized lenses, and three Cuban cigar boxes stocked with a full spectrum of filters. Clearly the man was serious about his picture taking.

I poked my head into the cubicle. A water closet/darkroom complete with developing bath, enlarger, safelight, everything he needed to process his own film. A black and white banner of blown-up prints were clipped to a drying line fashioned from a length of piano wire. Stepping inside, I marveled at the photos: a series of nudes, the two vahines posing together, entwined into one myth-like creature with two heads, four breasts, eight spidery limbs. The paradoxes were stirring—the young women at once beautiful and monstrous. Innocent yet erotic. Through the melding of their singular charms, the creator had made them not only twice as alluring, but also twice as lethal.

It was provocative, powerful stuff.

Backing out of the little room, I turned, and was methodically drawn to an old desk against the rear wall. It held a manual typewriter, and four thick manuscripts under a thin layer of dust, which I blew away to reveal four title pages:

Novel #4 (Final Draft)
Verse (Vols 1-5)
Apologue Trilogy
Essays (1990-2000)

Again no mention of the author.

I flipped to the first essay—"Eye of the Beholder"—and read aloud

> "It is highly presumptuous to proclaim one's self an artist. For the making of art is akin to the making of love. One's proficiency is subject to the opinion of another."

That's as far as I got. Cut off by a round of applause, I turned with a start, and there he was, standing in the doorway.

"Nicely done, Woody." Not a trace of French in his voice. He stopped the clapping. "I assume you can read between the lines as well."

I swallowed guiltily.

"I'm sorry it had to be done this way, sir."

"You can drop the "sir" tag." He walked toward me. "At this point I think you've earned the right to call me Ford."

"Ford . . . Sinclair." I'd said the name thousands of times, only it had a very strange ring to it now.

He said, "After twenty years it feels a little dated. Like trying on an old suit from way back in the closet. Doesn't quite fit anymore."

On the contrary, it seemed tailor-made to me.

"Judging from the artwork in this room, I'd say it still fits you to a tee."

He smiled at that. Those sharp blue eyes—the corners creased with inevitable age but remarkably undiminished in their brightness—intimidating as ever against the golden brown of his august face, under a shock of blond-gray hair.

"I'm tempted to ask how you found me but, really, what does it matter?" The smile got smaller, tighter. "The bottom line is you did."

He turned to a large block of raw black marble. Staring at it like he could see through the stone the statue inside, he asked, "Are you by any chance familiar with the *HMS Pandora*?

I shook my head. "No, sir. I mean . . . Ford."

"It was the ship the Royal Navy sent to bring back the crew of the *Bounty*. So they could be tried for mutiny."

He looked me squarely in the eye.

"Are you my *Pandora*, Woody?"

I held his gaze.

"Nobody sent me," I said. "I came on my own."

"Came from where?"

"Bird in Hand, Pennsylvania."

"Pennsylvania. And you said you're not a reporter, is that the truth?"

"Yes. I swear on my father's grave, I'm not."

He paused. Laughed. "Then it's no contest, is it? You are by far top dog in your breed."

"Huh?"

"The best damn autograph-hound ever to come *my* way."

"Oh. No. You got me wrong," I said. "I'm not that either."

He squinted, perplexed. "Okay. I give up. So what the hell are you?"

Good question.

"Well . . . uh . . . I guess you could say I'm just a . . . a hick from the sticks. Who's wet and tired and hungry . . . and looking for an answer."

He let it hang in the air for a moment as he considered the rock again, running his hand along the rough flat top. "An answer," he repeated. "Why? Is that what you want to know? Why did I do it? Why in the world would someone in his right mind leave behind the charmed life of Ford Sinclair?"

"A lot of people are still scratching their heads over it?"

"Tell me—what reasons have they come up with?"

"That you burnt out," I told him. "Or that you were afraid you couldn't compete with yourself. Or that you had nothing more to give. But I can see now that none of those are the case."

He seemed to be enjoying the confusion he caused. "Go on."

"Your sister thinks you ran away from the circus."

"You spoke to Alice Faye?"

"In New York City. And I promised Oats Sleet I'd tell you he's still kicking."

"Who else?"

"Olivia, Mara. Jack Buzbee believes you took off to keep from blowing your brains out like Hemingway. And your son Fletcher. He says he hates you."

"Then we'll just have to take him at his word. What about Deanna?"

"She lives all alone at the ranch. Waiting for you to come back to her."

"Yes, well, that's a shame. She's a sweet girl. And you, Woody? With all the insight you've gathered, what's your theory on my . . . *disengagement?*"

"To be honest, I don't have one. In fact the more I learn, the less sense it seems to make. And right now, well, I'm thinking it's not for me know why. That it's something best left between you and your conscience."

Clearly the last part of my reply surprised him. He blinked, his body stiffened like I'd landed a straight jab he didn't see coming; but it was only for a second. Quick to recover, he smiled again, this one, I thought, more genuine than the last.

"Bravo, Woody," he said. "For a hick from the sticks you have a certain, shall I say, savwahr faar."

"But I still don't have the answer I came looking for."

"Then by all means: If not why, then what—this question you so doggedly hunted me down to ask?"

"The question is *how*? I wanna know how you do it."

"And by 'it' you are referring to . . .'"

"How do you get a word to say more than it means? How do you turn a glob of paint into something with a soul? How do you change noise into music?

"How do you make magic happen, Ford?"

"Ah, so that's it. The querent. A seeker of artistic enlightenment."

"Please, before I go totally crazy—just tell me what it takes."

He breathed out a sigh, and then looked around the room, at the piano, the sculptures, the paintings, as if asking their permission to share the secret of their creation.

"You must be careful, Woody," he said mysteriously. "Illusions get burned when you play with fire."

As he walked across the room I followed him. He stepped up to a mirror hanging on the wall alongside the camera bench, and slid it aside, revealing a safe recessed in the paneling. Working the tumblers, he recalled the combination aloud. "Right 16. Left 22. Right 5." Then he pushed down the handle, and tugged open the heavy iron door. Reaching inside, he took out a long, thin, yellow-ringed cigar, and then slammed the door shut again. The looking glass returned to its place.

On the bench there was a box filled with matchsticks. He used his thumbnail to strike one, the flame dancing as he bit off the tapered end of the cigar, and spit it on the floor. To light the perfectly rolled Cuban tobacco, he took deep, deliberate, dramatic puffs, until finally he exhaled at length, a thick gray-white plume that blotted out his reflection.

"And there you have it, Woody," he said. "Smoke and mirrors."

He'd lost me.

"What do you mean? I don't understand."

"The secret," he said, "it's all about distraction, misdirection. You see, while the audience is watching one hand, the other is sneaking the rabbit into the hat. Then, once you've got them on the edge of their seats, you simply wave your shiny stage prop wand . . ." he circled the cigar in the air " . . . and *Presto*! You pull the little miracle out by its floppy pink ears. Magic, ladies and gentleman! Another standing ovation for the Amazing Sinclair." He took a hamy bow.

Only I wasn't buying it. "I don't believe that—that it's nothing more than a trick. And furthermore I don't believe you believe it, either."

"Welcome to the Island of Disenchantment, Woody." He puffed smugly on the cigar.

"If you think so little of it then what's all this?" I swept my hand, entering into evidence the substantiation of his artistry. "There's no audience to fool here. So why, why bother if there's nothing else to it?"

Tapping an ash to floorboards, he dismissed the work as "Old habits I can't seem to break. Only now it's just something to pass the time. The private puttering of early retirement."

"No. It's more than that," I contended. "It's who you are. You can never retire from it."

"What I am is an old tree, falling in the woods. Where nobody can hear me." He dropped the cigar, crushing it under his sandal. "Thus, I make no sound."

"What about me?" I replied. "I'm somebody."

"Are you?" he asked. "Is that really what you think?"

I braced myself, waiting for him to list all the reasons relevant to my nobody-ness. But he didn't go there. Instead, he picked up a camera, and removed the lens cap. "Because if you really believe that you're somebody, without even the slightest inkling of a doubt in your mind, then it may very well be, Woody . . . the answer you came looking for."

He shot from his chest. *Click!* went the camera.

The two vahines eyed me with distrust as Sinclair introduced us in a simple dining room. Mareta (the one who'd nabbed the fish) and Cecele were their names, and without saying a word they went into the kitchen to fix me something to eat.

On the walk to the house I'd asked Sinclair if the girls knew his true identity. He said no, that they were quite content with

Jean Roget, and in return he shared with them his home, all the relative comforts of his assumed life.

As they prepared my meal, he led me into a spare bedroom and gave me a pareu and dry shirt to wear. Left alone to change, I considered a large mask on the wall above the bed: a wooden, ceremonial-looking thing, frightful, no doubt intended to scare off unwelcomed visitors—like evil spirits, or long ago English ship captains. Not to mention present day snoops not entirely unexpected.

Returning to the dining room, I found Sinclair behind the wet bar, uncorking a bottle of red French wine. "A glass of vino before dinner, Woody?" he offered graciously.

"Just a splash, thank you," I said to be polite but wanting to keep my wits about me.

"It's been a while since I've entertained a guest. So forgive me if my social skills are a bit rusty."

"This is a very interesting house. Did you build it yourself?"

"I designed it. Hired a gang of locals to help with the construction."

"Have you been living here the whole time? Since you . . . disengaged?"

"No," he said, pouring. "Not entirely. I spent time on most of the smaller Society Islands, and then three years in the Marqueses, three in the Australs, and four on the Gambier Archipelago. In those days I thought it best to keep moving."

"Omoo," I recalled.

"Yes. You have done your research."

"So what made you settle on Huahine?"

"I've felt more secure here." He handed me a full glass of the wine. "Figured everybody had pretty much given up on me."

"Not everybody,"

He smiled, "You being the living proof of that," and raised a toast. "I salute your determination, Muss-yuh Washborn."

We clinked, and sipped to it.

"Have a seat." He motioned me to the table. "The ladies will be out shortly with your dinner."

We sat across from each other, under a slow revolving ceiling fan.

"So, how did you get away?" I asked. "I know you mailed the letter to Brimm from Mexico City. But after that?"

He rolled his glass, connoisseur-like, eyeing the red swirl. "I simply hopped on the next plane to Hong Kong. Within a week I had the all papers I needed. Several complete aliases, in fact. Though I've only had to use two of them. Maurice Malraux, and of course, Roget—a retired stockbroker from Paris."

"Like Gauguin."

"I take it you went to the museum."

I nodded. "He was kind of haunting me."

I told him about the Gauguin/Van Gogh conversation I had with Buzbee on Key West, and the peyote hallucination in the teepee in New Mexico. I was into the story of Gauguin's self-portrait on the coffee table book at the ranch when the vahines reappeared from the kitchen, bringing a long loaf of French bread, and a plate heaped with poisson cru.

It was so *dreamy*. I kept my feet apart, afraid if my heels clicked together I would wake up back home on the farm, and everything would be in black and white again, the wizard only my dad rousing me to go milk the cows after the storm.

"Am I eating alone?"

"Yes," Sinclair answered. "We had ours while you were lurking outside in the rain."

I looked at the girls. They stood bewildered by their beloved Roget's sudden grasp of English. Switching to French, he waved them off and they left us again; blaming me, I sensed, for bringing confusion into their happy home.

"Don't be shy now," Sinclair urged me. "Bonapatee."

Famished, I dug in. The fish so tender it melted in my mouth. The sauce ambrosial with fresh coconut. "This is really delicious," I said coming up for air.

"Not exactly a big menu item in Bird in Hand, I assume."

"I never even heard of it until Casa de Sol."

Deftly, he maneuvered off the subject of Palm Beach. "So, your life on the farm. What's the story there?"

"It would bore you to sleep."

"Try me," he insisted.

Obliging him, I started at the beginning. I recounted my first feelings of discontent, my unlikely fascination with art, how I'd washed-out on the trumpet, at being an actor, a painter, writer. He listened attentively while I spoke of my father: his death made even more tragic insomuch as he'd never really lived. Had never tried to do anything big, anything extraordinary. Not once had he ever reached beyond himself for a star.

"Tell me, Woody," Sinclair interjected, "what do you think of my barn?"

The question seemed a non sequitur but I suspected a point behind it. And, since he asked, the barn was something that bothered me from the moment I stepped inside. So I was glad for the chance to get it off my chest.

"The barn . . . well . . . frankly, I think it's a shame. It reminds me of that old saying—about hiding your light under a bushel. All those great works, stashed away where nobody can appreciate them. I believe some things are meant to be shared."

He nodded. "Then the true worth is in the sharing?"

"After you've poured your heart and soul into it, yes."

"And your father, he poured his heart and soul into his work, right?"

I paused.

"Yeah."

"And the fruit of his labor, the milk, he shared it, correct?"

"Yeah."

"Well, then, by your own definition, his work was truly worthwhile."

"But—"

"It sounds to me like he was a productive, selfless, satisfied man."

"Oh, he was satisfied, alright. More than satisfied."

"And that, I say to you, this from a chronically selfish and unsatisfied man . . . is *extraordinary*."

"But to what end?" I wanted to know. "After all the long

hours, the sweat and blood he poured into it—one loose shingle, one lousy slip, and it all died with him."

Sinclair smiled, sadly. "Perhaps therein lies the real tragedy. That nobody cared enough to make it live on."

"It's not that I didn't care. It's just . . ."

"Just what, Woody?"

"It's just that nothing great can come from always thinking small."

"Huh." A note of condescension in his voice. "If that's the case then I've been doing it all wrong. You see I always approached my work with the belief that the smallest details are what make the big picture great. Maybe that's the difference between you and me. I sweat the small stuff you find insignificant."

I had no ready reply. He was twisting the logic I'd settled on. I understood what was he was getting at—that I wasn't giving my dad a fair shake. It just never occurred to me before. Was I too hard on my father? Did I misjudge the length of his shadow against the seemingly endless pastureland I wanted only to escape?

As it tugged at my conscience, Sinclair sipped his wine. Then, when he was sure he had me, "Sometimes, Woody," he said, "you have to go halfway around the world to see the art in your own backyard."

In my own defense, I reminded him, "But playing with Oats, writing that letter to Mara, the portrait of Buzbee, you can't find inspiration like that in my backyard."

"Cezanne," Sinclair countered, "painted apples. Whitman found poetry in blades of grass. Duke Ellington made us dance to the A-train. No. It's not what you reflect; it's *how* you reflect it. Parnassus, Woody."

"Parnassus?" Then I remembered. "The mountain, where the Muses live."

"Know it when you see it and where ever you are . . ." he downed the last of his wine " . . . it will come to you."

He made it sound so simple. All I had to do was reconsider everything I thought I knew. Suddenly, it angered me. Who was he to preach? After all, he'd neglected a few things himself.

"What about your family?" I asked. "Don't you even wonder how they're getting along?"

"They've been provided for," he answered matter-of-factly.

"Paying their bills, you think that's enough?"

"Let's just say I've managed to keep my head above the guilt."

He got to his feet, and returned to the bar. I kept at him.

"And the milk in your barn—why not put it out, let people taste it and decide for themselves what it's worth?"

"Because their taste is too damn lazy to be trusted." He set two cups made from coconut shells on the counter. "Like you with your father, people don't want the inconvenience of having to change their minds. It requires an effort they can't be bothered to expend. So, when they slap on that blue ribbon—the genius tag—they're plenty determined to make it stick."

He started pouring, mixing some sort of cocktail.

"When it comes to me, Woody, their taste buds are hard-wired. They've been pre-programmed to swill anything I give them. Be it Grade A, Grade Z, or a snifter of cold piss—they'll lap it up like nectar from Heaven. Now you tell me: What satisfaction should I derive from that?"

I tried to grasp his dilemma, only it was too far beyond me to get my mind around. "Let me get this straight. Are you saying you split because everybody loved everything you did?"

"Imagine a gambler who's not allowed to lose," he said, using sticks of sun-dried vanilla to stir his concoctions. "After a while the game becomes very uninteresting."

"So you decided to play hide 'n seek instead."

"It seemed only fitting. To end the magic show with a vanishing act."

Again, I felt compelled to reassure him. "Well, you don't have to worry about me. I have no intention of blowing your cover."

"Ah, then you disappoint me, Woody," Sinclair replied. "Because a true artist must treat his experiences shamelessly. Right or wrong, he is duty-bound to exploit them."

It was the last thing I expected to hear out his mouth.

"Are you giving me permission?"

"Come." He smiled. "Join me for a little flavor of the island."

I got up and went to the bar. He handed me a shell filled with an orangish potion. "What is it?" I asked.

"Homemade Huanine Rum Punch," he told me. "Splash of mango, dash of lime, fresh vanilla, among other things."

I nosed it. "Smells good."

"It's customary to knock it back in one breath," he instructed.

"If you say so."

"That's the spirit. Together, on the count of three. Are you ready?"

"Okay. Yes."

"Here we go then. Ho'e . . . piti . . . turo. Bottoms up, lad."

I raised the shell to my lips and, as directed, chugged the punch like a sport, until the cup was empty. The drink warm, fruity, bittersweet. And stronger than I knew. "Whoa!"

Sinclair exhaled, rummy fumes.

"Yes. It really hits the spot."

He watched as I sucked air to quiet the sting; his cool blue eyes observing my condition with an odd anticipation. Like he was waiting for the punch to enter my bloodstream.

He didn't have to wait long. I could feel it coursing straight to my head. A heated, numbing sensation. "No more," I sniffled. "I've had enough."

"Yes, that should do it," Sinclair nodded. "But on a full stomach it'll take another minute or so."

I blinked. Suddenly there were two of him.

"Double vision," he said in stereo. "Don't be alarmed. It's quite normal."

"Normal?"

"It'll be easier if you sit down."

He reached for a chair. The movement set off a swirl of dizziness. My legs buckled, as though someone had dropped a heavy wet blanket, or fishing net, over me. I grabbed the bar to keep from folding to the floor.

"Here you go." His voice sounding far away, he eased me onto the chair. "Just lean back."

"I feel like I'm gonna pass out."

"It's nothing to be ashamed of," he said. "It's only natural."

"Natural?" I slurred.

"Yes. Organic, actually. A blend of several local plants. Various roots, seeds, extracts. You see, Woody, I knew, in all likelihood, this day would come. Exactly when, how, who—that I couldn't be sure of. So I had to be ready at all times, take certain precautions. Better safe than sorry, as they say. In other words, don't take it personally. It's not that I doubt your intentions. It's just that a secret can be a very slippery thing to hold on to. Sooner or later a good story demands to be told."

My eyes half-lidded, I managed to mumble, "I don't understand this story."

"Let's think in the detective genre. Noir. Pulpy. A la Dash Hammett, or Ray Chandler. With you playing the atypical hero: a soft-boiled Sam Spade, Philip Marlowe. Opposite me, the shadowy nemesis. Your 'Fat Man,' so to speak."

"Fat man?"

"The dialogue might go something along the lines of—Here's how it is, kid. Ya got too wise, too fast, and that makes ya too damn risky for my blood. So, in keeping with my part as the devious 'heavy,' I took the liberty of adding a little spike to your punch."

"Spike?"

"That's right, kid. I slipped ya a 'mickey'."

I tried to speak, to plead for my life but my tongue was now limp as the rest of me. Then my eyes, they slammed shut. My ears the last to abandon me—

"Ars gratia artis, Woody Washborn."

—before I faded into oblivion.

CHAPTER TWENTY-ONE

A darkness deeper than sleep.
Yet shallower than death. A drug punched black hole from which I slowly started to immerge . . . to the smell of something burning.

Mom frying up bacon extra crispy in the kitchen. Or is it the fireplace, Dad trying to cut down on the heating bill? Maybe it's both, and Christmas morning, and Kelly Ann will be here soon, and we'll open our presents under the tinseled tree after the cows have been milked, and then we'll all go to church together, dressed in our Sunday best, to hear the Reverend Sinclair deliver his celebrant sermon.

Sinclair?

Sinclair! My eyes shot open. Pained by a rush of sunlight, I turned away from the window, and came face to face with a screaming demon. "Ahhh!" I screamed back. Until I realized that mine was the only cry in my ears; that the frightful demon was in fact mute, frozen in its fearsomeness; carved, it finally registered, from the red-black flesh of a rosewood tree.

It was the mask I'd seen earlier, hanging on the wall in the bedroom where I'd changed from my wet clothes into the pareu Sinclair had provided me. Yes. The thin cloth was still cinched about my waist. I'd been neatly laid out on the bed. My head aching, throbbing with a hungover echo—

Ars gratia artis, Woody Washborn.

Art for art's sake.

It was all coming back to me now. *That's right, kid. I slipped ya a mickey.* But why? Shaking the cobwebs from my consciousness, I sat up, took a deep breath, my lungs filling with tainted air. It wasn't bacon burning but the smell of smoke persisted. I could see it now, a ghostly white haze softening the room, wafting in through the window screen.

I labored to my feet. My legs rubbery, I crossed to the window and looked out on the columns of coconut trees. Their high palm crowns were obscured by a thick gray cloud, through which I could see a strange yellow-red glow. It seemed to be burning brighter, and more sinister, than the sun.

I turned and staggered to the door. Was I locked in—a prisoner? No. It opened freely. I hurried down a hallway, looking for Sinclair, the vahines, anybody I could find, but the house was quiet, still, eerily so.

"Ford?" I called through the haze. "Mareta? Cecele?"

Receiving no reply, I rushed out the back door. The smoke heavier with every stride, I ran through the grove, and then down the narrow path into the woods. Above the treetops I could now see tongue-like flames licking greedily at the sky. A few strides later they stopped me in my tracks. It was the barn, Sinclair's studio—on fire. His secret trove of artistic treasures ablaze beyond any hope of salvation!

Truly a hellish inferno.

The repellent heat brought tears to my eyes, a sense of loss too enormous to comprehend. I dropped to my knees, conceding a sacrifice no god could justly demand—this cruel immolation of the human heart, soul—I could only kneel there in the mud, and watch in helpless horror as the fire brought down the roof, the crash bellowing a billow of black smoke and wicked red sparks. Aside from the death of my father, it remains the most sickening scene I have ever witnessed.

Not until the walls began to collapse did it occur to me: that I was alone in my grief. *Where* was Sinclair? The girls? Why weren't they here—cursing, in whatever language they pleased, the devastation?

Suddenly, above the dreadful crackling, I heard the sound of a motor. A high-performance growl, it turned me toward the sea. Rising from my knees, I pushed into the dense brush. The engine grew louder as I tore through the low branches and sharp briar. I could see daylight up ahead. And when I came out of the woods there was a narrow band of clearing along a high bluff backlit by sky and ocean. Hard to tell where the water blue stopped and the air blue began, just a subtle lowering in tone.

The roar of the motor was coming from below. I hurried to the edge and, looking over the cliff, saw a boat there at the bottom: a shiny sleek speedboat pulling away from a thatch-roofed wooden slip. Its cargo consisted of two seaman's chests secured to the fantail.

And at the controls stood Ford Sinclair.

It became painfully clear to me then. An unthinkable yet unavoidable conclusion. He'd done it. He'd set fire to the barn. The defiant son-of-a-circus had destroyed the evidence of his genius rather than risk a return to the spotlight reserved for the one and only Ford Buster Sinclair.

And now, again, (if not for the last time then until the next Woody Washborn arrived on his doorstep from out of the blue) he was making his escape.

Headed for open water, he turned to look back on what he was leaving behind. As Mareta and Cecele stood at the shoreline, like daydreams, waving a teary goodbye, au revoir, parahi, to the man they only knew as Jean Roget, he lifted his gaze—and when he saw me there, with the works of his artistry going up in smoke behind me, I believe I caught the distant trace of a smile on his face. *No hard feelings*, it seemed to say.

Then, above the din of surf and motor, he yelled out to me: "And for my next trick . . ."

In spite of himself, forever the showman, he could not resist an audience of even one. And, as always, he pulled the trick off. With a push on the throttle, the boat skipped over the gleaming surface of the water . . . shrinking against the endless blue horizon, until, like it was never there at all, it vanished, without apology, into thin air and thick sea.

Magic, ladies and gentlemen!
Another standing ovation for the Amazing Sinclair.

It took most of the day for the fire to finally burn itself out. The vegetation around it was green and still damp from the rain, so the blaze was naturally contained. It left only a black heap of ash where the barn had stood.

As Sinclair knew it would.

The girls appeared briefly; just long enough to give me my dried clothes and shoes. Their way, I understood, of telling me I was no longer welcome in the house. Their house now. Left to them, as too little consolation, by the previous owner, who I'd caused to abandon their lives.

They showed no interest in the fire, or the invaluable contents it had consumed. They'd lost a friend, teacher, protector, and lover. His art was unimportant, irrelevant to them.

Because that was the way he wanted it to be.

Without a word said, they walked hand in hand back down the path . . . fading into the sooty green lushness.

When the embers were cool enough, I trudged through the ashes. The only things still standing were what remained of the stone sculptures. Which wasn't much. They were broken, beheaded, defiled to little more than stumps of rock. A pre-arson sledgehammer attack, I suspected.

As for the woodcarvings, and the hundreds of paintings, they never had a chance. All reduced to a fulsome black dust. At the center of the devastation, I moved aside a jumble of collapsed ceiling beams to reveal the cremated remains of the piano, identifiable only by its scorched ivory keys. They grinned up at me like so many rotted teeth. I touched my finger down on one, but this time there was no sound to be heard.

The typewriter, the photo enlarger, everything, incinerated, slag, unsalvageable. A *total* loss. Because again that was the way Sinclair wanted it to be.

"Ars gratia artis."

Still, he'd taken it too far, to its fanatical extreme, a self-iconoclasm that betrayed an undercurrent of madness. Yet even that seemed a flimsy excuse—he was well aware of the consequences of his action. He'd premeditated it. He'd carried it out with a cool, calculating presence of mind, and for that there was no acceptable defense.

As I stood, judge and jury, over the atrocity, a last item of evidence caught my eye. A black box, half buried in the ashes. On closer examination, I recognized it to be the iron wall-safe from which Sinclair had removed the cigar to dramatize his smoke and mirror speech. The iron still warm, I rolled it over so that the door faced up. The steel tumbler was blackened by soot, but otherwise undamaged. I wiped it off to read the numbers. Then I remembered—the combination. Sinclair had made it known to me. Slyly, he'd pre-orchestrated this moment.

I worked the dial. "Right 16. Left 22. Right 5."

The handle moved hospitably. *Click!* And when I pulled the heavy door swung open . . . . At first, the safe appeared to be empty, just the lingering scent of cigars. But as I leaned over it, there was something in there after all—a thin rectangle of stiff paper—standing flat against a side wall. I reached inside and plucked it out, and, when I realized what it was, my jaw dropped. I felt a chill. Surprise. Gratitude. It took my breath away.

A *photograph*.

A sharp, perfectly framed picture—of me.

Only I wasn't alone in the shot.

The mirror that had hidden the safe hung just above my shoulder. And in the glass a clear, focused, cunning reflection: *Sinclair!* His full handsome face, and enough of his chest to see the camera in his hands, his finger on the shutter button. Unbeknownst to me, he'd captured us both. A black and white memento of our time together. Hard proof that I had, in defiance of the odds, found my way into his elusive company.

My reward. Validation.

I mooned over the photo—Sinclair and Washborn, Woody and Ford, a picture worth much, much more than a thousand

words, in any language—for I don't know how long, before I
thought to flip it and see what was on the other side.

When finally I did, a familiar handwriting jumped up at me.
One fluid, fateful line

Now you have the end to our story.

EPILOGUE

I took Alf's advice and flew from Huahine back to Tahiti. I got to Omai's house about ten o'clock that evening. When I told him I'd found Sinclair he asked if the encounter had lived up to my expectations. I wasn't sure how to answer the question. I'd expected to find a great artist, a genius, and I did. The rest had gone beyond anything I had ever imagined.

As for what I'd learned from the man, it was hard to put a finger on. It wasn't the neat, definable, clearly enlightening experience I'd anticipated. It was more like a dream to be interpreted from a convolution of seemingly contradictory parts. A mix of brilliance, darkness, creation, destruction, passion, indifference, bravado, insecurity, generosity, selfishness, idolization, disillusion, myth, fact, magic, trickery . . .

Too many components to fully comprehend. And even if they could somehow be separated, counted, analyzed, and assembled, I now understood that the whole would be still greater than the sum of its parts. That the secret I'd sought to discover was, by grand design, a ghost in the machine.

The next day Omai walked me to the airport. I tried to give him another ten thousand francs as a gratuity for all that he'd done for me, but he refused to accept it. It was not their way, he reminded me. So I slipped the money in his pocket when we hugged our goodbye.

"Bohn vwa-yahz, Woodywashborn!" he waved as I passed

through the departure gate to my plane.

Eight hours later I was back in Los Angeles. Then three days to drive the approximately twenty-seven hundred miles to Pennsylvania. Along the way my thoughts were kept more than occupied by what Sinclair had said about traveling halfway around the world to find the art in my own backyard; and how my father's life was more extraordinary than I'd realized. How the *real* tragedy of his death was that I didn't care enough to keep his work alive. It made the trip seem a lot shorter than it actually was.

On my return to Bird in Hand, I moved in with Mom. For six months. In which time I wrote this book. The manuscript, along with a photocopy of the picture of me and Sinclair, I then sent to Washborn Press, and they agreed to publish it. That was over a year ago now and, although it hasn't made any best-seller lists, it sold-out like hotcakes at the bookstore here in our little town, where I went to sign copies one Saturday afternoon. Mr. Coho was there, along with Mr. Crino, Miss Delripple, Doc Carney, and Mrs. Kincade. Even Kelly Ann showed up to get my autograph. She brought her baby son, little Jimmy Fry III. Her marriage to Jim Jr. having inspired the merger of Price Seed & Feed with Fry Hardware. I shop there often these days.

As a matter of courtesy, I sent copies of the book to Arthur Brimm, Otis Sleet, Keisha Mills, Olivia Sutton Sinclair Woolbright, Mara Sinclair Garcia, Jack Buzbee, Joseph Hightower, Fletcher Sinclair, Deanna Dees Sinclair, and Omai Teariki. In return I got congratulatory notes from New York City, Palm Beach, New Mexico, Los Angeles, the San Gabriel Mountains, and Tahiti. Still nothing from Key West, though. And sadly I received news from Harlem that Oats had passed away in his sleep before my token of appreciation was delivered. He will be missed, but not forgotten.

Fletcher, in turn, took the book to Howard Klein, who wasted no time securing the screen rights. So there is a movie in the making. With Fletcher, of all people, cast in the role of his father, a character he insists he still hates but was *born* to play.

At present they are holding auditions to find an actor bumpkin enough to portray me.

Incredibly, I was paid two-hundred thousand dollars for the story. I used that money, plus what was left of my inheritance, to buy back the farm. I like to think of it as a work in progress. If you're ever driving through Bird in Hand, you'll recognize it by the old weathercock on top of the barn. Also by the murals I painted on the outside walls. They show three generations of Washborn men—my great-grandfather, grandfather, and my father—working the land in proud succession. I reckon someday I'll put a self-portrait on the fourth wall. But for the time being I have enough to do: baling hay, mending fences, keeping the cows healthy and happy, the milk flowing.

As for Ford Sinclair, well, his whereabouts are again a mystery.

I have no doubt, however, that where ever he may be . . . the fish are biting.